JUL 2 5 1991

AF GATES
Gates, David
Jernigan

21.00

25¢ fine charged
for cards missing
from book pocket

Jernigan

Jernigan

a novel by

DAVID GATES

Alfred A. Knopf ✦ New York 1991

THIS IS A BORZOI BOOK PUBLISHED BY
ALFRED A. KNOPF, INC.

Library of Congress Cataloging-in-Publication
Data
Gates, David, [date]
Jernigan / David Gates. — 1st ed.
p.   cm.
ISBN 0-679-40237-3
I. Title.
PS3557.A87J47   1991
813'.54—dc20   90-53583   CIP

Manufactured in the United States of America
First Edition

Thanks to Dave Friedman for computer expertise, to Marjorie Horvitz for stern copy editing and to Garth Battista for making everything easy.

Thanks to Dolly Fried's *Possum Living*, regrettably out of print, for its account of suburban survivalism.

And thanks to those who have taught me, believed in me and saved my bacon: Sam Seibert, Patrick McKiernan, David Spry, Douglass Paige, J. D. O'Hara, Madeleine Edmondson, Meredith White, Sarah Crichton, Amanda Urban and Gary Fisketjon. And especially to Gene and Helen Gates, to Ann and to Elizabeth. And to Susan.

Jernigan

I

1

I ended up driving all night. The snow eased off after a while—or, more likely, I'd driven past the edge of the storm—and I just kept going. Stopped for gas where you get off the interstate, then followed the state highway on up through the woods and through the open lands and through the empty little towns as it began to get light. Church steeples. The first human, in a red plaid jacket, bending over to scrape his windshield, blowing out clouds of breath in early-morning sun. Two more towns to go. Then, in the center of the second town, a left at the church and up that road for probably five miles. And at what must have been eight or nine o'clock I finally got to the place where you turn off the town road to get down to Uncle Fred's camp. Just a gap between fenceposts. Blinding sun by now; this absolutely blue sky and snow all around. And so silent when I turned the engine off. This was as far as I could take the car: they hadn't plowed down to where the camp was. So I just pulled as far over to the side of the road as I could, passenger door scraping against the snowbank. And I thought, Before it snows again you better get a carlength of that track cleared so you can pull in there off the road. Otherwise, next time the plow comes through here, I don't know, no need to finish the thought.

My God it was cold when I opened that car door. Inch or so of gin left in the bottle, but then I thought No, save that for when you get the stove going and the trailer good and warm. I'd finished all but that last inch on the way up. Just drinking to keep drinking: it didn't make me any drunker. Or I guess any less drunk either. It wasn't supposed to be a good idea to be drunk and out in the cold, that was a common misconception. I mean, the misconception was that it kept you warm. Just hoped to hell there was some wood, and some paper to get it going, and maybe something lying around for kindling so I wouldn't have to try splitting logs in this kind of shape. Provided they hadn't stolen the God damn woodstove out of there too. Get that stove going and wash down about four five more Pamprins with the last of that gin, boy, and sleep the sleep of the just.

Now if only Danny had come along—I'd practically got down on my fucking knees—he could've been carving out that carlength of snow while old Dad was humping the wood inside and building the fire and getting the trailer warmed up for him to come in to. Heating up a can of beans if there was a can of beans. See, I would have had him sleep most of the way up, and then he could have stayed awake to feed the fire while old Dad took his rest. But, of course, stayed awake to do what? Oh, practice his guitar for a while, I suppose. Playing it through his Rockman so as not to wake old Dad. Well, fine, okay, but after a couple hours of that? So it might've been just as well.

The trailer was maybe half a mile in from the town road, down a pair of ruts. Though with the snow the way it was, all you could see was a gap in the hemlocks or whatever they were. Just pine trees, probably, but I had that thing going in my head—

And the hemlocks and the peacocks
And the peacocks and the hemlocks

—or however the hell it went. That Wallace Stevens thing about the peacocks and the hemlocks. Then I tried to make up some joke, in my head, about the hemlock maneuver. And then the hemlock re-mover. A chainsaw: that could be the hemlock remover, although how would you set up the joke? Some inner life, boy. That's about what it had come down to. At any rate, I grabbed a book of matches out of the dash, got out of the car, shouldered my shoulderbag, then reached in back and started trying to work the suitcase out between the front seats, banging it around the gearshift and the steering wheel. All the time thinking Fuck, wouldn't it have been easier just to bend down, release that little catch and flip the driver's seat forward?

So I started down through where I knew the road had to be, right up over my knees in all that God damn snow. I could feel it going down into my shoes. But at least nobody else had been down through here: the white surface ahead was utterly smooth. And so bright that the shadows under the trees were grateful to the eye. I wished right then for another storm to come and cover my tracks, if wished isn't too strong a word. And so quiet here. About halfway through the stand of hemlocks (I'm just going to go ahead and call them hemlocks) I stopped, let my breathing slow down to normal again, then held after an outbreath and started dropping into a silence without bottom. Though of course you can't drop far before you have to gulp in another breath, and there you are, back up in the old one two one two again. So I let that new breath out—you could see the big cloud of it linger; not for long—and went on again into the white.

At the bottom of the slope the trees ended and I looked out across a field of snow. I don't know acres, but say the size of two football fields. Once this was somebody's cornfield. Up in this part of the world they used to graze cows on the hillsides and plant corn in the bottom land, still do, there's some folkways for you. In case you're thinking, Well, Jernigan, fuck him, he just lives inside his own head. All around, hills forested in now-bare hardwoods and ever-dark ever-greens. I remembered the shape of every hill. At the far end of the field, near the edge of the woods, sat Uncle Fred's trailer, a faded blue, with snow halfway up to the doorknob and a white hump of snow on top, a stovepipe elbow poking out of a window. It seemed to be floating like an ocean liner. What do you know, white sea, blue ocean liner. Huh.

I started making my way around the edge of the woods instead of cutting straight across the field and fucking it all up. When I'd circled around behind the camp I could see firewood stacked under the lean-to that ran along the back of the trailer. A roof of green corrugated fiberglass propped up with two-by-fours. Weathered, wedge-shaped ends of split logs, stacked as high as my head the whole way along, except for a gap where the two-by-fours braced the logs away on either side so you could get in and out the back door. I had long since stopped holding Uncle Fred in contempt for being provident—no I hadn't—but right then and there I started praying Dear God, please bless Uncle Fred and thank You too, dear God. Praying like a five-year-old. I mean, *bless?* You picture somebody with this pile of things heaped on his back and still more things getting heaped on.

So I came out from under the trees and crossed the open snow to the back door. Stood under the lean-to, in the greenish shade, smelling that good sour wood smell. Then I tried the door. It was unlocked, as Uncle Fred had guessed it would be. I stepped inside, where the air was even colder because of no sun, and smelled musty. And the first thing I saw was that good old sheet-metal chunk stove, like a big old pencil sharpener standing up on end. The stovepipe still hooked up too, going outdoors through the sheet of galvanized metal in the window. And right next to it, the big old woodbox, with a few logs and a jumble of broken tree branches. And a stack of Sunday *Times*es about yea high. Thank You, dear God. And that book of matches right in my pants pocket. I patted and made sure.

2

I have Uncle Fred to thank, apparently, for making whatever arrangements were necessary to get me into this place. And for calling the state police, who carried me out of the trailer and rushed me to the hospital. I don't remember any of that, though I'm supposed to have been mumbling away on the stretcher. They got there too late for my thumb and forefinger—the surgeon almost had to do (meaning cut off) the whole hand—but the essential man was, and is, still intact. Which is the big thing, right, the essential man? Jernigan.

Suppose we start out by explaining that Uncle Fred's name isn't Fred and that he's not my uncle, that should stretch this out some. The name Uncle Fred had stuck because it just fit, though by that I don't suppose I mean anything more mystical than this: that even in his freshman year he looked like William Frawley on *I Love Lucy*. Though he used to say Edmund Wilson. I was the only other one on our floor who knew who Edmund Wilson was. Edmund Wilson, in fact, had once been dragged to one of my father's openings, and pronounced his work fraudulent. Or so their mutual acquaintance later took it upon himself to tell my father. Except the more I think about it the more I wonder if that story wasn't about somebody else and Edmund Wilson wasn't some whole other story. Anyhow, at some point in high school I'd bought the old gray Scribner's paperback of *Axel's Castle* and tried to read some of it. So Michael Warriner and I became friends.

We go back, in other words, to before he taught himself all that bluff Uncle Fred bullshit he does nowadays, where you can't get a straight word out of him. Oh, I can see the appeal: even during the drug years, he was still impermeably Uncle Fred. For which you had to envy him as well as hold him in contempt.

Right, how he got the name. Freshman year he and I took the train up to spend Christmas break with his family in Connecticut. That was the year my father was in Mexico. (My mother, of course, was out of the picture by then.) At Bridgeport I think it was, this little kid and his mother got on the train and the kid came running wide-eyed up to Michael yelling "Uncle Fred! Uncle Fred!" His mother couldn't talk him out of it. She had a Kelly green coat with big buttons. I remember her as a weary middle-aged lady, although I suppose, in retrospect, that she wasn't as old as I am now. You remember that song, *She was common, flirty, she looked about thirty*? It's like the difference between what that meant then and what it would mean today.

"I'm really sorry," she said. "He thinks you're his Uncle Fred."

"We'd gathered that," I said, snotty college kid.

"Timmy," she said, "this man is *not Uncle Fred*. See, his Uncle Fred"—she mouthed the word *died*. "We tried to explain it to him, but he doesn't get it. You know, he sort of gets it and he sort of doesn't."

"Time," said Michael. "In time these things become clearer." We were both pretty smashed.

"That's the thing of it," said the woman. "I don't think they really get it until they're a little older. When they're older they actually can get things. But a little kid?" She shook her head; he shook his head too. Big agreement reached about human nature. So it was Uncle Fred from then on.

The summer after freshman year, Uncle Fred and I and a kid named Kenny Angleton got a seventy-dollar-a-month apartment on East 10th Street. Angleton wore round wire-rim prescription sunglasses indoors and out, and always dressed in black jeans and black turtlenecks. No matter how hot it got—and this was a top-floor walk-up, right under the roof—he never rolled up the long sleeves that hid the tracks he didn't have. The day we moved in he went to 14th Street and bought a pair of ankle-high pointy-toed boots with Cuban heels. The heels were made of what looked and felt like cardboard, and they wore down in a week. So one night, about four in the morning, he bought a jar of Skippy at the all-night bodega and threw it through the window of the store where they'd sold him the boots. Or so he said. We'd all been up snorting methedrine and he came back in trembling, asking us if your fingerprints could be traced if you'd never been finger-printed. Not long after that he managed to get hold of some works, which he just took out and looked at for a week or so while snorting up as usual. The first time he tried to shoot himself up I watched until I got sick to my stomach, thinking if he could get it happening I'd maybe try it too. He tapped and tapped with his fingertip, trying not to hurt himself, then got impatient and howled when he jabbed the thing about half an inch in.

Although Uncle Fred and I never said so to each other, it was mostly to get away from Angleton and the people he'd started bringing around that the two of us went up to Connecticut to spend some time at his parents' house. Guilford had country roads to drive, in Uncle Fred's father's Buick, playing the radio loud: this was the summer of "Hanky Panky" and "Wild Thing." Not the "Wild Thing" they have now, where the guy just talks in rhyme the whole way through, but the real "Wild Thing," where he thinks she moves him but he doesn't know for sure. Woods to trip in, a village green to circle and circle and circle looking for girls, the beach at Hammonasset a couple of exits up the turnpike, New Haven with movies and Cutler's record store a few exits down. And Uncle Fred's fourteen-year-old sister always there when we got home: pretty enough to keep me stirred up, young enough not to have to do anything about.

We were still there when Uncle Fred's father got a four-day weekend because he'd had to work over the Fourth of July. He was going to spend it at their camp up in New Hampshire, putting up a lean-to to keep firewood under. (Right, same lean-to, same green fiberglass roof.) Mrs. Warriner said he'd do better to get going on the bathroom, and that all that hammering would give her a sick headache, and that she'd just as soon not go shacking all over Robin Hood's barn. Maybe Michael and his friend would like to go up and give a hand, and she and Diane would hold the fort and have a regular old hen party.

"Oh *man*," I said to Uncle Fred when I got him alone. We were supposed to have been getting together that weekend with some girl he knew from Clinton and some friend of hers whose parents were supposed to be away.

"It's cool up there," he said. "It'll be cool, promise. The old man just farts around and doesn't know *what's* happening." As if I'd had any choice anyway. My father had sold the house in the Springs—I think he let it go for twenty-five—and he'd sublet the place on Barrow

Street to somebody while he was in Mexico. So it was either stick with Uncle Fred or go back to 10th Street with Angleton sitting crosslegged on his mattress all night fucking around with his works and smoking Camels and scratching himself and jerking his head to the soul music on WWRL.

Late on a Friday afternoon, we bumped down the rutted track, kicking up a dustcloud, then straight across the big field, milkweed and goldenrod on both sides as high as the car windows. Right around the trailer itself the grass was kept down with a lawnmower, less grass really than dandelions and fuzzy pale-green lamb's-tongue. It was a plain old white house trailer, sitting out in the middle of things at the far end of the field. (It didn't get painted blue until years later, after Mr. Warriner died and Uncle Fred got the place.) A cinderblock for a doorstep. Behind the trailer the woods began, and above the treetops rose a hill shaped like the side view of the old Studebaker Grandpa Jernigan used to drive: a round peak, left side sloping away gradually, right side dropping steeply like the windshield of a car that was moving from left to right, the direction of time. Such a hill, I remembered from eighth-grade Earth Science, was called a *roche moutonnée*: that is, a sheep-shaped rock. Years later, when Judith and I had taken over the place on Barrow Street, we came in with groceries one afternoon and found the kitchen counter alive with cockroaches. "Well well," I said, always lightsome, "a roach matinee." She didn't seem to get it. And I thought, Oh well, so one more little thing.

But we're jumping all around here and losing track. Not that I mind losing track, far from it. But.

The camp had no electricity then: just kerosene lamps and an ice chest. An outhouse, since the bathroom in the trailer wasn't hooked up to anything yet. I was given Diane's tiny room, and I remember quietly sneaking her bureau drawer open and looking at her underwear and then feeling ashamed of myself. When everybody went to bed, I got stoned in there all alone, knowing it was piggish not to share with Uncle Fred. I was careful to light up by the window and blow the smoke out through the aluminum screen. Then, in that soft yellow light, I tried to read the Wallace Stevens book I'd brought, until the name Wallace started to sound funny: Wallace Wallace Wallace Wallace Wallace.

The Warriners had a croquet set and an aluminum rowboat you could put on the roof of the car and take to the pond a mile farther up the town road. And an old lever-action Winchester, the kind of rifle on tv westerns. They just left all this stuff there: no problem in those days with anybody coming in and stealing. Saturday afternoon Mr. Warriner knocked off work on the lean-to and we all drank beer out of the ice chest and shot the Winchester at the empty cans, each shot just echoing and echoing again off those hills. He turned out to be a great guy, Mr. Warriner, and not the Nazi I'd expected because he worked in a machine shop. That night he took us to a bar, a small cinderblock building with a big gravel parking lot, where they had a country-western band and didn't card me and Uncle Fred. The two of us by ourselves probably would've gotten in trouble because of our hair, but Mr. Warriner looked like everybody else in there with his burr haircut and his green work pants.

We got back to the camp drunk and Mr. Warriner went right to bed. Uncle Fred and I went into my room and took apart the last cap of the acid we'd brought from the city, divided the powder with a matchbook and washed it down with a beer from the ice chest. When the acid came on we prowled in the scary woods and walked what seemed to be miles of dirt roads under the full moon, the dirt still warm to our bare feet. Then the sun came up and we were swimming naked in a muck-bottomed pond somewhere and mist was rising from the surface. I thought of my breast-stroking arms as wings, and the water as viscous air through which I flew in slow motion. At some point I left Uncle Fred alone in the water, knowing in one part of my mind—I also knew it was a bad idea to think about your mind too much—that you shouldn't leave somebody alone in the water on LSD. I walked, naked, in the dewy grass, hoping it would feel like a dawn-of-man thing but actually shivering and worrying that the radiation in early-morning sunlight, slanting through the atmosphere at a special penetrating angle, would wither my dick or that some buzzy insect might sting it. Then I panicked about Uncle Fred drowning and went running back to the pond. Which turned out to be about ten steps away: the music I'd been listening to all this time, which I'd been assuming was just a pleasant hallucination, was actually Uncle Fred singing arpeggios—ha ha ha HA ha ha ha—slapping his palms on the surface of the water in rhythm and marvelling at the echoes. Of which there were many, many. I told Uncle Fred—and I wasn't trying to flatter him at all—that it was the most incredible music I'd ever heard, more incredible than, like, Mahler. Don't ask me why Mahler. Then we found our way back to the trailer, with the sun making jewels of dew in the grass, and managed to stay pretty much out of Mr. Warriner's way until we'd come down enough to get to sleep, which wasn't until fairly late that afternoon.

End of reminiscence.

3

I woke up in the cold, in gray light. So the fire had gone out while I'd slept the day away, on the floor, in this musty-smelling shithole of a trailer. I took my hands out of my armpits and put them over my cold face, cold nose especially. All that accomplished was to make the hands cold too. Left hand still hurt like a bastard, plainly not healing at all, and now that I was awake enough to think a little, I wondered if it wasn't the pain that had finally awakened me, and not the cold. Although it could also have been the other pain: the headache going in like a drillbit above the right eye. I threw off the blankets, squirmed back into my cold overcoat and got to my feet so as to be up off that cold floor. Better drag one of the mattresses in here; make a good little project for later. I switched on the floorlamp next to the sofa, but the son of a bitch didn't *go* on. I lifted the shade and tilted my head: oh, there was a bulb in there all right. I pulled the string hanging from the fluorescent ring on the kitchen ceiling: that wouldn't go on either. So no power, apparently. On the kitchen counter I found a kerosene lamp with a couple of fingers of kerosene in it. The wick was all fucked up, but I didn't feel like hunting around for scissors that I'd end up not finding anyway, so I just lit the thing and it seemed to do okay, considering. I located the bottle of Pamprin in my overcoat pocket. Only four left. I swallowed all of them, fuck it. Except then they got stuck in my throat and I could feel them caught down in there. So I went out the back door and knelt by the woodpile and ate snow until I felt the sons of bitches break loose and go down. I looked up and saw a last pulsation of sun behind Studebaker Hill: then it was gone and instantly the air got even colder although I was probably just imagining it. I brought in another few armloads of logs and finally got the stove roaring again.

Then I didn't know what to do next.

I tried sitting in different places: the stinky sofa, then a red-painted wooden dinette chair, then the stinky easychair covered in some kind of old brownish fabric with flowers or shrimps or something. The problem was, I didn't know how to be still. I got up and walked down the hall to the room that used to be Diane's. She'd gotten married to somebody years ago and they'd built a house on some island near Seattle where they still are for all I know. *Or* fucking care. There was a pinstriped single mattress, the old kind with buttons, still on the little maple bedstead. I hauled it off the bed by its handles and walked it back down the hall to where the stove was and flopped it down on the floor, puffing up dust. I lay down on it, still in my overcoat. On my side. On my back. On my other side. On my stomach. So much for the possibilities. But I couldn't get myself to where I felt like I was lying flat enough. I got up again and went looking for something to read. The table at one end of the sofa turned out to have books on its bottom shelf. Books that years ago Mr. and Mrs. Warriner must have thought of as light weekend reading for the country: Thorne Smith, Agatha Christie, P. G. Wodehouse, single volumes containing three Ellery Queens apiece. Unless of course this was more of the Uncle Fred touch, books he'd chosen to parody the idea of light weekend reading for the country. So I took the P. G. Wodehouse over to the easychair. To sit in this trailer and be able to fix your mind on Blandings Castle—hey, if only.

Well, I could stay with P. G. Wodehouse for about two sentences.

Then I got afraid the telephone was going to ring. It was the old kind you can't unplug. Not modular is what I'm trying to say. I picked up the receiver to check, and the phone was dead too. I mean, use your head: would Uncle Fred have left the phone hooked up, for Christ's sake, so people could break in, not even *break* in for Christ's sake, and call places and he's stuck with the bill? The power either. People coming in with, I don't know, electric space heaters or something.

I thought about trying to find a saucepan and melting some snow on top of the woodstove, as if on an Everest expedition. Now there's the real world for you, real factual information about what people do on Mount Everest. God damned good and tired around here listening to all this shit about how Jernigan only lives in his own head.

Thought, too, about trying to find some paper and writing to my son, asking his forgiveness. Oh, not for anything all that specific. It would be the thought that counted. Except what were you going to say after asking forgiveness? Pledge to do better? Right, I can see you now, doing better.

And then I thought about prostrating myself right that minute on the floor and just praying to be subsumed, if they were still subsuming people these days. The old *Not my will but Thine, O Lord, be done.* What I imagined I was hanging on to at that point I can't imagine. Same shit probably that I'm hanging on to now. The people who run the program here say I have to give it up. But as a matter of fact, I already—though I haven't told them this—I already made that surrender once, years ago. Sort of made it. The *last* time I found myself drinking a quart a day of whatever there was. Danny was two, screaming his head off about everything, and the walls of that apartment on Barrow Street were falling in on me, and an old friend of my father's took me to his AA meeting. Sculptor. He'd once suggested, years before, taking my father to one. (You can imagine.) At any rate, I'd apparently broken into this guy's studio and passed out on the floor. I was willing, at that point, to give anything a shot. Partly because it scared me that I really couldn't remember how I'd gotten into his studio. And partly for Danny, who hadn't fucking asked to be born. They said, *Keep coming back; it works.* I did. It did. So there I was holding hands with everybody standing in a circle and saying the Lord's Prayer, which I'd never learned as a child because Francis Jernigan was enlightened and my mother was an old party-line lefty. Well so of course I immediately loved the Lord's Prayer. But later it began to scare me what I was praying for. *Forgive us our trespasses as we forgive those who trespass against us?* I could hear an "insofar" in there, the catch calculated to keep me forever unforgiven. And was I really ready for God's Kingdom to come? I kept imagining a nuclear shitstorm. And of course eventually I became less keen on being led not into temptation. I finally got the thing down to *Our Father who art in heaven, give us this day our daily bread and deliver us from evil, amen.* And then I suspected there might be a catch even in *that*, that God could take it literally and you'd get nothing but bread. Anyway, by this time I was already telling myself Fuck it, you're on top of it again so so what's the big problem? I started having a beer once in a while and nothing terrible happened. So why don't you just keep your mouth shut, I told myself, and hope you squeak by.

They hate this kind of thinking here.

But who *isn't* just hoping to squeak by? Uncle Fred? Fine: let me tell you about Uncle Fred. This is Midsummer Acid Idyll Part II, okay? We're up all night tripping and so forth and so on and we get back to the trailer in the morning and so on, this part you know. So we go into Uncle Fred's room. Starting to come down, but hours from being able to sleep. And as the birdies sing outside the window, Uncle Fred explains to me exactly how he's going to kill himself. He's going to come up here in the wintertime, walk into the woods far beyond human earshot, chain and padlock himself to a tree and then toss the key away into the snow. He's got the chain and padlock there under his bed! He lifted a corner of the blanket and dragged them out to show me. So just remember that the next time Uncle Fred greets somebody by saying *Stand and give the password.* Or any of the rest of that hearty horseshit.

And in case you think that was just adolescence, here's another Uncle Fred story. Two summers ago I was up at the camp for a weekend. Or three, I don't know. I know it was when Judith was still alive, because I remember how quick Uncle Fred and Penny were to accept my bullshit explanation of why she'd decided at the last minute to stay home with Danny. At that time Uncle Fred had added a boombox to the amenities, and a bunch of Merle Haggard and George Jones tapes. Country music for the country: you'd have to know Uncle Fred to see that what he was doing was parodying the whole idea that things fit together. Except that he'd also started to like country music. Penny had gone to bed and we were sitting outside drinking Jack Daniel's under the bug-zapper. No other light but its purple glow, and a crescent moon just above the hilltop. Stars. We'd brought the boombox out, and Merle Haggard was singing a song about how a shrink gives him a Rorschach test and the inkblots look like broken hearts—kind of strained, I thought—when Uncle Fred announced that he, Uncle Fred, was an apostrophe. I thought that what he meant was *apostate* and I asked for some clarification on that. "It's like I'm what's there to show that something's missing," he said. Then he leaned forward and vomited. When he sat up again, he wiped his mouth with his hand and begged me to get a shovel and cover over the vomit so Penny wouldn't know in the morning. Which of course I did.

Well, the boombox didn't seem to be here now. Either thieves had gotten it or Uncle Fred had taken it back to the city. But sitting down on the sofa again I felt something and I reached under me and found the empty plastic case for *Serving 190 Proof*. It made me want to hear Merle Haggard's voice. I had my Walkman here somewhere, unless I'd left it back in the car. I thought about getting up and starting to lift sofa cushions and shit, looking for the tape itself. But the point is, here I was wanting one more fucking thing. And I could see that after that I was just going to keep wanting the next thing and the next thing and the next. Imagine thinking this was the end.

II

1

The Fourth of July had come around again. Even now, at eleven in the morning, you could hear firecrackers. Tonight, as dogs howled, they'd be setting off the big display over the lake.

Judith died a year ago today.

By way of commemoration I was going to mow the lawn and watch the Yankee game and try to figure out the evening from there. Oh, I know how bad this sounds: okay, fine. So what do *you* think would have been appropriate? There wasn't even a grave to visit. Her brother, Rick, had remembered her saying once that when she died she wanted her ashes scattered off Montauk Point. She was probably half in the bag, assuming Rick hadn't just dreamed the whole thing up. But once he'd said it, we obviously had to do it. Now *there* was a day, the day we drove out there to scatter the fucking ashes. Day after the funeral. We had to walk with this cardboard box for what must have been a mile of beach looking for someplace where there wouldn't be a hundred people on blankets watching you do this thing, which I think was against the law to boot. Just me and Rick along on this one. I thought it was something Danny could skip: he'd been taking the whole thing so calmly that it was scaring the shit out of me. By the time we found a spot, we weren't really that near Montauk Point anymore. Even getting the box open was more hassle than you'd expect—I ended up cutting through the tape with the Powerful Pete on my key ring—and then the ashes didn't scatter much, since there were chunks of bone and stuff and neither of us wanted to touch it with his hands. So I just kind of threw it out toward the water and some of the ashier shit came back down in a gray heap on the wet part of the sand where the waves didn't quite reach. We didn't know whether the tide was coming in or going out; if it was going out, the stuff was going to have to sit there for another eleven hours. Or was it another twenty-three? So I took the edge of my hand and brushed from side to side and they sort of smeared and we got the hell out of there.

Anyhow.

I went into the garage to get out the lawnmower, and there was my father's old scythe hanging by its blade from a spike in one of the studs. I hadn't had occasion to touch it since the day we moved here, when I drove the spike in, hung the scythe from it and steadied it with a fingertip to stop its swinging. Today I felt pity for the thing (yes, yes, displaced) and took it down. I hunted around for the whetstone, then spat on the blade and started honing, using the stroke he'd taught me: not back and forth, but going in little tight spirals, spitting and honing. A technique handed down, doubtless, to my father from his and so on. Unless my father had read it in *Popular Mechanics* or something. (He used to like *Popular Mechanics* for the pictures of machines, and the men wearing ties in their home workshops.) I will be the last Jernigan, most likely, to know the Jernigan scythe-lore. Which might go all the way back to when the Jernigans were landless scum in whatever dismal county it was. My father hated all that wearin'-o'-the-green crap, wouldn't even have Yeats in his library. Embarrassed, of course, by *his* father. Grandpa Jernigan. About whom I remember only the old Studebaker he drove, the liquor on his breath, and being taken to his wake and getting scared he was really going to wake up. So naturally my father hated having a grandson named Danny. The name was Judith's idea. She had a dead uncle or something named Daniel, and I didn't care one way or the other. At least not until that Elton John song came out about the scar that won't heal, and by then Danny was a year or so old. At any rate, my father used to greet him by singing out "Oh Dahnny Biiy!" in a Dennis Day tenor. And then he wondered why Danny never came to visit.

He was giving me the scythe, my father had said, in honor of my coming to my senses and getting out of New York. "Besides," he said, "*I* don't dare use the son of a bitch anymore." Talking about his heart.

"It's a God damn tract house in New *Jersey*," I said. "What am I going to do with a scythe on a quarter-acre lawn?"

"So what're you doing pissing your money away on a place you don't *like?*" he said. "Find yourself some handyman special in Westchester or something. Rockland. Something with a *little* charm to it. Christ's sake."

"Right," I said. "You price any handyman specials in Westchester lately?"

"All right, all right, it *has* to be Jersey, then. All right? Then you look for something on one of your older streets, even if the house itself is a little run-down."

"Pop," I said. "Forget it. I'm into the degradation, you know?"

"You think you're kidding," he said. "Here, you better take this with you anyway. It's a nice old thing. Even if you just hang it on the wall and think about mortality, for God's sake. Hell, you'll have *my* place one of these days. Then you'll need three of these sons of bitches to keep ahead of the God damn sumac."

I was wiping motor oil onto the now-silvery-edged blade when I saw Danny standing in the door to the breezeway. "Hey Dad?" he said. "You got a minute? Can I just play you this one neat thing?"

The anniversary didn't seem to be getting him down any, though with Danny you never knew. If he'd forgotten—though how could you forget the Fourth of July?—*I* sure as hell wasn't going to bring it up. But wasn't it my fatherly duty to draw him out about what he must be feeling? But on the other hand, might it not be my fatherly duty to shut the fuck up and let him handle it his own way? Certainly that was a more comfortable view of my fatherly duty. I followed him back into the house. In his bedroom, he handed me the Rockman I'd insisted he get as a condition of having an electric guitar in the house. So now I worried that he was deafening himself with the earphones. And worried, too, that I was a bad father for trading his hearing for my tranquillity. Such as it was.

"No way," I said, handing it back, afraid of a blast of noise God knows how loud stabbing my eardrums. "Put it through your amp, why don't you. Let's hear what you got."

"Sure, great," he said. He unplugged and replugged cords; the amplifier gave an echoing pop, warning of the vast deep silence about to be filled.

"Just not *too* loud, right?" I said. "The old man doesn't have mutant ears."

He picked the guitar up off the bed and slung it around him on its strap. "Okay now, watch," he said. "I just learned this. Ready?" And he ripped off an ascending snarl of notes, both hands tearing away at the strings. It certainly sounded plausible. Even exciting in that cheap way.

"Yeah," I said. "Sounding good on that, big guy."

"Yeah, but did you see it?" he said. "What my hand was doing?"

"What was I supposed to see?"

"Watch me again," he said. "No, look. Watch my *right* hand." I watched, trying to ignore the godawful studded leather thing on his wrist, a gift from his little girlfriend. He played exactly the same sequence of notes again, as far as I could tell. (I'd wondered the first time if it had just been some random gabble spewed out any old way his fingers had happened to move.) "You see it?" he said.

"What am I missing?" I said.

"That last note," he said. "To get it you have to come up *here*, see, with *this* hand. That's what's normally your picking hand. But you could never get your left hand all the way up from here to here that quick."

"You're really serious about this, aren't you?" I said. "How come you don't want to be in a band?" Mistake: asking Why Questions was just a way of giving people shit. Judith and I had learned that in cognitive therapy. One more thing we'd tried.

Danny said nothing. I stared, as I always did when I was in here, at his poster of blank-faced Elle Macpherson just about to rip open the front of her bathing suit. A Grecian Urn for the Dannys of the world. Well, at least we hadn't made him a homosexual, although of course I knew that you didn't *make* someone a homosexual. But thinking about Rick you wondered if Judith might have been carrying a homosexual gene or something that was in the family. I was relieved that it had stayed recessive (if it existed) although that was wrong too, to feel relieved, because homosexuality was just another way of being. And this guitar business was something else to be relieved about. True, he was getting C's in school, but sitting down and actually working out something like the little move he'd just showed me argued that he wasn't without some self-discipline, and that his attention span was all right even though I had taken LSD and he had watched so much television. Who knows, maybe the guitar might actually get him something. Oh, I know better than to think it's all emperor's new clothes and that you can be a rock-and-roll star without any talent whatsoever. But neither do you have to be a commanding genius; we all know that too. So why not Danny? And all that watch-me stuff: he seemed to be enough of a ham to get up in front of people. So why *wasn't* he in some little band? And why wasn't it all right to ask?

"Forget it," I said. "Look, I'm not trying to tell you how to have fun. The only thing I want to say about it is, if you ever do want to have some kids over to the house to play or something, it's fine with me." Part of why I was offering this was that he was spending too much time at the girlfriend's and I had an idea the girlfriend's mother wasn't providing much supervision. Though *I* was a great one to talk.

He shrugged. "Okay," he said. I marvelled at the fine balance of his mind: my offer had just enough of an undertone so that to have thanked me would have compromised his dignity. It was neurotic to worry that he'd been born with something wrong.

"Okay," I said. "Listen, the lawn beckons. If you want to keep playing, you don't have to bother with the headphones, 'cause I'm going to be making some noise myself."

"Okay," he said. "Except if you're mowing the lawn I might put 'em on so *I* can hear."

"Up to you entirely," I said. "Catch you later." And I went back to the garage, feeling satisfied with my son, despite everything.

I hefted the gasoline can: that plus what was already in the mower ought to be plenty. But if I went now and filled the can up again, I'd be all set the next time I had to cut the grass. Nothing like being all set. So I took the funnel off its nail, topped off the lawnmower's tank, then carried the can out to the driveway. I set it on the blacktop next to the Datsun and went in for my keys, worrying about an explosion. This is how it would happen: black retains heat, therefore heat from the blacktop would touch off what gas remained in the can, which would touch off the gas tank of the Datsun. "Hey Danny?" I called from the kitchen. "I'm going over to Hamilton Ave, to get some gas. Need anything?" But he must have had his earphones on.

At the Gulf station, I stood uselessly watching as the guy filled the gas can—here in the Garden State they actually don't allow you to be a man and pump your own; some union bullshit—and the digital display raced from cent to cent to cent. And I started thinking about the time I was over at Philip Adler's with my father and asking, little Irish boy that I was, why he had a candle burning in a jelly glass. Philip Adler said it was the day his grandmother had died. I was confused about whether his grandmother had died that very day, and if so, why things seemed so normal, but I was cagey enough to wait until we left before asking my father.

So after all, I couldn't just let this day go by.

So I stopped at the mall and found a Hallmark Cards, and sure enough: Yahrzeit lamps with bar-coded labels. Back home, I got out matches and a saucer to set the thing on. I considered calling Danny out to light it with me, but then I thought No, let him be. Out of fear, I imagine. (What fear? Fear that he would finally snap and I

wouldn't know what to do. Fear that he would, finally, accuse me.)
So I took the whole setup into the bedroom, shut the door, lit the
wick and said a prayer while staring at the flame: Dear God, please
bless Judith wherever she is, or whatever she is. All very theological.
And in such terrific taste, too, standing there God-blessing a wife
who might still be alive if you had, or hadn't, done this, that or the
other thing. And all the time my father probably looking on from the
spirit world with amused contempt, though at least it wasn't a Catholic
candle. This one would keep going for twenty-four hours, and probably then some. Less dazzling than starbursts over a lake, but more
lasting. Three or four seconds of starburst compared to twenty-four
hours of candlelight, I thought, made a good, graspable analogy to
the soul's short residence in the body as against its duration in eternity.

$$\frac{a}{b} = \frac{c}{\infty}$$

Let a = the starburst, let b = the candlelight, let c = the thirty-five
years of Judith's life. Though isn't it true that once you've put infinity
on one side of your equation you've got an equation that no longer
makes any sense? I stood looking at the flame, thinking how ignorant
I was of mathematics. Then I went out and got busy on that lawn.

It really didn't need mowing out back by the pool, but since I was
doing the front anyway I thought I'd keep it all the same length. It
was an easy lawn to mow: none of this shit where you had to go up
on two wheels to trim around rocks or what have you. It all broke
down into squares and rectangles; I marched around and around,
diminishing them. It was a chance to think, that's what I didn't like
about it. But it was repetitive, which tended after a while to soothe.
So, six of one. By the time I'd finished, I didn't feel any worse.

I put the lawnmower away and headed through the breezeway for
the kitchen, forcing myself to stop once and smell the newly cut grass
for a second through the screening. On the theory that it was the
little moments that counted. A drop of sweat from the end of my
nose splatted on the cement: was that splat, too, an event to be cher-
ished? Fact was, the only moment that I really gave a shit about just

then was the moment I could feel that first gulp of cold beer in my mouth, my throat, all down inside. So I went on into the kitchen, letting the screen door slam behind me, and a few seconds later I heard Danny's door close, way down the hall. Then I realized I didn't hear the guitar going. So he was probably in there reading. (Little joke.) Then I remembered: headphones. I got a beer out of the refrigerator. I had thought there were four left, but there were only three in there now. Well, so Danny was sneaking beers: okay, could be worse. Probably *was* worse. At any rate, I didn't feel like confronting him about a God damn bottle of beer, especially when I wasn't absolutely sure there was one missing in the first place. Be wrong just once about something like that and your kid would never trust you again.

The Yankee game ought to be just about getting started. I turned on the tv and the image gave a little twist as it jerked into focus: green grass, brown earth, white lines. No wonder my father had loved to watch baseball. Assuming it was the shapes and colors that appealed to him rather than the idea of himself preferring baseball to, say, an opera. (This would have been a typical Francis Jernigan move, like the way he used to make the argument that *Peyton Place* was greater than *Madame Bovary*, I forget exactly why anymore.) Me, I just used baseball to numb myself. You know, like everything else. Overhead shot of the infield from behind the plate. Cut to the pitcher, seen from center field, leaning in for the sign. Cut to batter (right-handed), catcher and umpire, seen from field level, near the dugout. Catcher in white, batter in gray. Therefore still the top of the first: imagine knowing this. So the next couple of hours were taken care of. The batter swung and missed, the catcher bobbled the ball, tagged the batter and tossed the ball away and everybody trotted off and they went to the first commercial, for Chevrolet, the Heartbeat of America. I liked the little tune they had in this one, and I also liked knowing that I wasn't so easily worked on as to want to go out and buy a new Chevrolet just on the strength of some fucking little tune. My shitheap of a Datsun would do fine, and when it stopped doing fine I'd get some other shitheap to get me to and from the station. So at least this was one vanity with which I didn't have to tax myself.

Then I realized that I was beginning to smell something, if I wasn't just imagining it. Smelled like pot, except now I didn't smell it anymore. Then I smelled it again. Fuck, now this really *did* have to be checked out. I put my beer down on the floor (God damn carpeting in here so thick a bottle wouldn't stay standing on it) and now I saw I'd tracked grass clippings all over the fucking place. Well, so who was going to come in and be scandalized.

I knocked on Danny's door. You could definitely smell smoke, boy. "Yeah?" he said.

"I come in a second?"

Pause. "Okay," he said. "If you want to."

I opened the door and he was sitting, as before, on his bed, guitar in his lap, headphones around his neck like a dog collar, the padded earpieces touching at his throat. Now that I could really smell it, I could tell it was just tobacco. Impaled on the snipped-off end of one of the guitar strings, a filter cigarette smoldered away. At least he hadn't humiliated himself by trying to hide it.

"How long have you been doing *this*?" I said, pointing.

He looked at his feet, shrugged. "I don't know," he said. "A year. Am I going to get in trouble?"

"I guess not," I said. "I mean, not from *me*. It's not a moral issue." Which might have been true, but I didn't really think so. I found something indecently sexual about a fifteen-year-old smoking a cigarette. What I must have meant was that it *shouldn't* be a moral issue. "But," I said, "it's a truly stupid habit. I mean, I know how boring all this Voice of Experience shit is, but believe me. I had a hell of a time quitting, and the fact is that I didn't even really enjoy the things. Smoking *dope* makes more sense, you know? Not that I want you to be smoking dope, but that at least *does* something, you know? All this does is make you feel lousy."

"It relaxes me," he said.

"*Relaxes* you?" I said. "Christ's sake, you're fifteen years old. Relaxes you from *what*?" Oh, I know, another mistake. I knew it even as I was saying it.

He just looked at me, with contempt.

2

Judith and Danny had enjoyed each other more before he reached puberty, big surprise. Though I don't know how much you can actually attribute to puberty, since those were the years she enjoyed everything less and less. But when he was a kid Judith used to teach him kid things she thought he should know. Shake Spear Kick in the Rear. Your Teeth Are Like Stars They Come Out at Night. It wasn't that she was so full of life: what she liked was that the hilarity could go out of these things and leave the shape behind. So she and I understood each other. In that respect. Take the Powerful Pete she gave me. Chrome-plated disk that goes on your key ring, with screwdriver tips at each of the four compass points and a cartoon strongman stamped in the center. The kind of thing a kid would get a bang out of. Its appeal for us was that here was this thing practically begging you to get a bang out of it yet you were too jaded to get a bang out of it. Which was in itself a species of bang. I don't know, maybe this isn't so remarkable. Big deal, we both had a sense of camp. Of course with the added fillip of giving Powerful Pete to somebody named Peter. Who supposedly had a powerful peter. Which was getting to be an issue along about then.

She gave me the Powerful Pete on her thirtieth birthday, which she had forbidden me to do anything about. In part for the obvious reason, and in part because we hadn't been getting along. We were in the car outside the Robinsons' house, waiting for Danny's Cub Scout meeting to be over so we could go out to dinner. If you could call Roy Rogers out to dinner.

"*Your* birthday and you're giving *me* a present," I said. None too pleased with all this martyrdom. Roy Rogers had been her idea.

"Old hobbit custom," she said. "You give other people gifts on your birthday and that way you get lots of gifts back and they're spaced out during the year." She and Danny were reading Tolkien together.

I rolled my eyes. "Oop, sor-*ry*," she said. "Pardon the enthusiasm." I had refused to have anything to do with the Tolkien project.

When Danny found out where we were going he wasn't any happier than I was. He said Roy Rogers was rotten and why couldn't we go to McDonald's like everybody else did. Judith told him it was Mommy's night to howl, and went *ah-OOO* like a lonesome ki-yote and that cracked him up. He had fried chicken and an iced tea; Judith had a cheeseburger, french fries and a chocolate shake and said Roy Rogers was her favorite place to eat in the whole world. I had two biscuits, the only trustworthy thing at Roy Rogers, and a cup of coffee.

"Did you ever read *The Answer Is God*?" she said. She was holding up a french fry with thumb and forefinger, considering it from different angles.

"I must have missed that one," I said.

"*You* know," she said. "About their re-tard kid?" She turned to Danny and said, "No offense." He cracked up again.

"Who had a retarded kid?" I said. She looked at me pityingly.

We'd only had a couple of glasses of wine before leaving to get Danny, although Judith had a way of getting more into her than you were aware of, always sipping lightly from a glass that was always full. After Danny went to bed, she polished off the rest of the bottle in the refrigerator and opened a new one. I helped her polish that one off, and we'd gotten most of the way through yet another by the time the eleven o'clock news was over. The late movie was *The Girl Can't Help It*, and we'd been telling each other all evening that we were looking forward to it. When the Little Richard part came on, Judith jumped up and insisted on being danced with. "Are you kidding?" I said. "I want to *watch* this. Look at how fucking scary he is."

"You pathetic, life-denying—" She shook her head. "I can't even think of a right noun. A *noun* is a verb of *being*, and you don't even *have* any being."

"Okay," I said. "Sounds like time for beddy-bye." I don't suppose I really thought that once her head hit the pillow she'd pass out and that would be the end of it. Probably I just wanted to get the subject of bed stirred up again so she'd really start behaving unforgivably, so I'd have another thing not to forgive. And sure enough. See, we really *were* partners.

"Beddy-bye to do what?" she said. "So you can roll on your side with your limp dick between your legs?"

"Right," I said, getting up and facing her, all charged up now to throw the Don't Argue With Them When They're Drunk rule out the window. "You make yourself so *appealing*, I can't understand why I'm not hard for you twenty-four hours a day."

She picked up her glass from the coffee table. "Oh *Peter*," she said, in her mock in-love voice. "Wouldn't it be romantic if we had a fireplace right on that wall?" She pointed, then threw the glass. Overhand. I thought the noise would bring Danny out of his room, but he must have been far down in Stage Two sleep, or whatever stage it is. Either that or he knew better by now. She flopped back down on the couch and stared up at me. "As usual," she said, "you're just totally the master of the situation. Judith behaves herself so badly, and all *Peter* is doing is *blamelessly* trying to keep things under control."

"Whatever," I said. "I'm going to sleep. Good night."

"It's so thrilling," she said, "the way you *dominate* me. Oh Peter, I'm your *dog*. Rip my clothes off and *fuck* me." She bared her teeth. Then she laughed, and kept laughing, which was scarier than the teeth. "*Oh* my," she said, finally. "In the morning I am going to be *so* contrite. And that won't touch your heart either."

3

One year ago today.

We had invited people over for the Fourth, and I'd put in the invitation that the theme of this year's party would be entrepreneurship. Entrepreneurial foods would be served—Perdue chicken, Ben & Jerry's—and everyone was to come dressed as an entrepreneur. When they called up to ask what the fuck *that* meant, I got to tell them just to wear whatever they'd normally wear because in America anybody could be an entrepreneur. All so clever. This was the kind of fun we used to affect to like, Judith and me. Penny and Uncle Fred put off their weekend in New Hampshire for a day and came out from the city. And a couple from here named Steve and Sandy, who were about the only people in town we socialized with. Judith had met the wife at yoga. And Rick, Judith's brother, and Rick's friend Rich (which she and I agreed was probably a little narcissistic on both their parts), who were visiting from Minneapolis. Steve and Sandy, it turned out, almost didn't come because Steve had been offended by the invitation. He had his own business, a store in the mall called Bedford Falls Video. I don't know why I thought he'd have a sense of humor about entrepreneurship. In fact I probably *didn't* think it. Probably I was doing something I knew would piss him off because Sandy was Judith's friend and I resented having her friends foisted off on me even though she endlessly put up with having Uncle Fred foisted off on her. At least that's the way Judith saw it. Or said she saw it, once a fight got going.

It had become clear over the years that Judith shouldn't drink. But one glass of wine had never been a problem, and it didn't lead in every case to another glass and another. We were drinking Gallo that day because the only entrepreneurial beer we could think of was Coors and Judith refused to have Coors in the house. And because Ernesto and Julio Gallo embodied the immigrant spirit. And because drinking white wine, even Gallo, on the Fourth of July was another fuck-you touch. We were all sitting around the pool in bathing suits—it was an aboveground pool with this redwood deck going around it on three sides—and I suppose I wasn't watching Judith as closely as I might have been because I was talking with this Sandy and thinking about how much better I liked the shape of her breasts than the shape of Judith's, an awful thing to remember now. Judith also made several trips back and forth to the house: to fetch food, to carry back dirty dishes and leftovers. I should have helped. Not just out of simple decency, but because she was probably sneaking gin in the kitchen every time she went in. The alcohol level they found in her blood argued that she'd had much more than the few glasses of wine we'd seen her drink.

This shitbox house of ours didn't have any back door—just a blank wall with a couple of small, high windows—so you had to walk all the way around the fucking garage to get into the kitchen through the breezeway. I couldn't imagine how the people who'd lived here before could have gone to the expense of putting in a pool—I hope you didn't think *we'd* put it in—and then not bothered to put a lousy screen door on the back side of the breezeway so you could get out to it. Then again, we'd been here, what, ten years and hadn't bothered either.

So after several of these trips back and forth, Judith just lay back on her lounge chair not talking to anybody. Peaceful day. Sandy sitting between Steve's spread legs, lucky guy. Rick and his friend holding hands and pretending not to be self-conscious, Uncle Fred looking away from them. Me listening to Penny talk about going back to the Ph.D. program part time. She was talking away and I was thinking about how she called it "her" Ph.D., as if it were somewhere waiting for her, when Judith got up, came over, stood staring down at me and said, "Is there anything you *can't* fuck up? I mean, once you really set your mind to it?" She started out on Steve and the entrepreneur thing—I looked over and I saw him start whispering to Sandy—and then she went on to no sex in the marriage, which wasn't even true, technically. By this time everybody on fucking Heritage Circle could have heard her. Finally she gave me the finger and dived knifelike into the pool. Everybody stood up. She swam to the shallow end, stood up, unhooked the top of her suit and hurled it at me. Then she peeled the bottom down her legs, stepped out of it and hurled that too. I climbed into the water to get hold of her and she hauled herself out, naked, dripping, and ran across the deck in front of everybody, down the steps, across the grass and around the garage.

I got into the kitchen in time to hear the front door slam. I looked out the kitchen window and saw her, still naked, getting into the Honda. (We had a new Honda Civic in addition to my shitheap Datsun.) She started the engine and revved it to a roar. I ran back through the breezeway and out to the drive, grabbed for the door handle and missed as the car leaped into reverse. She backed into the street at what must have been twenty miles an hour, looking not over her shoulder but right into my eyes: with hate. Hornblast, shriek of tires. The van that hit her, it had no chance to stop.

When I looked again I could see her hair, and one arm draped over some metal. Not moving. The driver of the van, either. He had gone through his windshield and was jackknifed at the waist, his legs still in the cab, his arms and head hanging down, fingers just touching his own bumper, as if he were diving.

I ran into the house but Rick was already in there shouting into the telephone, and back outside a crowd had gathered around the car and the van. But nobody was getting too close. It looked like a scene out of an old *Twilight Zone*, neighbors on some little suburban street looking at the flying saucer whose arrival would soon reveal what fascists they all were. Pretty inappropriate thing to be thinking, but. The whole thing, in fact, looked as if it were in black and white. I should have gone and pushed through the crowd and done something. Later they told me it had been over instantly: no blame. Right. But at any rate, I walked around the end of the garage instead and back to the pool, now deserted. I climbed the steps up onto the deck, felt like I was going to black out, quick sat down on something, and when the shiny flecks stopped swimming in front of my eyes I looked down and saw her wet footprints fading.

They questioned us at the kitchen table, a cop with a heavy gun in a heavy gunbelt sitting in my usual place, from which I had carved turkeys and asked blessings, rolling my eyes ceilingward so nobody missed the irony.

"It was just a family party," I said. Except Rick was actually the only family. "I mean family and friends."

"Must have been some family party," the cop said. "Doing a little coke to celebrate the Fourth? We'll be getting a lab report, but you could save time."

I shook my head. "It was just a normal thing," I said.

"This is a normal thing to you, your wife out driving the car without her clothes on?"

Rick spoke up. "What are you saying?" he said. "You're talking to him like this was his fault. I'm her brother, you know? We *all* thought she was all right, and she *was* all right and everybody was just having a good time and it was normal like he *said*."

"And you're her brother?" said the cop. Looking at Rick's too-trim body and too-neat mustache.

At least Danny hadn't been home. He'd gone off with his friend Warren Robinson and Warren's family for a picnic at the lake. I say at least, though in fact it might have been better for him to have been there and seen it happen and know for sure that there was nothing anybody could have done. Although on the other hand, if he'd seen it he'd have those pictures in his head. The hair, the arm. Not that he doesn't probably have pictures in his head anyway. But at least they're probably not accurate. Oh, at least at least at least.

I called the Robinsons' house but of course got only the machine. So the thing to do was to drive out to the lake and try to find them, if that was the thing to do.

"Michael," I said to Uncle Fred. "What am I going to do about Danny? Should I go out to the lake right now and go looking all over hell for him and break up the Robinsons' picnic? You know, there's like a million picnic areas. Plus the Robinsons are going to shit. I sort of feel there's nothing anybody can do anyway, so why not let 'em, you know, have their day?"

"Fuck the Robinsons and their fucking *day*, man," he said. "Whoever the fucking Robinsons are. You let Danny fuck around all afternoon at some picnic and he will never forgive you, man, I'll guarantee."

So we left Penny at the house to answer the phone and Uncle Fred drove me out there. We pulled into pine grove after pine grove, kicking up dust. Eventually we found Henry and Suzanne Robinson (Suzette?) sitting across from each other at a picnic table, drinking Bartles & Jaymes wine coolers. Thank you for your support. Henry Robinson spotted me coming his way and put down his bottle.

Danny and Warren Robinson and Warren's sister, whatever her name was, were in swimming. Henry Robinson pointed to a cluster of yelling heads and splashing arms. "I got my trunks on under these," he said. "I'll go out there and get him in for you." I shook my head no. This much, these few more minutes, I was damn well going to let him have, no matter how much he might make me pay later for having let him have it.

4

I woke up in my chair. On the screen, that commercial was going where the dogs' jaws flap open and they sing, "Lies! Lies!" The idea being that their owners can't bullshit them into eating inferior dogfood. A song Danny will always know as a dogfood commercial, just as I'll always know that waltz tune—whatever the hell it actually is— as Think of Rheingold Whenever Y'Buy Beer. I had my usual thoughts about everything being debased.

What had awakened me, apparently, was the kitchen door slamming—was the ballgame over?—because in came Danny, who gave me a pitying look right out of his mother's repertoire. "You fall asleep again?" he said.

I picked up the remote control and hit MUTE just in time to avoid hearing the strongman bellow, "I'm not gonna pay a lot for this muffler!"

"Maybe you work too hard," Danny said, without a lot of conviction. There I was, stubble-faced, shoes off, stinking t-shirt, and beer bottles all over the floor. Which really gave an unfair impression, although there it all was. On the screen, something that looked like a Fourth of July sparkler was welding a muffler in place, and I could hear the God damn Meineke Muffler March in my head even with the sound off.

"You been out?" I said, still looking at the screen so as not to miss the thing where they show the Meineke logo with the pronunciation: Mine-a-key.

"Just over Clarissa's," he said. This was the girlfriend. A depressed little dyed-platinum blonde who only came up to about here on him; you saw her in black jeans a lot, and a denim jacket with Grateful Dead patches. I didn't know if that still meant you were an acid head or what the hell it meant anymore. I remember seeing a thing in the paper not too long ago about some asshole who made his living tie-dyeing Grateful Dead t-shirts; he said the skull meant we were all the same under the skin. I couldn't imagine whether or not I would have understood that when I was fourteen, or whatever the hell this Clarissa was. Assuming it made any sense to begin with. At any rate, she was obviously a piss-poor influence on Danny's schoolwork and general attitude. So what could you do. I wondered sometimes if they talked together, and if so what about. In addition to the obvious things to wonder. She was pretty, this Clarissa, in a brutalized kind of way.

"Hey Dad?" said Danny. "Wake up, okay?"

"Sorry," I said.

"Listen," he said, "do you want to come over?"

"Come over," I said. When I repeat something that way, it means What do you mean?

"Clarissa's house. Her mom said you could. She's real nice and everything. She's having this party in the backyard." Backyard party on the Fourth of July, and even that didn't seem to be reminding him. Well, hey, fine, more power to him.

"*Kind* of party?" I said. "Kids, grownups?"

Danny shrugged. "Whoever wants to," he said. "It's not any big deal or anything."

"Sounds like it's about my speed," I said. "She told you to invite me?" This sounded like a pretty casual way of doing things for someone who was an adult and a parent, sending a message through the kid. We were in the phone book, for Christ's sake. I mean, *I* was in the phone book. No: come to think of it, we *were* still in the phone book. One of a bunch of things I hadn't had the heart, if that's the word, to see about.

"Sort of," he said. You could see him thinking. "It was like, Clarissa and I asked if you could come and she said sure."

"Very gracious," I said.

"Come *on*, Dad," he said. "You're not doing anything."

"Out of the mouths of babes," I said. "Yeah. Well. Why not. I suppose it's time I met this alleged woman." Not to be outdone in graciousness. "When does the gala event get under way?"

"Right now," he said. "Or whenever you want to come. It's real casual."

"Sounds real inviting," I said. I was giving him shit about the way he talked, but either it went right by him or he was being tolerant. "Can you wait'll I take a shower and put on some clean clothes?"

"That's cool. You know, if you even feel like coming," he said. Then I got it: he was being *too* casual. So this was obviously a command performance, for whatever reason. Well, I was game. Well, maybe not game, but I did recognize my duty when I could no longer ignore it.

Clarissa's house was at the end of a cul-de-sac off Maple Avenue. You went down into a little hollow and there it sat among a lot of trees, with only one other house in sight. Fake Tudor, two-story, stucco, which meant probably '30s or '40s. It had obviously been the only house on the street for years. Most stuff around here was built after 1960; Heritage Circle went up in I think '64. At the time I was born, this house must have been sitting here alone in its little dell like Snow White's cottage. Sort of. The gray paint was peeling now, the stucco was cracked, the picket fence was missing pickets the way cartoon hillbillies are missing teeth. But at least this house had something to it. Though maybe I mean *therefore* instead of *but*. That a house with character could produce a little girl as bombed-out as any kid from a split-level shitbox like mine made you wonder if you could ever make anything right.

I parked next to a faded mustard-colored VW bus, if you can imagine, and in front of a blue Reliant, doing my best to get so I couldn't be blocked, and Danny led me across the crumbling blacktop, through the gate in the picket fence, around the house and into the back. He was right about this being no big deal. I counted six people, three and three, my age pretty much. Two women in shorts and t-shirts, one in shorts and halter top; two men in jeans and t-shirts, one in cutoff jeans and t-shirt. Then a couple more men and another woman came out of the house laughing about something. The women were still looking okay; the men had begun their bellies. Two of them had beards, which of course didn't tell you anything anymore. A net was stretched between a maple tree and a clothesline pulley attached to the frame of the kitchen window; a volleyball sat in the grass, which needed cutting. In a galvanized washtub, cans of beer and Diet Pepsi; the necks of screwtop wine jugs sticking up out of the icewater. Taco chips in a wooden bowl, guacamole in an earthenware bowl. Two stereo speakers, each on a metal folding chair, the wires leading back into the house through another window. "My Guy" by Mary Wells bravely playing out of them. My kind of scene all right.

"She's probably inside," said Danny.

He led me into a kitchen, then into a living room. Funky in a way you wouldn't mind sitting around in. Big oatmeal sofa, bottom sagging. A Morris chair, for Christ's sake. The tv covered up by a white tablecloth with a pattern of red cherries. Even an old woodstove, which looked as if it got used. A woman in shorts was down on her knees, bare heels denting her buttocks. She was flipping through a red plastic milk crate full of LPs, going at it with both hands like a dog digging. Strong arms, strong legs, maybe a little overweight. But not unpleasingly. Her t-shirt had shrunk, or she had bulged, so you could see below the shoulder the—what would you call it?—that arc of skin, that ridge beyond which lies the armpit. I wanted to see what she was like in the face, now there's a crude way of putting it. "Mrs. Peretsky?" Danny said, touching her shoulder. "This is my dad."

She turned her head. Wide, pretty face. Eyes farther apart than I liked. She got to her feet and came toward me, tugging down one side of her shorts.

"Peter Jernigan," I said.

"Martha Peretsky," she said. Hands went out. As I do with women, I clasped firmly but did not shake. (With men I pump up and down.)

"Clarissa's in her room," she said to Danny, and he started upstairs. It hurt me that this house was so obviously familiar to him. "I think my daughter is part vampire," said Martha Peretsky. "It's like if sunlight touches her . . ." Cracking rubber letters on her t-shirt read DAMN I'M GOOD.

From upstairs came a quick blast of rackety music that was not "My Guy" by Mary Wells, then a door slammed and you heard "My Guy" by Mary Wells again. Martha Peretsky shrugged. "I don't even want to *know* what they do up there. At least they're not glued to the tv. Clarissa and I are at a little impasse these days—I won't buy a color tv and she won't watch black-and-white."

"What *do* they do up there?" I said.

"Oh," she said. She seemed to remember that I was an interested party. "Not drugs or anything, I don't think. Danny's been very good for Clarissa in that respect. You knew that she—I mean, we both did, but Clarissa in particular went through a very hard time when her father left." First I'd heard, of course, about any of this.

"Now when was that?" I said. I meant it to sound like a keep-it-rolling kind of thing. I could hear that I sounded like a cop grilling somebody. (That cop. Grilling *me*. One year ago today.)

"Was it *two* years ago?" she asked herself. "I was—Clarissa was twelve. So it'll be three years in October."

"This coming October," I said, getting it absolutely nailed down. I mean, who *gave* a shit.

"Right," she said. "Time flies when you're having fun. Listen, would you like a beer? Soda?"

"Beer'd be good," I said.

She smiled, a nice combination of open and sly. "Follow me," she said, and kitchy-kooed with her index finger. I didn't mind. I wondered what her breasts would look like. I mean, decent-sized, obviously. But specifically. Except for one throwaway fuck about two months after Judith died—a woman client I'd gotten drunk with; I never called her afterwards and the sale never went through—I'd seen no breasts in a year.

Back outside, I plunged my hand into the icewater and came up with a can of Old Milwaukee. Made my hand ache to hold it. I ripped open the top and was brought over and introduced to the friends. There was a Jerry with a *j* and a *y*; another, unattached to him, was a Gerri with a *g* and an *i*. Much merriment over this. Also a Dave and a David: the two beards. And a Tim who didn't look timid, with rimless glasses. So it was Rimless Tim. See, I'm bad at names; shit like that is how I try to keep them straight. This Tim had the Gerri and another woman laughing and laughing. He was one of those men with a pointed nose and a wolfish grin. So you could think of a timber wolf. I sat down in a lawn chair whose seat and back were made of crosshatched wire about the gauge of a coathanger. I'd seen these chairs on sale at Caldor's; this Martha Peretsky had actually bought them.

She went over and said something to the Tim person. He said something back, and they both laughed. Then she came and sat on the grass beside my chair, gave her knees a hug and looked up. "You really *are* nice," she said. Based on what? On my saying that a beer would be good? "Danny said you would be. We've become great friends, Danny and I."

"Well," I said, "always nice to hear. That your kids, you know, think you're nice."

"God, I always say the wrong thing," she said. "Say what you *mean*, Martha. What I mean is, *I* am a nice person too, and I think the nice people in this world should stick together. Because bro-*ther*."

"To the nice people," I said, raising my beer can from collarbone level to chin level. But not actually drinking. To have taken a belt right then would have been crude, wouldn't it? Suggesting this world was so awful that we should all immediately get drunk. So I just raised the beer can and lowered it, as if crossing myself. Then, after a couple of seconds, I went ahead and took a belt, as if someone had changed the subject.

But we were still on the subject, apparently.

"Actually, Danny didn't *need* to tell me you were nice," said Martha Peretsky. "He's so nice himself, I knew that he had to have been raised by—" and here she hesitated, for reasons she must have hoped weren't obvious. "I mean, a boy that nice, his father had to be nice too."

To the human intellect, I felt like saying. *And its capacity to reason shit out.* "Yeah, I'm proud of Danny," I said, looking over to make sure I could see my car from here. I was slow today, boy: how could it have taken me this long to see that she was absolutely shitfaced and trying to keep it together?

"That's what I mean," she said.

"To meaning," I said, and took another good belt. So why not get shitfaced myself?

She narrowed her eyes. "You're very bright," she said. "I am not doing a very good job of establishing that I'm bright too."

I tried to think what to say. Finally I went with, "Is that important?"

"If we're going to be *friends*, yes, I think so," she said. "I would like very much to be friends with you. Oh *God* am I losing it. Martha *ma chère*, why don't you just *taisez-vous* for a change, *n'est-ce pas?*" She shook her head; her straight blond bangs, in accordance with some principle of physics, wagged in the opposite direction from the way her head was going. I got interested in the way that looked. To avoid, I suppose, having to pay attention to the chatter.

"Sorry," she said. "Sorry sorry sorry. See, I have to tell you. Or else you are going to think the absolute worst of me. Clarissa gave me this pill. Because I was getting nervous? With people coming over? And she warned me not to drink on top of it and I'm like give me a break here. What is a fourteen-year-old going to give you that you couldn't have a beer with?" She shook her head. "Whew."

"How long ago did you take it?"

She shook her head again. "Before everybody show up. Show-da up. Couple hours ago?"

"Well look," I said, "just don't have anything more to drink and I'm sure it'll wear off pretty soon." As if *I* had any idea what the hell her kid had given her. "You like to go for a walk?" I said. "Walk it off a little?"

"Feel like lying down," she said. "So maybe I should walk. Boy oh boy oh boy." I stood up, she raised her hand like a student who has the answer, and I pulled her to her feet and we walked. The way we worked it out about the hands made me think there were possibilities: each kept holding the other's hand for longer than necessary, then each let go as if we'd counted one two three. This Martha Peretsky must be very wise in the body, I thought, if she could manage this while drunk and stoned on what was obviously some powerful downer. I felt a jolt of heat to the penis. Machine that I was.

We went through the gate and up the street, avoiding potholes as if they were puddles. Which of course they must be when it rained. "I wonder are there any frogs," I said, which couldn't have made much sense to her.

"Mmm," she said.

We got as far as her nearest neighbor's house, a gabled box, probably early '60s, with windows wider than they were tall. Like mine. "Ugly," I said. I was criticizing her neighborhood.

"Ugly people live there," she said. Then she said, "I'm deserting my guests."

"Not your *favorite* guest," I said, old smoothie. I sort of remembered now how you did this.

"You," she said. She smiled a pacific smile and took my arm. I considered considering where this was all heading, but found I didn't feel like considering. On one beer? I must have wanted not to feel like considering.

"This is a little crazy," she said. "What are we doing?"

"Taking you for a walk," I said. "Ostensibly. But I don't see that anything beyond the ostensible would necessarily"—smoother and smoother, boy—"be so crazy. I mean, okay: we have our kids in there doing whatever they're in there doing. Which does *not* mean—"

I tried to think how to say what it didn't mean.

"But there isn't any *music*," she said.

I dislodged my arm, assuming this was her trite way of saying she was having second thoughts.

"Better get back there put some music on," she said. "You can't give a party and then neglect it. Any more than you neglect your own *child*." She seemed much in earnest about this.

"Are you in any shape to deal with your party right now?" I said.

"Dealing with my party," she said, "will get me in shape to deal with my party." She took my hand and pulled. "But you have to come help."

It was the first husbandly duty laid on me in a year. In exactly a year. To the fucking hour. Give or take. And clearly I was the first husbandly help this Martha Peretsky had had for a while too. I thought about her kneeling by that crate of records. Trying, unadvised, to come up with the song that would get things going.

5

Martha Peretsky's bedroom was unrecognizable by morning light. It was full of all this detail, whereas the night before it had been, I don't know, whatever. A long-legged old dresser, painted glossy black, with an oval mirror. A flower decal on each drawer, centered between the many-faceted glass knobs. On top of the dresser, jars and jewel boxes and hairbrushes. A wicker laundry basket with a pantyhose foot dangling from under the lid, as if someone were being swallowed. On the wall, in a too-ornate silver-painted frame, an old chromo of a hula girl with ukulele. Our clothes here and there on the floor. Outside, birds sang and a faraway lawnmower was going.

Martha Peretsky was asleep, or pretending to be asleep, face down. Shoulders swelling and subsiding. I got out of bed, found the jockey shorts where they'd ended up—I remembered now her taking them down and my not caring what became of them—and crept to the door. Then I remembered the girl, Clarissa, and went back and put on trousers. Glanced at stomach. Put on shirt.

In the hallway I met Danny, in just his jockey shorts, coming out of the bathroom. He gave me thumbs-up, and a grin I would never have given *my* father, no matter how much of an old bohemian he was. But what was the point of trying to be on your dignity when you were getting up from doing the same thing he was getting up from doing? I decided fuck it, and gave him thumbs-up back, the canny old veteran who could still come off the bench and move the runner along with a perfect bunt. Greeting the rookie who'd raise his average fifty points and still hit almost as many home runs if he'd just cut down on his swing. Then he went into what I gathered was Clarissa's room and closed the door behind him, back to whatever moody pleasures she gave him, and I went into the bathroom. Should I really be countenancing this?

Back in the bedroom, Martha was lying pretty much as I'd left her: on her stomach, bent arms making a diamond around her head. I undressed again, got under the covers, lay against her, caressed her awake. Sleepily she rolled onto her side, facing away, and my penis slipped between her buttocks. Then she reached around behind and pulled me in tighter. So. If she was ready for refinements this early along, it meant what? Probably that it would run its course even quicker.

"Mmm," she said. "Do you like that, is that good?"

"Listen," she said, after another little while, "I hope this isn't too shocking of me, but I think there's still a little thing of Vaseline in the drawer of that night table." Right she was. I got the cap off, hands trembling. A few seconds later she said, "Oh my God. I know you're

not supposed to do this anymore, but I just"—she inhaled sharply—
"do not care." Later we both lay staring at the ceiling. "You're
probably completely scandalized," she said. "Rusty sort of gave me
a taste for that." She snorted. "Literally *and* figuratively." We stared
some more.

"I guess you probably don't need to hear about Rusty," she said.
I reached over to pat her thigh, and my hand collided with hers
reaching over for me.

When we finally got up, the kids had gone off someplace. She made
coffee and brought it to me on the living room sofa, pretty good brewed
coffee with cinnamon in it. I couldn't decide whether cinnamon was
a good idea or whether it was in bad taste because you should want
the true flavor of the coffee. She pawed through the records again and
came up with Webb Pierce, which got her some points. I mean, Webb
Pierce? You would've thought Billy Joel or something. Or would you?
Consider the woodstove and the black-and-white tv, and just the house
in general. So maybe that t-shirt had been an aberration, or even a
very twisty irony. Then there was the thing she'd said about her
husband giving her a taste for that: had this been tactlessness or air-
clearing openness? She did seem to know the difference between *literally* and *figuratively*. I was having trouble getting a handle on this
Martha Peretsky.

"Have you ever heard him?" she said, lowering the needle.

I considered saying yes and said no. So whatever the first lie was
going to be, it wouldn't be that. Unless I'd told one last night at some
point. I thought I remembered maybe fudging some things.

"If you end up liking it," she said, "I'll stick a tape in the thing."

"Great," I said. "Friend of mine's been getting me into country
music a little."

"Why isn't anything coming out?" she said. "I've *got* it turned up
to five."

"I can *sort* of hear it," I said.

"*Oh* my God," she said. "I forgot to bring the speakers inside."

"Your neighbors like Webb Pierce, do they?"

She jerked the needle off the record.

"Why don't I go out and hand them in to you through the window?"
I said.

"Would you? That would be great."

Another beautiful day out. And full-grown trees around: on Heritage Circle the trees mostly weren't big enough yet to give shade. Here I was in the backyard of some woman I'd been fucking. Whereas a year ago today—I don't know, enough with the year ago todays. "Your yard looks kind of partied-upon," I said, handing her the first speaker. "I'm afraid our cleanup last night was kind of superficial."

"And whose fault was that?" She actually shook a roguish finger.

"I'll make it up to you," I said, queasy at having to coquette back, but wasn't it a lover's obligation not to break the mood? "It actually shouldn't take that long."

"Come in and have your coffee first," she said, probably meaning Let's go back to bed first. Or at any rate, that's how it turned out.

We got to hear the Webb Pierce later.

"Yeah, I really like it," I said. So maybe *that* lie was the first. "How did you end up getting a taste for this?" Phrased about as maladroitly as possible.

"Long story," she said. "You really want to know?"

"Sure," I said. The second.

"When we were growing up, outside of Washington, my dad had this country-western band? The Stony Davis Show." She said this announcer-style.

"That was your dad's name, Davis?" I said, wondering about the Peretsky.

"Yeah," she said. "I just sort of kept my married name. So anyhow, his big thing was imitations, I mean he could do Johnny Cash and Ernest Tubb and, I don't know, Eddy Arnold. Webb Pierce, of course. And he really had them down, and that was part of his show. And see, he *looked* a little bit like Webb Pierce. Kind of jowly? So about once a year he and the band would drive someplace like Pennsylvania or New Jersey where he wasn't known, and they'd call some little nightclub and give them this story that Webb Pierce's bus had broken down on the way to somewhere and that since he was stranded in the area he'd put on his show that night for—I forget what he'd ask, but something that would've been really a lot of money then. And they really used to fall for it. And he'd comb his hair the exact way Webb Pierce did and go in there with this real fancy cowboy suit on and sing, you know, 'There Stands the Glass' and everything."

"He actually got away with this?" I said.

"For years," she said. "And that was money he would never spend. He used to say Webb Pierce put me through college."

"He made that much on this thing?"

"No," she said. "He always liked to exaggerate. But I guess it might have covered a year or something."

"He still alive?" I said.

She tapped her lips with index and middle finger. "Two packs of Luckies a day," she said. "I really wish Clarissa could've known him."

It wasn't until late afternoon that we got around to filling brown plastic trash bags with paper plates and beer cans. I emptied one can into a withered geranium in a pot on the mossy back steps, figuring kill or cure. And wondering if I'd be around to learn which. The kids had come back by this time, but they'd gone right up to Clarissa's room. Of course. I spun the bags, twisting the mouths into tight ropy spirals which I tied with paper-clad lengths of wire. Then we dragged them out by the mailbox.

"Garbage day isn't till Wednesday," she said. "I hope the raccoons don't get into this stuff."

"What's today anyhow?"

"Sunday."

"Really Sunday?" I said. "It feels so much like a Sunday I thought it couldn't actually *be* one." A feeling I'd forgotten: Sunday with a wife, and work the next day. "Jesus," I said. "Is that twisted thinking or what?"

"Not really," she said. "Do you always assume everything you think is so crazy nobody can understand it?"

Odd that after all that bed it made me angry that she was getting personal. Odd unless you thought about it.

"Hmm," I said. "Am I a snob, in other words?"

We were about that close to getting nasty.

Then she laughed. "I would never *suggest* such a thing."

By six o'clock I'd had enough of it. I pleaded chores, unspecified, to finish up around the house before another workweek began, then knocked on the door of Clarissa's room. After much rattling and clicking of bolts, the door opened to the exact width of the girl's white face. "Daniel?" she said. And his face appeared above hers.

"Petals on a wet black bough," I said. The faces didn't look any more or any less blank. "Listen, Danny?" I said. "I've got to get back to the hyacenda." Now, where hyacenda came from was one of Fitzgerald's Pat Hobby stories, where Pat is writing a western movie and gets *hacienda* wrong. *Ext. Long Shot of the Plains. Buck and Mexicans approaching the hyacenda.* One more of my obscure things that Danny had no way of understanding. He probably thought it was really hyacenda. "I'll see you back there, what, before eleven, huh? And if you want to come home for dinner we'll call Domino's or something, okay?" Don't be fooled by how casual this all sounds: I was issuing a command.

"Okay," he said, looking down and away. I was sorry for him, being ordered around by his father, however collegially, in front of his girlfriend. Or perhaps he was embarrassed by a belated sense of having gone too far with his cheeky little thumbs-up this morning.

Back downstairs, Martha stuck a cassette in my shirt pocket. A long kiss at the door—each bending a knee to insinuate a thigh between the other's thighs, a voucher for unfinished sexual business—and I was out of there.

The house looked, as I pulled into the driveway, the way a house looks if you've been away for a month: that is, the angles and proportions had gone all funny. Or something. Maybe just more distant than I'd expected, as if through the wrong end of binoculars. But there was the lawn, all freshly cut. By me. Yesterday.

I got a beer out of the refrigerator, took it into the bathroom, and finished it while taking off my clothes. The tape in my shirt pocket was labeled WEBB PIERCE in awkward handwriting. I stayed in the shower a good long time, soaping and rinsing everything twice. Then to the bedroom, where the Yahrzeit lamp was still going, pale in the late-afternoon sunlight. I gave the plastic rod a twist to close the blinds, then shut the door, and the candle threw a shaky shadow of me on the wall. I thought how amazingly sick it would be to jerk myself off, after this day, in this candlelight. Then I thought, You'd better stop scaring yourself. So I put on clean clothes, got another beer out of the refrigerator, went into the living room and turned on the tv. Another ballgame, with two thirds of the outfield in shadow.

I was still sitting there when Danny rolled in, during the Independent News. In fact, just as they were rerunning the highlights of the same ballgame, how about that. He sat down on the sofa, crosslegged, with his God damn running shoes still on. Though I don't suppose I really gave a shit. He sank at once into the tv trance, as if that were his real life in there and the rest was shadows. Well, like father like son. Some commercials came on, then the weather, then the commercial where the pretty woman eats Frusen Glädjé and you wonder whether or not you're supposed to think she really feels shame. Then the muffler strongman came on and Danny said, "So you going to see her again?"

What he was really asking, I imagined, was the following: A, was his father the kind of man who wouldn't see a woman again after spending the night with her? B, was that the kind of man to be? C, how would this complicate his life? And perhaps D, was he going to get a new mother? Hey, I could have used the answers too.

"Well," I said, "we certainly liked each other a lot—I mean, obviously." Idea: Why not put it on the kid? "But how would *you* feel about it?" I said. "You and Clarissa? I mean, it's sort of a strange situation for you to be in, right? All of a sudden your father and her mother. . . ."

He shrugged. "I don't know."

"Well, at least unusual, okay? You'll grant me unusual?"

"I don't know," he said. "We kind of knew it would happen and everything. When we finally got you guys together."

I stared at him. This was sitcom stuff. Well, of course. These were kids who'd spent their lives watching shit like this, widower with houseful of girls meets divorcée with houseful of boys, and some William Frawley type around too, in an oh-so-improbable apron.

"She's real nice," he said. "And you two have a lot of stuff in common, right?"

What, like being old?

"You're kidding me," I said. "I mean, it was a nice thought, but didn't you think through the consequences? You know, suppose it really got serious with the two of us and then you and Clarissa broke up. Or vice versa." I was a great one to talk about thinking through the consequences.

Now he stared. "But Dad," he said. "If you thought that way about everything, you wouldn't ever do anything."

Hey, welcome to Heritage Circle.

He got up off the couch. "I'm gonna go practice."

"Fine," I said. "Just use the things, okay? The earphones? And don't stay up all night." The shit you're obliged to say.

After the news they had some paid program on about being an entrepreneur, with people like Famous Amos. I zapped the sound down almost to inaudible and picked up P. G. Wodehouse. If I ever needed Blandings Castle, boy, tonight was the night. The lawns and gardens that you could practically see before you as your eyes moved along through the words, and Psmith winning the hand of Eve Halliday entirely on charm and eccentricity. Without so much as a kiss.

6

Although I'd had enough of it by Sunday afternoon, on Monday morning I called her from work. Partly because it was the call you had to make if you didn't want to seem heartless, partly because I wanted her again that night. Hey, partly because it would put off for another few minutes having to start calling more prospects about this dogshit office space I'd just listed in the too-far-West 30s, next door to an SRO. I mean, I was *saying* I'd just listed it. And in fact it *was* my most recent listing.

Nobody answered the phone, and I hurt like a three-year-old at the thought that she had a life of her own.

Danny wasn't home when I got back from work. Called over to the Peretskys', got Clarissa. Yes, Danny was there, but her mother wouldn't be home until eight. Did I want to talk to Danny? Did I want her mother to call me when she got back? No, no, not important.

I called again at nine-thirty. Not back yet. Tell her . . . tell her I'll try to reach her later in the week. Nothing important, tell her. Catch up with her eventually.

Went to work the next day, came home. The phone was ringing as I unlocked the door; son of a bitch stopped just as I got to it. Danny, of course, wasn't home. Phone rang again ten minutes later. Her. "Clarissa is such a space case," she said. "She didn't tell me you'd called until this *afternoon*. I could've *killed* her. So"—deep sigh—"how *are* you?"

III

1

Eight days before my father died, I had driven up to Woodstock to see him. Oh, no premonitions; just the routine visit I'd been making every couple of months. Better quickly say Woodstock, Connecticut. He bought there in 1970, convinced it was going to be discovered, like the Woodstocks of New York and Vermont. Certainly it became unaffordable, like everyplace else, but as far as I could see it hadn't been discovered in the sense he meant. Just another pretty New England town with no reason for anybody to be there.

"So how do things march down there in America?" he said, pouring a glass of George Dickel for me and a smaller amount for himself. America, in his code, meant New Jersey. The whiskey glugged, as it will out of a new bottle. His face seemed redder than ever, and his belly forced gaps between the pearloid buttons of his denim shirt.

"A lot *you* care, you old beatnik," I said. "I bet you don't even watch *Wheel of Fortune* up here. What do you do with yourself, anyway? Read Emerson all day?"

"Emerson?" he said. "What do you think, I'm going native? Emerson tv, maybe. Actually, I was thinking about trying to get my Latin working again so I could read the *Eclogues*. Or maybe it's the *Georgics*— what the hell am I trying to think of? There's one about shepherds and one about farming. One I want is the one about farming."

"Then you want the *Georgics*," I said. "I think."

"Let me write this down," he said. "So you still remember all this business."

"You can take the boy out of the academy . . . ," I said. "So what have you been up to?"

"Here you see it," he said, raising his glass, which was almost empty already. "Nah, I do this and that. Work a little bit. You want to see a couple things? Don't say yes just to humor an old man. On the other hand, don't say no."

"What can I say?" I said.

"And mind you praise 'em up," he said, getting to his feet and setting down his empty glass. "No matter how much they secretly depress you."

"This must be hot shit," I said. "Assuming I'm uncrumpling your ironies correctly."

"Well," he said, obviously pleased with himself, "you'll see what you think."

I got up and followed him. "Leave it," he said, pointing to my glass. "House rule. No bringing sauce into the workplace. Unless," he said, patting his stomach, "it's already on board."

The studio had been a henhouse. He'd paid some contractor too much money to move it from up behind the house and attach it to the north wall of the kitchen on a new foundation. Now it had a wall of glass where chicken wire used to be and skylights let into the roof. A potbelly stove sat on a podium of salvaged bricks.

"Looks neater than usual in here," I said. "I thought the creative impulse was supposed to thrive on disorder."

Instead of answering—or by way of answering—he laid a hand on my shoulder and turned me around. It was a giant painting of my mother's face, as it was when I was a child, on a yellow field squirming with brushstrokes. Big: the top of the head was level with the top of my head, the chin down around my navel. And absolutely photo-realistic, except for the eyes: like most of his recent people, she had two pairs. And a dagger-shaped piece of paper, a foot or so long, that was glued or lacquered over her mouth. You had to look closely, but you could see it had been ripped out of a blown-up print of the Mona Lisa: you could make out the smile, the chin, an ear, and some of that crumbling landscape. The way it was slapped across the bottom of her face, it looked as if she were being gagged. It looked like a smirk too. Or a scream.

Then I stepped closer: at two feet away I could see that the whole *thing* was painted. At the instant I caught on, he laughed his little two-note laugh. "Trump your oil, did I?"

"You old goat," I said. "So you can still get it up."

"Try to," he said. "Couple more here someplace." From behind the sort of stand-up screen artists' models used when they undressed, he carried out five more canvases, all in the same series.

"Jeez," I said. "Should I try to strike the Greenbergian note here, or just tell you they're wonderful?"

He shook his head. "Detail," he said. "Go into a lot of detail about why they work so well. Then I want to hear about how Trina is going to sell 'em for a hundred grand a pop and how that little shit Julian Schnabel is going to get his *ass* kicked."

"Well," I said, gearing up.

"And then maybe throw in a word on your own behalf, and tell me what the *hell* you're doing as an assistant vice shoeshine boy at some outfit that's doing its bit to help squeeze the working man out of New York City. Not to mention the painting man."

"Ho boy," I said. "Do we have to do this again?"

"I worry," he said.

"About *what*, for Christ's sake? The money is fine, as long as you don't try to live in Manhattan on it. I mean, it beats junior-professor money. And it's, I don't know, soothing. It's all this *business* that has to get done, you know?"

"It depresses the hell out of me," he said. "Underneath all those layers of bullshit, what you've basically got is a bunch of self-pity. And what you've got underneath that, presumably, is rage at *me* for whatever it was you think I did to you."

Don't worry, he wasn't going to catch me that easily.

"Aha!" I thundered, levelling an accusing finger. "All the father's fault!" I blew on my finger and holstered it. "I mean, come on. Being Francis Jernigan's son isn't like you have Down syndrome, for Christ's sake." This much was true, no matter how I felt. "If you want to blame somebody, then blame what's-his-name, Hofmann."

"What Hofmann? What are you talking about?"

"The LSD guy," I said. "Somebody Hofmann. Hans Hofmann."

"Not Hans," he said.

"Little joke," I said.

He shook his head. "How anybody could take that stuff *twice*," he said. "That God damn little pill of yours cost me six months of work."

"So that was your atonement, okay?" I nodded at the paintings. "So. What did you work from on these?"

"Ah," he said. "Sheer inspiration. See, she appears whenever I rub the bottle. Those George Dickel ones seem to work best these days. You rub it and . . ." He suddenly got tired of his *jeu d'esprit*. "Old picture I had around," he said. "You ever see this one?"

He went over to his work table, opened an Edgeworth tobacco tin and handed me an old black-and-white snapshot the size of a playing card. "I had this blown up so I could see it better, you know? And just took her head off it."

It was the three of us, in bathing suits, with a lifeguard's tower in the background. Me standing between my mother and father, holding their hands. I looked to be about three or four, short enough so that to reach their hands my arms were raised like a strongman's. My mother's face was the face in the painting, all right. I avoided looking at the breasts. Across the years, her eyes met yours.

"Where *was* this?" I said.

"Florida."

"I vaguely remember," I said. "There was a big cockroach or something where we were staying." I looked again: all three of us. "So who took this picture?" I said.

"Ah, that's what makes it so special," he said. "Jack Solomon."

"You're kidding," I said. "He was there with the three of us?"

"Sure. Him and Margaret. Poor old Margaret. You think *I* look like shit. You ought to see *her* these days. As I remember, we only dug out these bathing suits for the picture so we wouldn't scandalize 'em back at the drugstore. Most of the time we were running around buck naked. You remember he used to walk out into the water with you on his shoulders?"

I shook my head. "I hope I shit all over his hairy back," I said.

"Nah, you and he were big buddies," he said. "Hell, he and *I* were big buddies."

"This was before anything was going on? Or don't you know?"

"During," he said. "In the middle of. As nearly as I can tell. Six months, a year into it. I suppose I didn't figure it out because it was so obvious. The Purloined Letter. I can remember just like that"— he made an artist's half-frame with a right angle of thumb and fore-finger—"when this picture was taken. Him standing there naked pointing that big old box camera and his dick hanging down."

"Jesus," I said.

"Taken me all these years to see that I could just go ahead and use the image and not worry about, oh, *narrative* or anything. I guess I decided nobody gave a shit anymore. Including me."

"Well," I said, "it made you a hell of a picture. Hell of a series."

"And only a part of my long legacy of joy and light." He opened the door. "What do you say we go in and get pissed? I already gave myself the day off tomorrow to watch the playoffs. That's what kind of Emerson we got up here. Emerson tv." He seemed to have forgotten he'd made this joke before.

"Suits me," I said. "Judith took Danny with her up to her mother's, so I'm not expected. I can go back down in the morning, if you've got a bed for me to pass out on."

"Couple of 'em," he said. "So how come *that* old cow gets to see her grandson and I don't?" He filled his glass, then topped off mine.

"It's not that he doesn't like you," I said. (He's lying. Joe Isuzu.) "He likes going up there because they've got this big music store around the corner from her house. What do you have around the corner that can compete with that?"

"Cows," he said. "Four-footed ones. And a damn sight better to look at. And a lot more useful to the human race. And not a whole lot stupider."

"What can I say," I said. "Next time."

Which turned out to be his funeral. Not the heart attack for which I'd been preparing myself, but a fire that burned the whole place to the foundation. First the studio, then the rest of the house. The oil and the turpentine and the woodstove and him probably in there drunk. At any rate they found a bottle, shattered by the heat apparently.

2

Whatever money Trina could have gotten him for the new work probably wouldn't have helped much.

The day after his memorial she invited me for a drink. It turned out there wasn't much business to wrap up. She had a few small pieces she hadn't been able to get rid of; he'd owed her a few thousand dollars for a few years. My father had distrusted Trina on principle, though she'd been his dealer since his first show, in 1949. I'd always assumed she'd done what she could. It wasn't her fault the stuff from the early '50s kept going up every time it got sold again, and she genuinely seemed to admire the post-'65 stuff: she gave a muted wail when I described the paintings destroyed in the fire. "Don't tell me any more," she said. Her eyes darted around the tabletop: finally she tapped her cigarette ash into her empty glass. "Ah well," she said. "At some point they simply weren't tracking him anymore, and of course what can one *say*?"

"He never should've stopped with the squiggles," I said.

"That couldn't have lasted forever, either, darling. What you've told me—I can't even think about it. And that *stunning* old house.

Though at least you'll have the insurance. Is that crass of me to say?" She lit another cigarette and raised her hand; when the waiter looked over, she scribbled on a phantom credit card slip with a phantom pen.

His lawyer called the following day. How much had I known about, ah, "the situation"? I said I hadn't known there *was* one. Hmm, he said, how shall I begin? Seemed my father had been days away from being turned out of the stunning old house. He'd taken out a second mortgage to get the henhouse converted and, apparently, to get money to live on and to keep up the payments on the original mortgage. When the money he'd borrowed was gone, of course, he was left with even higher monthly expenses he couldn't meet. After the insurance company cancelled his homeowner's policy—they'd been dunning him for three months—the bank had been forced to step in.

Judith took the news like a champ.

"It's a relief, sort of," she said. "Isn't it? I would never have known how long a face to pull while we were going through the money, you know?" She laughed. "God, listen to me. *The* money. There never *was* any money, right? Isn't that the gist?"

"If not the gist," I said, "certainly the bottom line."

"Well," she said, "we can still be happy." This was 1982. "Probably more happy, don't you think? In the long run?"

"*Quién sabe?*" I said. "And on the other hand, *que será será.*"

"*Kissez moi,*" she said. One of our better days.

3

When I got around to telling Martha the story—it wasn't until we'd been together for a couple of months—she was angry that my father hadn't, as she put it, provided for me.

"Christ," I said, "he provided for eighteen years. Fuck was he *supposed* to do? *Plus* four years of college. I mean, at *some* point, you know?" The rest of the thought was something like, Sons have to take responsibility for themselves. Not exactly the way I felt, as a son, but the way you ought to feel. As a father, on the other hand, I was all for sons getting their shit happening at their earliest convenience. All for it some of the time.

She picked up something in my tone. I was learning that you had to watch yourself around Martha. Assuming you had stuff you didn't want picked up. Though really, how intuitive did you have to be to pick up something in somebody's tone when he starts yelling at you?

"I didn't mean to touch a sore spot," she said. "It's just that all that money could've changed your life. I hate to see money that could really, really help somebody just go up—"

"In smoke?" I suggested.

"Sorry," she said. "I didn't mean that."

"What nobody seems to understand," I said (meaning her: Judith had understood), "is that this money never fucking *existed*. I mean, he was Francis Jernigan and everything, but all the real money got made off of stuff he'd let go for a couple of thousand dollars in like 1952. My mother split in '56, he boozed from then until '64 or '65. . . . You know, what can I say? By which time it was all Andy Warhol or something, or whatever it was after Andy Warhol. Believe me. There was . . . no . . . money."

Without asking, she poured more coffee into my cup and pushed the milk carton my way. Morning sunlight warming the gray-painted top of the old pine table.

"Anyhow," she said. "I still think it's possible to live a more rational life."

"*Quién sabe?*" I said. "It's easy to talk theoretically about the rational life, but when that ole lonesome whistle blows on that ole lonesome 7:48—gal, I just get that ole commutin' fever in my blood. Cain't set still nohow."

"There are ways to make it work," she said.

"And *speaking* of work," I said, looking up at her old electric wall clock. The clock part was set into the belly of a rooster. Why were second hands always red? To tell you, in case you hadn't fucking figured it out, that seconds went by quickly? Oh, probably just so you could tell the second hand from the minute hand. "The light of common day," I said, alluding to something or other, "reveals to me that I've got about a half hour to collect Danny, drive him over to the bus, get back to the station, find a place in the lot and get my ass onto the platform."

She looked at the clock. "I had no idea," she said. "I guess you really better run along. We can talk when you get home, okay?"

Home?

Well, wasn't I sleeping here most nights? And Danny had pretty much moved in. He'd even insisted on having his birthday party here, such as it was. The four of us and a lopsided chocolate cake from Martha's unlevelled oven: this was how he chose to turn sixteen. When I'd asked him what friends he wanted there, he just stared me down.

Mornings I dropped him at the corner by Heritage Circle so he could get his old school bus, and he took the same bus back in the afternoon to practice his guitar in the empty house. But he was back by dinnertime. And no wonder. Where would *you* rather be: Martha's house with the cooking smells and the corny old braided rugs and the black-and-white tv with the tablecloth thrown over it, or Heritage Circle with the painted walls, cool to the touch and smooth as an eggshell? And, always, that place where the driveway met the street.

On the train, I sat down next to a *New York Times*, across from another *Times* and a *Bergen Record*. Pawed around in my shoulderbag for *Northanger Abbey*—that's the one where it turns out the creepy old house isn't creepy and there aren't any dark secrets—and found a magazine I certainly hadn't put there. What the hell was *Suburban Survivalist*? Same size as *Time* or *Newsweek*, with this airbrushed cover of the American Gothic couple, dressed in camouflage fatigues and looming in front of a split-level house, oh so original. Instead of the pitchfork, the geezer with the glasses held a golf club; a kid at their side was sitting at a camouflaged PC. I opened the magazine flat on my lap, so the people across couldn't see I was reading such a thing, and found "A Letter from the Editor."

Despite the name, this magazine hopefully isn't for paranoids or gun nuts—though we do recommend you think about getting a firearm for home protection—but for ordinary folks who want to live more simply without giving up the benefits of the suburban lifestyle. We don't advocate any radical transformation of society—not that we wouldn't welcome some improvements!—and we don't think you should count on it. We're

*not into proselytizing. Only you know if you're discontented enough with
the way you're now living to start making some changes for yourself and
your family.*

 *Have you ever been in an old house where the mice have really gotten
a foothold? They've got their own little spaces behind walls, under floors,
above ceilings, secret passages going all over the place. Call us the New
American Mice. We can show you the secret ways of getting around
everyday suburban America. We're not about taking over the whole
house. We're about living there on the sly, keeping out of harm's way,
and, hopefully, getting some fun out of it!*

Who was this "we," dangling his *hopefully*s right and left? The man-
ifesto was signed "Adam Newman," transparently somebody's idea
of a joke. I paged around and found the masthead: it listed Adam
Newman as Editor in Chief, Managing Editor, Art Director, Copy
Editor, Business Manager and Ad Sales. The thing was purportedly
put out by Orbit Publications, whose address was a post office box
in Metuchen and whose logo was a sputnik with a smiley-face and
three little curved lines to the right of it to suggest it was moving in
a counterclockwise circle.

After "A Letter from the Editor" came "The Rational Life: An
Editorial," by Adam Newman. The rational life according to Adam
Newman was spent foraging for unrotted produce in supermarket
dumpsters, running a perpetual yard sale, eating rabbits you raised
in your basement and making moonshine instead of paying for "government liquor," all the while taking advantage of such suburban
amenities as good schools, relative freedom from crime and squalor,
and easy access to cities. All this prefaced by a bunch of boilerplate
about soul-killing jobs, the credit trap and the folly of working a
lifetime for a retirement you were too old to enjoy.

Then an article about living space—by Adam Newman—which
advocated doing all you could to own your own home free and clear
so you didn't have to work to come up with that monthly nut or pay
some bank its ruinous interest. Adam Newman seemed to think that
could be done by going to sheriff's sales, or by fixing up an old store
or gas station for living quarters. "Architectural distinction," he wrote,
"is where you find it."

Did you know the first McDonald's stand, once an eyesore, is now a landmark building? So before you turn up your nose at that flat-roofed cinderblock building (former home of Moe's TV Repair), remember: it may be a precious specimen of vanishing Americana!

By the time the train got to Penn Station, I'd skimmed the other articles. I read about heating with wood ("Make friends with the guys at your local tree service"), living without a telephone ("If Aunt Tilly dies, Express Mail will still get you to the church on time") and buying clothes ("Nobody you need to impress will see you rummaging through the shirts at the thrift store"). I sort of liked the fuck-you spirit of it all. But Jesus.

For Martha, though, as I learned that night over dinner, *Suburban Survivalist* was a trustworthy call to action. One more way you knew she was a little scary, despite the food smells and braided rugs. "But why not?" she said. "Wouldn't you like to get out of the money economy?"

"Wouldn't I like to be twenty-four years old and have a twelve-inch dick," I said. I didn't want to have to hear how seriously she took all this.

"Perish forbid," she said, kindly. (Clarissa and Danny, I should have explained, had taken their dinner into Clarissa's room, or I wouldn't have been talking about dicks.)

"You know," I said, "this actually is good." I'd never tasted moonshine before.

"Tim's is the best," she said. "Clarissa and I tried to make our own once." She gave thumbs-down.

"*Quién es* Tim?" I said. When I talked Spanish like that, the little Spanish I knew, it was because I thought Spanish sounded streetwise and I was parodying the notion of street wisdom. But it was too many moves. It just sounded crazy.

"You met him," she said. So she knew a little Spanish too. "At the party? He had on—forget it, men never notice what anybody's wearing. But he's sort of tall, glasses?"

I shrugged, dismissing this Tim. Then I remembered. The timber wolf who wasn't timid. "I mostly remember *you*," I said, gallantly.

"We all of us tried to talk him out of that stupid name," she said.

"What's wrong with Tim?"

"So funny," she said, reaching over and pinching my cheek. "*Suburban Survivalist.*"

"I'm lost," I said.

"Peter," she said. "I *told* you. It's Tim's magazine."

"Somebody you *know* puts out that thing?"

"I did tell you, Peter. You must not have been paying attention."

"Listen, I'm sure you did," I said. I'm sure she did.

"Tell me something," she said. "Has Danny given you any idea of what goes on around here?"

"Why?" I said. "What, do you sit around—" I was going to say *levitating*, but I needed something more improbable. Nothing came to mind that was too weird to imagine her maybe actually doing; that's how much I trusted this Martha Peretsky. So what was I doing in her house all the time? Right, but I mean besides that.

"You look so *stricken*," she said. "It's not anything deep and dark. It's just that this is a sort of a two-woman survivor community here. Who, disguised"—trying to deepen her voice to a Don Pardo baritone—"as an everyday broken home, fights a never-ending battle." Back to normal voice. "Though I sometimes wonder why we bother. You've never even asked me what I do for money."

Huh. Yeah. Well. Certainly had me nailed on that one. I really should've shown some minimal curiosity, especially when she was seeing me off in the morning and showing no signs herself of getting ready to go to work. Fuck, I really should've *felt* some minimal curiosity. I must have assumed she was on vacation or something, assuming I was assuming anything. I mean, a vacation that goes from July into September? What did I think she was, a college professor? Maybe I just assumed she was my mother, seeing me off to school and not existing until I came home again. (After third grade, of course, it was a sequence of nannies and shit that I forgot about every day. Whole other story, though.) But I was certainly wrong not to have asked what she did for money. Well, I hadn't. Though on the other hand I wasn't about to eat shit for it, either.

"Well?" I said. "Do tell."

"I can see you're fascinated."

"I'm curious, yes. What *do* you do for money?"

"Nothing," she said, pretty clearly expecting me to smite my brow like a Three Stooge. "I might temp once in a while if I'm really strapped, and over Christmas I usually work at Alexander's if they need extra help. But basically . . ." She waved her hand around in air as if twirling a lariat, to suggest her freedom from the everyday. "The house is paid for—it actually was Rusty's parents' house. But it was sort of part of the agreement when he left that Clarissa and I would just keep staying here. Anyhow, so with a good big garden and this and that, Clarissa and I can just sort of . . ." She lariated her hand again. Old Martha here seemed to be pretty popped on that moonshine. "I call her my little cash cow," she said, "because Rusty sometimes kicks in some money. When he's feeling guilty enough, basically. You know, maybe she'll be the next Madonna, support me in my old age. She has the look down, if she just knew how to *do* anything. But you know, we do fine. And we do it pretty much outside the money economy. I can't believe Danny didn't tell you any of this. Did he tell you about Bunny Hell?"

"Is that like Benny Hill?" I said. I just really didn't feel like getting into all this.

"I think it blew his mind a little at first. You know the way he never lets on, but you could sort of see it. I mean, I guess it blows *my* mind a little if I think about it the wrong way. But he doesn't seem to mind eating the bunnyburgers."

I got serious. "You mean you really raise rabbits? Where the hell are the rabbits?"

"Bunny Hell," she said. "You want to see?"

She stood up and kitchy-kooed. She opened the door next to the refrigerator and I followed her down the cellar stairs. Fluorescent lights were already on down there, as if it were a business office; black plastic was stapled over the chin-level windows. "I thought we better cover the windows over," she said, "so people wouldn't see the lights on all night and think we were growing sinsemilla. Anyhow, *voilà.* Bunny Hell."

I counted five cages, made of two-by-fours and chicken wire: three on the built-in workbench, two on a ping-pong table, one on each side of the net. Each cage had three or four rabbits. White, black, piebald; bright, trusting eyes. Martha stuck two fingers through the chicken wire and smoothed between the ears of a chocolate-brown rabbit the size of a roasting chicken. "You want to hold one?"

"I'll pass," I said.

"Look," she said, "I know. But they really do have a good life. You know, for a bunny. Lots of other bunnies to hang out with and fuck—we definitely encourage fucking—and good big cages that get cleaned all the time, good stuff to eat, sunshine all day every day"—she pointed up at the fluorescent lights—"and when their time comes they never know what hit 'em."

"What *does* hit 'em?" I said.

"Twenty-two," she said. "Look it's absolutely no more immoral than going to the supermarket and buying a chicken that somebody has killed *for* you. You want to see?"

"Christ no," I said.

"I don't mean a *demonstration*," she said. "Here." The basement was divided by a partition; she opened a door into a room that smelled of . . . some smell from my childhood. She pulled a string, and a bare bulb lit up. One corner was stacked with haybales. "Used to be the coal bin in here," she said. Coal: that was the smell. Grandpa Jernigan's basement. "Before Rusty and I put the oil burner in, his parents had this big-ass old coal furnace sitting in the middle of the basement. With all the ducts going all over the place? When Clarissa was a little girl, I used to tell her it was a tin tree for the Tin Woodman to cut down."

She squatted down and lifted the top of an old metal tool chest. Inside was a little automatic pistol and a box of .22 shorts. "In case you're here alone," she said, "and the Revolution starts or something."

"This is the death chamber?" I said. "What do you do, shoot 'em against the haybales?"

She looked surprised. "Huh," she said. "Yeah, Tim told me to make sure and use a haybale. Otherwise probably the first one I would have done, the bullet would have ricocheted off the floor and killed somebody. See, what I do is just sort of get a good grip on the bunny, and then I just put the thing right against the back of the, the thing's head, so I'm shooting into there like. We use the hay for the little guys' bedding, too."

"Waste not, want not," I said.

"Believe me, I know how all this sounds," she said. "But it's actually more moral than going out and buying chicken or something. Do you know how those chickens *live* that you get at the store? You know how they *die?*"

I didn't, exactly, but I nodded yes so I wouldn't have to hear about it. Of course she was right, although you had to wonder if all those millions of miserable chicken lives outweighed a single ruined human life, ending in a drunken human death by automobile. Apples and oranges, probably.

Walking past the cages again, I gave the deathbound bunnies a crisp salute, thinking of the old *morituri te salutamus*, although in fact I had it all fucked up, since I was doing the saluting and they were doing the moriturying, at least right now. Good and popped on that moonshine myself.

4

But the next morning, hauling myself up the steps of the train with a headache going above and behind my right ear, I'd lost what zest I'd had for all this. It was clear this morning that I had gotten myself involved with another crazy woman: this time, a crazy woman who shot rabbits in her basement. And who would shoot me if I now tried to extricate myself. Who would shoot my son. Shoot herself. Through inattention, through indifference, through—shall we for once just cut the crap?—through deliberately looking away from a father's responsibilities, I had first let Danny become involved with this crazy woman and her damaged daughter, and had then allowed myself to be pulled into their delusional world.

I nestled between two men in charcoal pinstripe suits, each reading the *Times* C section. The theme was Home: today, therefore, was Thursday. Like *The Mickey Mouse Club*. Tuesday, Guest Star Day; Wednesday, Anything Can Happen. I opened up *Northanger Abbey*.

At work, a nice hello from Miranda, Kelsey's pretty secretary, except these days you have to call them assistants, with whom it would never go beyond occasional eye contact. Imagine Jernigan making eye contact: that should give you an idea of this Miranda. Three pink While You Were Out slips on my desk. All business calls; not one saying Martha. Everybody was going to have a normal day here at work.

Except that it turned out to be a disastrous day. I mean, to the extent you could take things at work seriously. Although you do. Especially when people are that angry with you. What happened was this. The week before—I'll try to keep this brief; a bunch of work stuff is too dreary even for *Life of Jernigan*—the week before, I had apparently misplaced a decimal point or something while figuring up the cost of ripping out the internal walls in four floors of some building in NoHo. (Not even my listing, for Christ's sake. I did the numbers as a favor to Coleman, since I'd had a little down time. A lot of down time. But again, whole other story.) With my rough and very much mistaken estimate in hand, the client had gone to his people, and the estimate prompted them to move some money they wouldn't otherwise have moved. I mean, basically, who gives a shit. But at any rate, today was the day this whole thing came out. So. Big meeting with Coleman and Kelsey and our lawyer. Another big meeting, with the client and his lawyer and Coleman and Kelsey and our lawyer. I sat there like a bad boy, cursing Uncle Fred in my heart. As I had, pretty much every day, for ten years. With his fucking friend Coleman in the fucking real estate business. With his fucking *helpfulness*. The last meeting of the day was a one-on-one with Kelsey. During which I basically told him mistakes happen and what can you do. Which didn't seem to fly all that well. I left his office thinking *Ten years of this shit*. Hey, like they say. Day at a time.

I had planned to take the 5:46, go over to Heritage Circle and mow the front lawn before it got dark. Even this late in the year, the front part grew like a son of a bitch. Watered by a martyr's blood, I suppose. That isn't funny. The back didn't worry me so much: only three neighbors could see it anyhow, and then only if they stuck their neighbor noses right up against the chain-link fence, interwoven with green plastic ribbon. Well, I didn't make the 5:46. I ran like a bastard through Penn Station and just barely caught the 8:37. That late a train, at least you could get a window: this was the kind of thing you were reduced to thinking was a big fucking deal. I thought about Uncle Fred saying, "What the hey, do it for a year. The worst that can happen is teaching will start to look good to you, and you'll go back with some money in the bank. Besides, it could be a goof."

When we came up out of the tunnel and into New Jersey, night had fallen, and all the salmon-pink highway lights were on. I glanced around the compartment. All the men looked like me. Human basset hounds in wrinkled suits. Except they were drunk, lucky bastards, from their after-work stop-off at Charley O's or something. Ties loosened, breathing through their mouths.

Once I was off the train and safe in my own car, I put the seat all the way back and just lay there, as if in a dentist's chair, in the station parking lot. Only a few other cars left, in all that expanse. I closed my eyes and pictured the empty house, eggshell walls. Put the seat back up straight, finally, got the car going and went left on Hamilton Avenue. Instead of taking the right, which was how you got to Heritage Circle. Heading for Martha, however crazy she was.

"*Hey*, stranger," she said, opening the door. "It was getting so late I didn't know whether to expect you." Thanksgiving smell in the kitchen—sage and onion?—and Martha's breasts swelling under a forest-green reindeer sweater. One of her thrift-shop jobs, I imagined. It must have been her idea of an autumn thing to wear, and I found myself touched by the way she did the best she could. "Danny's in watching television," she said. "And Clarissa's upstairs sulking. We didn't wait supper, but there's some macaroni and cheese left. Or if you'd rather, I just finished a stew for tomorrow night. It's actually better if it sits for a day, but."

"Macaroni and cheese," I said. Not ordering it up, but in wonderment.

She jerked a thumb over her shoulder. "Danny insisted," she said. "Apparently they had something on tv about Mom Food. You just going to stand out there?"

"Macaroni and cheese, please," I said. "But could I have something else first?" Jernigan, being oh so winning.

These were still the days when, if we could, we'd spend a couple of hours in bed. I mean, a good part of why I was there in the first place was just the weird novelty of having sex again. Something I'd pretty much given up on. Embarrassing as hell even to think about it now, but we'd gotten into this business where she was pretending to be a one-woman harem, working permutations on her name to match what we were doing. Martha>Marty>Martina>Tina. Sullen Marty was the boy, meaning I was to turn her over; bossy Martina was the lesbian, meaning I was to go down on her; reluctant Tina meant straight missionary, her arms at her sides. Whatever *that* was about. One afternoon we had experimented with Mr. T (Marty>Mr. T), which was her fucking me with a finger. When she got the second knuckle in I squirmed away, and her growls gave way to giggling. "Okay, okay," she said. "We had to *try* it, right?" Meaning *she* had had to try it.

Tonight was particularly intense.

"So what's it like, Mr. Jernigan?" she said when I absolutely couldn't do any more. "Having your own little private cathouse at your disposal? Is it nice for you?" Dabbling a finger in the sweat on my chest.

"*Oh* yeah," I said. "Though I do sometimes wonder where it all leaves Martha, you know?" As polite a way as I could think of to say that I was no longer sure that some of this might not be a little over the edge. Apparently Peter Jernigan had come to believe in edges.

"Oh, fuck Martha," she said. "She's a drudge and a drag. Who cares, you know? The world is full of unhappy women."

5

Eleven-thirty or so I finally got up and had macaroni-and-cheese dinner. Then still more bed, a good big glass of moonshine, and off to sleep.

Three in the morning I was back awake. Got up and crept down the hall to the kitchen. A line of light glowed at the bottom of Clarissa's door, faraway music rasped and clattered. My son was here. And all was well. Or so I was willing to think. In the refrigerator I found tomorrow's stew. In a copper stewpot, yet: before opting out of the money economy, old Martha hadn't done *too* badly for herself. I lifted the lid, dripping with condescension, condensation I should say, and went and got a wooden spoon out of the dish drainer. I stood there eating and eating. Rabbit stew, with still-firm quarters of potato, still-firm logs of parsnip. The stew part was gray and thick, and not at all disgusting.

IV

1

By October neither Danny nor I had spent a night in our own house for over a month.

"Has it occurred to you," Martha said, "that this is getting silly?"

"I'm not complaining," I said. I was sitting on the edge of the bed, in shirt and trousers, pulling a sock over my right foot. Martha was lying face-down, cheek against my left thigh, pulling down the sock I'd just put on my left foot. I wasn't complaining, true, but this wasn't the time for her to be proving she was still seductive. I was already going to miss the 7:48, and I'd be lucky to get the 8:04. Although I was probably misreading simple playfulness.

She caressed my bare left foot with both hands, burrowed her head into my clothed crotch and kissed, rolled over onto her back and then sat up. "I don't mean us being together," she said. "I mean you and Danny shuttling back and forth with your clothes and everything. At least you're not rousting him out of bed at the crack of dawn anymore to drive him over to your house for the bus." She cocked her head, stuck out her tongue, crossed her eyes and made crazy-circles around her ears with her index fingers.

"I still think I was right about that." I picked up the other sock from the floor and pulled it back on. "I don't think you're taking into consideration how weird this whole arrangement is," I said. "Somebody's going to start burning fucking crosses on the lawn." This was Peter Jernigan talking, taker of twenty-three acid trips (I had kept count) and sworn enemy of convention.

"Well if anybody's freaking out," she said, "*I* haven't heard about it. Nobody here even knows anybody."

"Isn't it pretty to think so," I said.

"Why pretty?" she said. Oh well.

"Dear Peter," she said. "If we could only get you to quit worrying about what people are going to *do* to you."

"And live the rational life?"

"I like it when you're angry sometimes," she said, rubbing the small of my back. "I'm not saying stay home and fuck me"—she slipped a hand down into the back of my trousers and fingered my coccyx through my shirttail and jockey shorts—"because I know you have to go to work. But just think if you didn't have to."

"The unlived life," I said, raising an Uncle Fred forefinger, "is not worth examining." Neatly turned, I thought. Sailed by.

"But it's so stupid," she said. "You said yourself it was like being in high school."

"Right," I said. "Builds character. Teaches citizenship."

She worked her hand inside the jockey shorts and poked with a nailed finger. "Mr. T says think straight."

"Hey," I said. She reached in further, up to her elbow, hand all the way between my legs and up the front of me. "Hmm," I said.

"But promise you'll always wear a business suit," she said in my ear, undoing my belt with her other hand. "I like reaching around in baggy pants."

"If I quit my job," I said, lying back and letting her, "even my *jeans* are going to be baggy." I was alluding, obscurely, to starvation.

"I would never let you go hungry," she said, somehow understanding.

A knock on the door. "Dad?"

"He went to *work* for Christ's sake," I called. "You think the bread-winner can lollygag around the house all day?"

"You want me to come back later?" said Danny.

Martha nodded yes.

"Nah, hold on," I called. "Be with you in a second." Martha shook her head and silently booed me. "He's got to catch the bus," I whispered, standing up and zipping my trousers. "Back in a trice."

"Drat," she said.

Down in the living room, Danny had spread out the tablecloth I'd forgotten to put back over the tv the night before, and was sitting on it in full lotus position, the soles of his sneakers turned to the ceiling.

"*Shantih shantih*," I said. " 'S'up?"

"Listen," he said, uncurling. "Do you mind if I use the house after school for something?"

"For *something*?"

"Well, like, for band practice?"

"What band?" I said. Thinking of gold braid and tubas.

"It isn't really like a *band* band," he said. "I was just talking to this kid that plays bass? And he doesn't like the band that he's in and we were just going to get together and jam or something."

"Great," I said. "I'm glad. Sure. By all means."

"And Clarissa can maybe sing," he said, looking away. "Or I was thinking maybe about starting her on drums if we can't get a real drummer."

"Well," I said, determined to encourage, "at least you could have her shake a tambourine or something."

"Do you think it'd be okay if we turned up kind of loud? I mean not real loud, but it would sound better if we could have it a little loud."

"Okay by me," I said. "You might want to keep the windows shut so old Mr. Howard doesn't call the cops on you." (Cop with holster sitting at the kitchen table: *This is a normal thing to you?*) "He doesn't strike me as a heavy metal kind of guy."

"It's not *metal*, Dad. You know, it isn't anything yet. Dustin's into the Smiths and stuff." Whoever the fuck the Smiths were. "I mean it probably won't even work out or anything. I never even *played* with this kid, okay?"

"Well, whatever," I said, ignoring the tone. "*Mi casa su casa*. I mean, obviously. Now, should I call and tell the power company they might have a brownout in the area of Heritage Circle?"

He looked at me. "Is that a joke?"

"Yes," I said. "Hope it amused you."

"Sorry," he said.

"One more thing," I said. "If you plan on smoking dope—of which I firmly disapprove—do it in your bedroom or something, so when the cops *do* come about the noise you don't end up in the hoosegow."

He raised his eyes like a persecuted saint.

I heard a door close upstairs, and down came Clarissa. She drifted into the living room, stinking of pot smoke. When she noticed me, she shrank back, but she couldn't very well turn tail. So she just stood and blushed. Which was something, to see that pale face go red.

"Sorry, Mr. Jernigan," she said. "I thought you went to work already."

"What can I say?" I said. "Sometimes your mind will play tricks with you, you know? What we used to call your my-yind." Small-time cruelty, I know, I know. I wasn't her father, thank God, so it wasn't up to me to come down on her. But she might as well know I wasn't an idiot.

"We're gonna be late, babe," said Danny. Though only after saying this did he take his eyes off Clarissa to look at his watch. "Got everything?"

She had nothing but a purse the size of a wallet, black leather with silver studs, dangling at her hip from a disproportionately long shoulder strap.

" 'Bye, Ma," she called. (" 'Bye, honey," from far away.) Danny took her hand and led her out the door. I checked *my* watch. So much for the 8:04.

Back upstairs, I found Martha under the covers with only her head sticking out. Oh surprise surprise.

"It's seven forty-five," I said. "Do you know how smashed your daughter is?"

"Oh shit," she said. "I knew she'd been backsliding a little on the weekends."

"Well," I said, "I'd hate to be in her little Reeboks when they get to quadratic equations."

"I don't think they have anything like that *this* year," she said. "But I take your point." She smiled what was meant to be a wicked smile. "And speaking of taking your point . . ." She lifted one arm free of the covers and kitchy-kooed. And what do you know? The arm was bare to the shoulder!

I sat down on the edge of the bed. "Is this something we should be doing something about?"

"Not right now," she said, trying to preserve a mood clearly slipping out of her control. She writhed a come-hither writhe.

"Don't *you* ever wonder," I persisted, "what goes on in that room?"

This made her sit up, not caring anymore whether I saw breasts or not. "What?" she said. "My little girl's corrupting your little boy? Is that what you're worried about?"

"I worry about *both* of them," I said.

"Right," she said.

"If you recall," I said, "you gave me this big speech about how Danny was so *good* for Clarissa, and how all this was a problem from the distant past."

"So it just goes to show you, right? Love works miracles and they don't last."

"Meaning what?" I said, as I was clearly expected to. I remembered from Judith just how to do this.

"Meaning you seem to be finding me increasingly resistible."

"So now what is *this* about?" I said. "Because I want to talk about something that legitimately worries me? And *should* legitimately worry *you*?"

"And you don't think I'm worried?" she said. "What, in your wisdom, do you think I ought to be doing about it? Put her in Fair Oaks because she smokes a joint? I know you think I'm a shitty mother. You, of course, are a world-class father."

"I can't believe this shit," I said.

"Which is why Danny has in effect been living here for six months. Because his *father* is just such a warm *guy*."

"Maybe the fact that he can fuck his brains out every night and nobody says jack shit about it has something to do with it too," I said.

"I wouldn't go by that," she said. "It doesn't seem to cut much ice with *you* anymore."

I shook my head. "This is a really grotesque situation, if you think about it for one minute. Them in there and us in here? That ever strike you? That this is deeply fucked up?"

"So change it," she said, tearing off the covers and standing up. "You think it's *grotesque*, why don't you change it?" She strode naked to the dresser and began brushing her hair, buttocks bobbing with every stroke.

And so on.

2

That day I didn't make it in to work at all.

Next morning I got up and took the 7:31, rolled into the office bright and early. No smile from Miranda, who looked up, then went back to her typing.

"How goes?" I said.

"All right," she said.

"That's good," I said. She typed another burst of characters, then said "Shit" and reached for the white-out.

I said, "I myself am feeling better, thank you." Keeping up the pretense that I'd been sick the day before. She leaned forward and blew on the sheet of paper where she'd brushed on the white-out.

"You know," I said, "Dr. K should really break down and at least get you something with backspace erase. This is like one step up the evolutionary ladder from the stone tablet and chisel." Dr. K was my little name for Kelsey.

She looked at me then. "I really hate this, okay?" she said. "But he told me to tell you he wants to see you. Like as soon as you came in?"

"You're trying to tell me something," I said.

"I'm really sorry," she said.

"Ho-*ly* shit," I said. "Hmm. Yow. Well."

I had never been fired from anything before.

"Sort of bizarre," I said. "It's like in Dagwood or something, you know?" Right, this Miranda was really likely to know about Dagwood; what was she, twenty-five? Unless they still had Dagwood.

What exactly did they say when they fired you, in the real world? Surely not *You're fired*. In Dagwood I think they tossed you out by your shirt collar and the seat of your pants.

"Guess you might as well buzz," I said, hoping Miranda would at least admire the sang-froid. Office romances were a bad idea, not that I hadn't had one, and almost a second one, while Judith was alive. But now that I was apparently out of here, maybe I could call Miranda sometime for a cup of coffee. Although there was now Martha to be thought of.

"Send him in," went Kelsey's voice from her desktop.

Miranda salaamed the squawkbox, both palms aloft, then said to me, "Keep your chin in."

I shadowboxed a little for her, to show my insouciance.

"Sit," said Kelsey.

I sat.

"This may or may not come as much of a surprise to you," he said, "but it's been decided to let you go. Very frankly, it just hasn't been a good fit."

"I guess I'd been feeling that for some time," I said. Hey, you always said you were into the degradation: dig it now. *Degradation*: I played with the word as I looked at Kelsey's hands, his hands being as far up as I dared look. Gold wedding band pinching into the bloat. I came up with *Dagwoodation*. As if Elmer Fudd were saying it.

"Damn it," Kelsey was saying, "you actually have a lot on the ball. You're smart, you're presentable . . ." A third attribute seemed to escape him. "All this has really accomplished is to keep you from doing"—he shrugged—"whatever it is that you should be doing. And I'm a great believer in this, that people do have, each person, a right job or a right niche or what have you." He pronounced it *nick*. "I wish we were big enough, frankly, to where if a guy wasn't working out in the one job, move him over, try something else. But fortunately or unfortunately . . ." He spread his hands, to show his despair. "So all we can do is just say Godspeed, work out some kind of a severance package that's fair to everybody and . . ." Out went the hands again.

"What kind of severance thing specifically are we talking about?" I said, all business. In fact, I'd forgotten that part of what made a decent job a decent job was that they didn't just shove you out the door with your last paycheck.

"Well, what we were thinking of offering," said Kelsey, "and if you don't think it's equitable please say so, is two months at full salary, plus use of the office for the next week, say, to get yourself on your feet, make some calls, whatever you need to do. We're also willing, if need be, to keep you on the health plan for the next month, month and a half, so you'll have time to make other arrangements."

It was plain even to me that he could be talked up. Two months? Even for a cheeseparing operation like Kelsey and Chittenden, this could only be an opening gambit. Christ, hadn't he invited me to bargain? He sat there watching me, thinking whatever shit business-men think. Probably trying to anticipate how I was going to react, so he'd know which way to fuck me. I really didn't have the energy for this.

"Two months?" I said. "Is that the usual?"

"I suppose in this case we could stretch a point," he said. "I think we could probably justify an additional couple of weeks on a sort of hardship basis. Justification being the sudden termination and the years of service. Beyond that, I'm not sure we're prepared to, in a sense, prolong things in a way that's not productive for anybody."

So apparently all I had to do was keep myself from saying Okay and I could watch the free money pile up.

I fetched a sigh, which I hoped he might read as *I had in mind something more like three months.*

"So we're agreed," he said.

So much for Jernigan the crafty negotiator. At this point I just wanted to get the fuck out of there. "I don't know," I said. "Whatever."

"Now," he said, and took in a breath through his teeth. So there was more. "In regards to recommendations. I'd be perfectly happy to tell any and all comers just what I've told you, that you're bright, well-spoken—but I'm not certain to what extent that would really be of great help to you."

He waited for me to say something.

Finally he said, "It's a sort of a horns-of-a-dilemma situation in regards to the ethics of it. On the one hand, you don't want to hurt anyone's chances, as I'm sure you can appreciate."

"That bad," I said.

"I'm going to tell you something for your guidance," he said. "This had been contemplated last year, at the time you had your tragedy. And we felt at that time that A, it simply wouldn't be right at such a time, and we also wondered very frankly, and forgive me for saying this, which I don't mean any disrespect, if you might not have been having problems in the home which might in turn have a bearing on the other problems. And that conceivably, given time . . ." Which was as far as he got in imagining Jernigan transformed. "But," he said.

"Well," I said.

"May I be frank?" he said. "I really don't like you. And if I'd been listened to when Mr. Chittenden wanted to take you on, you would have never *been* taken on. I just thought I should pass that on as part of the total picture."

"So that's what this is really about?" I said.

"No," he said. "But of course you're welcome to think whatever makes you feel better."

"Ten years," I said.

"Long time," he said.

I decided to try that thing you always heard about in high school. Absolutely nothing to lose at this point. "Well, fuck you very much," I said.

And damned if it didn't work. "For what?" he said.

Back in the outer office, Miranda looked up and raised her eyebrows by way of question.

"*Son cosas de la vida*," I said, a phrase I picked up from *Naked Lunch*. Commute for this long and you'll read pretty much anything. I'd been through the P. G. Wodehouse period, the Chesterton period, the fucking Lamb–Hazlitt–De Quincey period. *Naked Lunch* was from the Reread Everything You Read in High School period. Though I mostly just reread the dirty parts, still half afraid they'd make me a homosexual.

"You're going to think this is a really inappropriate time," Miranda said, "but I think I have to tell you that he isn't actually being cheap or anything. This actually does erase, but I sort of use the white-out for moral reasons. Because I don't think you can just backtrack and undo your mistakes like that."

This got my attention. In all the months she'd been here, I'd never understood that Miranda was crazy.

Well, so maybe crazy enough to see you outside the office.

"Interesting," I said. "Interesting way of thinking about it. Listen, they've offered to let me come in for a few days more, but I think I'm just going to clean out some stuff now and bag it. Otherwise I think it's just going to weird everybody out, including me. But I was thinking, sometime when I'm in the neighborhood why don't I give you a call and we can go grab a cup of coffee or something."

Fired after ten years and just coming out and blithely putting the moves on this Miranda. To the extent it was moves. To the extent it was blithe.

3

By noon I was back at Martha's house. On the train, I'd gotten into this thing in my head that she was one of those Housewife Hookers you read about (though technically not a wife) and that this explained where the money came from. It made complete sense.

Inside I could hear music going. I rang the doorbell and whapped the knocker. Footsteps came trotting, Martha yelling "Just a minute!"

The other idea I had was that she was cuckolding me (if an unmarried man can, technically, be cuckolded) with Tim the Untimid: author, editor, moonshiner, New Adam and all-around timber wolf. Thinking, I suppose, of my sainted mother.

"I'll huff and I'll puff and I'll *blow* your house in," I cried, Jack Nicholson in *The Shining*.

"Peter?" she called. She opened the door a crack.

"The wand'ring O'Jernigan," I said. "Make my bed soon, for I fain would lie down." Oh, I had the bitch dead to rights. Noon, and she was naked, apparently, under her baby-blue terry-cloth robe.

She opened the door wide. "What are *you* doing home?"

Home?

I could hear now that the music was Webb Pierce. Which she'd given up trying to play with the kids in the house: Clarissa and Danny thought it was funny to howl along like lonesome ki-yotes.

"Fair question," I said. "And now, my turn. What's the door doing locked?" This was the same Jernigan, remember, who'd just been putting his approximation of moves on poor Miranda.

"You're going to think this is really stupid," she said. "I was just about to jump in the shower, and I still always lock every door in the house because of *Psycho*. And bolt the bathroom. Nowadays it actually makes some sense, but I was doing this when I was like thirteen. So how come you're home, sweetie?"

"You haven't invited me in," I pointed out.

She gave me a look, then took my hand and led me inside.

I listened for the sound of a man scuttling out a window, or rustling in a closet as he waited for a propitious time to make his getaway. Like maybe while the faithless bitch was seducing me. If she now reached for old Dr. Johnson that would be a shit-sure sign. (I call it Dr. Johnson because I read it in Auden's list of names for the genitals in *A Certain World*. Jernigan the Colorful.) Webb Pierce sang, *But the one that I'm tied to was the first to be untrue.* And I understood that she was defying me to pierce her web of deceit.

Of course it was just that I'd gone off on that thing in my head.

It must've been because I had just been fired. Odd as it seems that I might actually have taken to heart a thing anyone else would have taken to heart. Well, hell, anything to anchor you to the planet, right? Here's how I reconstruct it: losing the job—ten years of having a place to go and things to do there—made me afraid nothing else could be counted on either. Except maybe afraid's not right: maybe the opposite. *Wanting* everything to fall apart under me, leaving me in deep space. Wanting what you dread to come true. The twists and turns of Jernigan: what could be more interesting?

"You're kidding," said Martha, when I'd settled down enough to tell her what had happened. "How come?"

I shrugged. "Turns out they were going to get rid of me last year, only they took pity on me when, you know, there was the little incident." Bound to bother another woman to hear me speak of it so slightingly. Though better that than to have to hear myself saying, oh so solemnly, *when my wife died.*

"Well I think it's *great*," she said. "And I think we ought to celebrate. Like to help me take that shower?"

So why not be human.

"Good God, woman," I said, trying to get playful. "Don't you realize that losing one's job robs one of one's symbolic manhood?"

"I'm not thinking about your *symbolic* manhood," she said. "Ooh, I made him blush."

"Don't be vulgar," I said. "This is serious, symbolic business here. See, for a real man the maw of unemployment is the symbolic equivalent of a big, snapping *vagina dentata*. Snap snap." I made my hand into a mouth (thumb as upper jaw) and snapped at my crotch.

"You really *do* think that, don't you?" she said, putting a companionable arm around me.

I shook my head. "Irony, irony," I said. "With me, always assume irony."

"Even when you say 'always assume irony'?"

"Hey," I said. "You've heard of the Liar Paradox? Well, this is the Ironist Paradox."

"I love you," she said. "Sans irony."

"Well," I said, "since I've been sent to the showers anyway . . ."

"Do you love *me*?" she said. "Oh God, you should *never* ask that. Withdraw the question. Sorry."

"Slow down," I said.

"No. I really don't want to hear it right now. Even if you *do*."

"Suit yourself," I said. I knew how to get around this one. Easy: be oh so winning. "But can we still have that shower?"

"Yes," she said. "That we can do."

Afterwards, in bed, she said, "So this is really true?"

"As a ploy to get my ashes hauled," I said, "it's a bit elaborate, no?"

"Are you really freaked?" she said, grabbing a pillow off the floor and tucking it behind her so she could sit up. "I sometimes can't tell with you." Apparently we were now to have a conversation about it.

"Heavens to Betsy *no*," I said. "I'm sure the bank will be understanding about it when I stop sending my mortgage payments. Power company? Pretty loose guys over there. Supermarket—"

She put a hand over my mouth. "Hush," she said. "Why don't you sell that awful house and move in here? You live here anyway. What'd you pay for it?"

"Fifty-seven. That was, like, ten years ago."

"Ten years," she said, and scrunched her eyes to figure. "So you put it up for probably one seventy-five, one eighty, you pay the bank what you—how much *do* you owe them?"

"I don't know. A lot. Probably forty-five. We didn't put all that much down."

"Okay, so say forty-five. Even less commission you've got well over a hundred thousand dollars just *sitting* there."

"Right. Which the minute I touch I then lose half of in taxes."

"So you find some tax-free thing to put it in, and you don't touch it for a while. Keep a little back for yourself, don't get another job, so you can income-average your next year's taxes. . . . You'll be fine. Hustle together a little money when you need it, you know, odd jobs, this and that."

"Fine until I get sick," I said. "Or Danny. What am I doing about health insurance and shit like that? I mean, what if somebody has to have *root* canal?"

"Well Peter, you can't just live your life in a cringe, *waiting* for stuff to happen. I really believe that's a way of *inviting* stuff to happen. You could be living here for practically nothing—"

"I.e., on whatever money your ex-husband sends you."

"So?" she said. "What? It's good enough to slum around in, but you wouldn't lower yourself to live here?"

"Christ, give me a *break*," I said. "I got fired from my job, what, three hours ago? I mean, that's enough to absorb. Would *you* be ready to change your life just like that?"

"You betcha," she said. "If it needed changing as much as *yours* does. Sweetie." She got out of bed and walked naked to the door. "I have to go pee," she said. "When I get back, you tell me what you want to do."

I lay there and tried to figure out what I ought to think. I thought I probably ought to think I was being pressured by a crazy woman. If she kept after me about it, then I would know she was evil and meant me harm, wasn't that right? And then I would know not to do anything she said.

When she came back she had the robe on again.

"Okay," I said. "Now what *is* this?"

She got under the covers, robe still on, and stared at the hula girl. "I'm sorry," she said. "That was meant to be just sort of an exercise that I thought might help you. I guess it was stupid to use shock therapy on somebody who's shocked already. What I mean is, you're welcome to come live here, Peter. You and Danny. You know that already. I think it could be a nice life. And it could be really good for Danny to have a woman around. *And* Clarissa to have a man. Or if you want, you could look for another job and we can just keep on the way we've been doing. Or you're at liberty to change that part of it too. I mean that's pretty much giving you, I don't know, whatever you want."

This didn't sound like someone who meant me harm. Though actually what could be more hostile than giving you whatever you wanted? Thinking about the *Twilight Zone* thing where the guy says he's going nuts in heaven and won't they please send him to the Other Place and this guy tells him this *is* the Other Place, nya-ha-ha-ha-*hah*.

She looked at me. "I just think you could have a more satisfying life for yourself, Peter," she said. "You were talking the other night about how you used to want to write poetry. You know, you could *do* it."

"*Madre de dios,*" I said. (The other night we'd gotten popped on that moonshine again and I'd been telling high school stories.) "I was talking about when I was fourteen years *old*, for Christ's sake. Every kid in my little *clique* wanted to be a poet. Like with a *beard*, you know? Because we thought Allen Ginsberg was this great romantic figure. I mean, this was just after I wanted to be Roger *Maris*, okay?"

"Sounds like I hit a nerve," she said.

"You didn't hit a fucking *nerve*," I said. "I would just like to be spared the final degradation, you know? Being a fuckup and a burnout I can deal with. Being a fuckup and a burnout who's starting to write *poetry* at forty years old, or learning to play the fucking *saxophone*, no."

"You know," she said, "it actually sounds like I'm picking up fear of failure? I think that's so cute."

"*You're* a twisted fuck," I said.

"Isn't that the way you like 'em?" she said. "You're only thirty-nine, by the way, unless you've been lying about your age."

I did the bang-zoom gesture. Channel 11 had *The Honeymooners* just before *Star Trek*, which was just before *The Twilight Zone*.

"I'm serious," she said. "Really, no wonder you like demeaning jobs, Peter. You ever thought about being a desk clerk? There's that nice Holiday Inn that overlooks the whole Meadowlands. Would *that* be depressing enough?"

"Martha dear," I said, and put a finger to my lips. "We've made our point?"

She tapped her forehead and nodded, then crossed her hands over her chest mummy-style and lay rigid, staring at the ceiling.

"Oh for Christ's sake," I said.

"Shhh," she went.

"Okay, fine," I said. "Listen, I'm going out for a walk." Knowing I was just being a huffy asshole. Since she was acting out of love, apparently.

4

Against that cobalt-blue sky, the leaves looked morbidly colorful: the hectic yellow, orange and red stages of a wasting disease. You were supposed to think they were beautiful. I hadn't even noticed them this morning while walking to the car, or driving under the arching trees all the way out to Hamilton Avenue. Oh, completely my own fault: simply having a job needn't numb you. Obvious example: Wallace Stevens. Any deadass drudge can feel even worse about himself by thinking about Wallace Stevens.

At least this much was clear: to move into Martha's house with no job and no other place to go was to lose power, imaginary hundred thousand dollars or no imaginary hundred thousand dollars.

If even that much was clear. I mean, if at some point you *wanted* a job, then fine, go get a job, right?

Though like what? And how would you explain when they asked you what you'd been doing for the last year or whatever?

Which in turn was a whole other question: what *would* you do with yourself all day long?

Though on the other hand, just getting some job merely to avoid having to figure out what to do with yourself all day long—Christ. This hand, that hand, the other fucking hand.

I walked left on Maple, went a block and took Nottingham over to Oakdale. This part of town beat the hell out of Heritage Circle. Big old one- and two-family houses, mostly wood-shingled still, though more and more with new aluminum siding or brickface. Big old trees in the strip of earth between street and sidewalk; their roots, swelling and swelling through the years, now tilted up every third or fourth square of concrete.

On the sidewalk up ahead, a woman was pushing a baby carriage toward me; stroller, I should say. Thing where the kid has to sit there with the world coming at him. Young woman, green colleen sweater for a fall day. A little plump, as a mother ought to be, now what kind of a thing is that to say? Pale, pretty face, straight reddish bangs. Map of Ireland, if Jernigan's any judge. Still a bit of a flirt, it seemed to me, but now only occasionally wheedled into sex, as is proper for a mother. I can't believe it's Peter Jernigan coming out with this stuff.

It bothered me that I really knew nothing about the neighborhood except that it looked like it was still 1953. Which seemed pretty irresponsible, to change your life (to say nothing of your son's life) without even looking into stuff like that. Well, here comes your chance: a totally disinterested party.

"Hi, excuse me," I said, and then didn't know how to go on. Having trouble deciding what tone to try to strike. I'd been going to ask if she lived around here, but that was patently a rapist's question. I also thought about asking her if she was Irish and noting that I was Irish too. That might sound deranged, but not rapisty.

She stopped, glanced down at her baby, then gave me a quick smile, off-on-off, apparently a sign of attention.

"Sorry," I said. "I'm sort of new to the neighborhood here, and in fact I'm actually thinking of . . ." It seemed weird to say moving in permanently, because what would that mean to somebody who didn't know the situation? Absolutely nothing. "Thinking of buying here," I said.

Boy, never lie: do you see what a mistake this was? New to the neighborhood implies you're already *in* the neighborhood; thinking of buying implies you're not. What was she supposed to assume, that I was renting? Oh, probably it all just sounded to her like friendly gabble.

"But what I was wondering," I said, "I assume you live around here"—sneaking the rapist's question by her—"and I was just wondering if this is, you know, a good place to be."

Her eyes were narrowing and narrowing. "You're talking about safetywise?"

"Well, sort of," I said. "I mean, not *just* that."

She looked over her shoulder, then said, more quietly, "You mean is it going black? I would say not at all."

It had taken, what, ten seconds to find the ugly place in her? Probably she was nice on the whole and this was just something that was being discussed around here a lot. So now I would have to manage some way of not embarrassing her for having said a racist thing without being complicitous myself.

"I guess not so much that," I said, "as just, you know, is it okay in general?"

"I wouldn't really know what you're talking about," she said, reaching down and adjusting the baby. "Christopher sit *up*. Excuse me?" And she pushed past.

I would have called "Sorry" after her, but what for? To acknowledge openly that I'd given her the rebuke she already knew she'd been given?

Well, so much for checking out the neighborhood. Not that a bunch of thoughtful pros and cons wouldn't have been even less helpful. I mean, at least I'd found out that this was a neighborhood where blacks weren't moving in, however you were supposed to feel about that. Uh-oh, no cultural diversity. Though in fact all I'd really found out was that this was a neighborhood where people didn't want blacks moving in. However you were supposed to feel about *that*. Uh-oh, be coming after me next.

I kept going on Oakdale in the direction of Hamilton Avenue (east, I guess it was, though I'd never entirely gotten my bearings anywhere in New Jersey), thinking I really ought to check out how long it took to walk to the nearest shopping. In case I lived to see gasoline go up to ten dollars a gallon, I suppose. After walking for fucking ever I finally got to the E-Z Mart, just around the corner from Hamilton Quik Dry Clean. It was quarter to four, which told me absolutely nothing since I hadn't looked at my watch when I left. I went in and bought a Diet Coke I didn't want.

I was obviously going to do this crazy thing. Why Martha, rather than some other woman? Because she was there in front of me. Although I was probably refusing to acknowledge some dark psycho-schmycho thing, probably having to do with my mother. What else did anything have to do with? I'd probably just decided to think it could be made to work, since basically anything could be made to work if you took it a day at a time, so why not this.

Probably not the most caring decision I ever made in my life. If you could call it a decision.

Back at the house, I found Martha down in the cellar feeding her rabbits.

"Listen," I said. "Before I really say I'm going to do this I've got to talk things over with Danny. He's in this too, you know?"

"Oh, absolutely. I wouldn't expect you not to. Here, babe," she said to a piebald rabbit. "C'mere, hon." She picked him up and he burrowed his head into her armpit. "This guy feels about ready," she said, stroking him. "Easy, buster. You know, it's funny, but I'd sort of come to think of Danny as part of the household already. Easy, babe." She put the rabbit back in its cage.

"So when is *his* rendezvous with destiny?" I said, turning a thumb toward the rabbit.

"Next couple days, I think. The cupboard's pretty bare, and he's ready to roll. Much bigger than him and I don't think they're quite as tasty."

"Then look," I said. "Why don't we celebrate tonight and make him guest of honor?"

"Sounds reasonable," she said. "Let's go upstairs, I'll get us both a drink, then I'll come back down and do this and we'll just—do it. Okay?"

"Listen," I said, "would you like *me* to? I really wouldn't mind doing it, and it seems to me the guilt ought to be spread around a little here. I've been *eating* enough of these guys."

"My, you *are* going the whole hog," she said.

"Hey. Man's gotta do what a man's gotta do."

"It's nice of you," she said. "But really. I've sort of got it down now, and I'm used to doing it."

"You hate it," I said. "Why don't you let me for a change?"

"Are you sure about this, Peter?"

"Stand aside, wumman," I said. "And fetch me mah hogleg."

This got a smile. Which made me realize how inane it had been.

"Seriously," I said. "It's a godawful job to have to do, and I'm tired of watching myself slink off while you're doing it. And then showing up at the table smacking my lips, you know? Now, should this get done right away, or should it wait a little closer to dinner?"

"For your sake," she said, "I wouldn't do it much closer to dinner than this. Take it from one who knows."

"Then go on up and do your preparations, and the deceased and I will join you presently."

"And you're sure you know how?"

I pointed to the stairs. "Out."

"Thank you," she said.

I went into the death chamber and got the pistol out of the toolchest. Loaded? I popped the little catch at the bottom of the handle and took the clip out. Sure enough. I pushed the clip back in, felt it click home, and stuck the gun in my pocket. I had worn these same trousers to Kelsey and Chittenden this morning, and now there was a gun in them. Went back into the other room and took the piebald rabbit out of his cage. He burrowed his head into my armpit; I stroked his fur and told him Good boy, good boy. Not looking at him much.

He was warm, this rabbit. A mammal like me. I searched for the right word and came up with lapsarian. Marsupial is what I was trying to think of. Although rabbits, according to the dictionary here, are not marsupials. I probably got lapsarian from *lapin*. I carried him into the death chamber, sat us both down on a haybale and, holding him with my left hand, sneaked the pistol out of my pocket with my right and put it next to my right hip. With both hands I lifted the rabbit, sat him down on the other side and pressed him firmly against my right thigh, my left hand gripping his shoulders, cruelly now, as I took the right hand away. He tried to squirm out of my grasp but I had him too tight, and I picked up the pistol with my right hand, jammed the muzzle between his ears and jerked the trigger, hoping to God a haybale was really dense enough to do the trick. The gun went snap and the rabbit gave a shiver and just turned to meat.

5

By the time Danny and Clarissa rolled in, maybe a quarter past ten, Martha and I had had our dinner and done the dishes together. (She washed, I dried, though she said not to bother.) Now I was pretty well into the bottle of Gordon's gin I'd gone out to get special. Store-bought liquor tonight, boy. I was looking forward to *Star Trek* later, which I'd come to think looked less cheesy in black and white. Not that I minded its looking cheesy, that was part of the appeal. Oh what a sense of fun.

"Hey guys?" said Martha. "You do something about dinner? You're hungry there's some pretty dynamite bunny *à l'orange* left over."

"Dynamite," I said.

"We ate already," said Clarissa.

"Hey Dan?" I said. "I know it's late and you do have school to-morrow, but you and I need to have a talk, okay?"

"What about?" he said.

"Relax," I said. "I'm not after you about anything. What it is, I actually need your advice on something."

"Like what?"

"Ladies?" I said. "You'll excuse us? We're going to have a man-to-man here. The old *mano a mano*, whaddya say?" He probably didn't even know it didn't mean man to man, that's what kind of a quote unquote education he was getting at that God damn school of his. He looked at Clarissa and she looked at him. Like a scene out of fucking *West Side Story*. "Dan," I said. "Dan my man. What do you say we go out for a ride, bud?"

He shrugged. "You okay to drive?"

"Nice mouth," I said. "What is this, the Contract for Life or some-thing? *Trust* the old man." Not remembering, of course, that he might be just a leet-tle sensitized to parents' getting behind the wheel drunk.

Chilly outside. This reminded me. "You over at the house all this time?" I said. "You remember to turn the heat back down to forty?"

"Yeah, Dad."

"How'd you get home, anyway?"

"Dustin gave us a lift."

"Dustin," I said.

He didn't seem to understand I was asking him a question.

"Is Dustin the one who plays the drums?" I said. I opened the car door for him.

"Bass," he said.

"Bass is what I meant," I said.

We got in and I started up the car. He just sat there. I felt like taking him by his uninformative little throat. "So how did your practice go, Dan?" I said.

"Okay," he said. "So what did you want to talk about?"

I backed the car out and started up the hill.

"Lights," he said.

"Okay, tiger," I said, turning on the headlights. "Just testing to make sure your head was in the game there." He tugged to tighten his shoulder belt.

"So," I said, "are you and Clarissa getting along okay?"

"I guess so. Why?"

"You guess so."

"Look, Dad. If this is about AIDS or something—"

"Oh Christ," I said, "I'm fucking this whole thing up here. Listen, all this is about, Clarissa's mother and I have been talking about all of us sort of moving in together. And we're concerned that, I don't know, that it might turn out to be weird for the two of you. You know, say you two broke up or something and your parents were still, you know, everybody in the same house sharing the bathroom and everything. Or, I don't know, even if you *didn't* break up it could be weird. And I just thought it was something we ought to talk about."

"Is Mrs. Peretsky talking to Clarissa about it now?"

"I assume so. Though I don't frankly know."

"Do we have to move away someplace?" he said.

"No. No, our plan—I mean, to the extent that it's a plan at all, you know? I would imagine that we'd just keep living in *their* house and that we'd put our place up for sale, and that was one of the things that I thought we needed to talk about. See, I found out today that they're letting me go at work, and—"

"You got *fired*?" he said. "Dad. Why did they *fire* you?"

"Apparently thing was in the works quite some time," I said, as if it had been an answer.

"What are you gonna *do*?" he said.

"Listen," I said, "you want to go sit somewhere have a Coke?"

"If you do."

I took Nottingham over to Oakdale and made a left, heading for Hamilton. Same way I'd walked this afternoon. The headlights picked up leafpile after leafpile, spreading out into the street. I could've sworn they hadn't been there earlier. (But a whole neighborhood just happening to rake their leaves the same evening? Not likely. More plausible explanation: Jernigan on a disconnect.) The tires crackled through the leafpiles' outermost reaches. Huh: they'd called it Oakdale and it actually had oak trees, assuming these were oak trees. Those were the days, boy.

"Getting pretty nippy nights," I said, rolling my window the rest of the way up. Danny had no comment. "That pizza place down on Hamilton probably open this hour," I said. "Suit you okay?"

He considered. Probably judging the chances of being seen by friends when he was out with a father. "I guess that's okay," he said.

"Anyplace you rather?" I said. Push push push.

"It's all *right*, Dad."

The pizza place was a low cinderblock building with PIZZA in the window in angry red neon. Fluorescent light inside, stained-plywood booths with coat posts. We took possession of the one farthest back, then I went up to the counter and brought back a can of Diet Pepsi for Danny and a coffee for me.

"How about a slice while we're at it?" I said.

"Okay," he said.

I went back to the counter. "Couple slices," I said. "Just regular."

"Two?" said the kid. He looked like the kids who scared me when I was Danny's age, their faces all stubble and pustules. A cigarette smoked away in a round aluminum ashtray next to the ivory-colored plastic bucket of shredded cheese.

"You got it," I said. This was how you had to talk to get by in places like this. The kid lifted out two triangles from the pie sitting on the counter—not the two biggest, I noted—flopped them onto a pizza pan and thrust it into the oven.

I went back to Danny. "Anyhow," I said.

"So you're going to sell the house?"

"Well," I said, "that's something we have to talk about. You know, it's not just *my* house. I'd always thought of it as something that someday, you know, would probably come your way when I was out of the picture."

"*That* place?" he said.

"So you should've picked a Rockefeller for a father," I said. As if he even knew what a Rockefeller was.

"I didn't mean it that way," he said. He didn't elaborate on how he *had* meant it.

The kid called, "Slices ready." I went up and fetched them.

"I guess you can sell it if you want to," said Danny. "We could practice just as easy over Dustin's." He picked up his slice and blew at the molten cheese creeping over the point.

"We don't have to decide this in any big hurry," I said. "You know, it's where you grew up and everything." And everything.

"I guess it's okay," he said. "So are you going to marry Mrs. Peretsky?"

"We've talked about it," I said. Christ, had we? I certainly didn't remember it. "See part of the thing is, if we went ahead and sold our place, we could probably find all sorts of interesting stuff to do with the money."

"Like what?"

"Well, *travel* for one," I said. Right, I could see the four of us in the fucking Piazza San Marco. I was really winging it now. "Could even buy some place up the country go there summers, you know? I realize it's been—and this is completely my fault—you've had a very, very, very complicated life so far. I mean, to lose a parent." Which was about as close as I was willing to come to talking about it. "The thing is, you know, I guess my life was pretty complicated, too, by the time I was your age, I mean actually even before. Third *grade* or something. And, you know, here *I* am." And if *that* didn't buck a kid up, I ask you: what would?

I had lost the thread.

"I just want you to know," I said, "that I would not be doing this if I didn't think it was going to make life better for us." (He's lying. Joe Isuzu.)

Well, so take the worst case, all right? Danny was already sixteen; in two years he'd be eighteen and off to college someplace and out of whatever this turned into. Provided his grades got better. Provided there was any money left.

"It's also been in the back of my mind," I said, "that the money from that house might come in handy for your college." I'd only thought of it that minute. "How you coming getting your grades up, by the way?"

"Okay," he said.

"Well," I said, and then just stopped. I didn't have the energy for a whole thing on grades just now.

"Your pizza's getting cold," he said, the crafty little fuck. Or thought he was. I picked it up and took a bite.

"Good," I said. "You want the rest of it? Looks like you got outside of yours pretty fast." He shook his head no. I took another bite. It either was or wasn't good.

As we walked to the car, I put a fatherly arm around his shoulder. He let me. He stared at his feet. Cold as a bitch out.

"So you think you're going to be okay about this, bud?"

"Sure, I guess so," he said. "I like Mrs. Peretsky and everything. So it's not going to be all that different, right?"

"That's it," I said. "It really won't be. Good God, would you look at that." I pointed.

Big scary orange moon, low in the sky.

6

"Glad you got back," said Martha when we came in. "Weatherman just said we could have a really big-time frost tonight. Can you believe it? Anyhow, we've got to get all the rest of those tomatoes in or we're going to have tomato paste in the morning."

"Shit," I said. "Can't just cover 'em up?"

"I really don't want to risk it," she said. "They said it was supposed to get down to twenty in the northern suburbs."

"This is a northern suburb?"

She sighed.

"Okay, okay," I said. "There any coffee?"

"Isn't it going to keep you awake?"

"That was the idea," I said.

"I mean after."

"Little joke," I said.

She lit a burner and clanked a saucepan of cold coffee down on it. "Anything else out there perishable?" I said. Now I was being oh so helpful.

"Not very," she said. "I guess I'll throw some plastic over the herbs and hope for the best. Danny, would you go get Clarissa, please? If we all help out, maybe we can get this done."

He trudged off down the hall.

"How'd it go?" she said.

"Okay," I said. Christ, I sounded like Danny. "I mean, he *says* it's fine with him. I don't think he's really focussing on—I don't know. Maybe he's got the right idea. You talk to Clarissa?"

"Clarissa and I made up our minds a long time ago," she said. "Don't know what took you *fellas* so long."

Nice lighthearted thing to say. Now be lighthearted back.

"It just took us a while to believe our good fortune," I said. "Beauty

and utility we could have believed, but beauty and economy . . ."
Was this lighthearted? Or labored and obscure?

"Well, I'm glad you've both come to your senses," she said, "however belatedly." And kissed my neck. Feigned biting.

"Speaking of belated," I said, getting a coffee mug out of the dish
drainer, "where *are* those lazy little shits?"

She drew in her breath in mock horror. "Your own childring," she
said in her comic hoity-toity voice. "Hey Clarissa?" she called. "Let's
move it, okay? We'll be out in the garden."

She put on the suit jacket I'd left hanging scarecrow-style on a chair
at the kitchen table—I'd been fired in that jacket this morning—and
grabbed the flashlight and a bunch of plastic grocery bags with paper
bags inside them. I poured a little milk into the mug, then filled it
with coffee. I drank while pawing left-handed through the closet for
a warm coat and followed her outside.

The moon had risen, paled and shrunk: now it was just your normal
white moon in a dark sky, except the sky was never really dark here.
Pink everywhere, though pinker off in the direction of Newark and
New York.

"Yow," I said. "It's really getting down there."

"Weathermen," she said. "The only men who never lie to you."

"That's because they know you're going to find out anyway."

"That would never stop a *real* man," she said. "Here. Why don't
you hold the light, *and* the bag, and I'll pick."

"Outstanding," I said. "Outstanding in his field. And that's where
we found him. Out standing in his field."

"Oh *God*. My father used to say that all the time when I was a little
girl," she said. "I used to think it was an absolute *howl*. Hold the light
steady, please?"

"Sorry," I said. "Listen, you don't suppose the kids are going to
fuck the dog on this?"

"I don't?"

"They're not down here in about one minute," I said, "I'm gonna
by Jesus go in there kick some *ass*."

"Let's just get this done," she said. "While we're asserting our
authority we'll be losing our tomatoes."

"Lapidarily put," I said. Thinking of the postlapsarian *lapins* again, probably. "But if by the time we're done . . ."

By the time we were done, the light was off in Clarissa's room.

We managed to catch the end of *Star Trek*—it was the one where Kirk splits into his good and evil selves and finds that without the evil part he dithers too much to command the Enterprise—and went to bed. Martha fell asleep, an arm across my chest. I lifted the arm away and lay there, thoughts racing. From the God damn coffee, plus of course everything else. What I was going to do about money, what a failure I was as a father, whether or not I should extricate myself from this whole deal with Martha.

Finally I got up, put on shirt and trousers and went into the living room to read. Noticed on my way down the hall that the light was back on in the kids' room, the music faintly going. I began again— how many times had I read it?—the long and winding story of Psmith passing himself off as the poet Ralston McTodd, and everyone trying to steal Lady Constance's necklace and Lord Emsworth wanting only to be left alone among his flowers. Maybe if I drank a little more gin, I thought, I might get drowsier faster. So I got out the bottle from under the kitchen sink, thinking about the residuum of puritanism that had led Martha to put it away with the Mr. Clean and the Brillo pads. Maybe it was a Southern thing, something she got from her father.

The bottle was still about half full: ought to more than do me. I set it down next to the Morris chair, tucked my feet under me to sit sidesaddle and began reading again and sipping right from the bottle. A much more generous feeling than doling it out to yourself by the mingy glassful. I was satisfactorily drowsy, if drowsy is really the word, by the time I got to the part where Freddie Threepwood finds Psmith's ad in the newspaper (CRIME NOT OBJECTED TO). But now I didn't want to stop reading. So I went back to the kitchen, drank off the inch or so of coffee left in the saucepan (not bothering with milk this time), then filled the pan with water and made a fresh pot. Not to drink all of it myself; it would be a nice surprise for Martha to wake up and find coffee already made that all she would have to do was heat up. Those old husbandly nice surprises. Oh what a feeling, Toyota, not to have to work tomorrow, and to be able to stay up and do whatever the fuck you felt like doing as late as you felt like doing it.

So I sat curled up in the Morris chair, reading again the familiar deceptions and revelations, taking now a sip of gin, now a sip of coffee. At some point I looked up and saw branchy webs of frost on the windowpanes. I tried to remember how Coleridge's "Frost at Midnight" went, or at least what the fuck it had been about besides frost at midnight, but all I could remember was the title—and this was one of the seminal poems of the Romantic period! Unless I was getting it mixed up with the "Dejection" ode. The old *In our life alone does nature live*. Then it began to turn gray outside, and most of the coffee was gone, and most of the gin.

So: My Big Wild Night, by Jernigan. Now, probably at the same time I was up reading P. G. Wodehouse in the Morris chair, some rock-and-roll star in New York was speedballing coke and heroin and getting sucked off, as flunkies stuck needles into both arms, by a groupie in a leather skirt. Okay. But who's to say I wasn't as close to my edge as he to his?

The gray gave way to full daylight, but I didn't turn the light off: I liked the yellow glow off the page, giving the illusion that darkness still surrounded. Martha appeared in her robe and said, "Hi, you been up all night?" Not even judgmentally. And nonjudgmentally, she put the tablecloth back over the tv.

I picked up my coffee mug and raised it as if to toast. Meaning, I suppose, Here's what kept me awake and here's *to* it. She whittled her index finger at me and said, "You want some breakfast?"

I shook my head.

"Listen," she said, "were you going to speak to the kids about last night? Because if you're not up to it, I'll be glad to say something."

I stared at her. "Be assured," I said, "that Jernigan is up to it."

She looked doubtful. "Well, I guess that settles that." She picked up the gin bottle and raised it to eye level. "Whew," she said. "If you're sure."

"I would like some toast," I said with great dignity. "And I will come to the table."

She put down the gin bottle and saluted, then went into the kitchen. I listened to the breakfast sounds: burners lighting snat snat snat snat, pans clanging, cupboard doors squeaking open, refrigerator door thumping shut. Two soft pings—slices of bread being dropped into the toaster!—then the springy snap of the toaster's lever being pushed home. I got up then and went into the kitchen myself, so I wouldn't have to hear my name called. And there I sat as she bustled.

"Are you all right?" she said.

I nodded.

"Maybe you can get some sleep once the kids get off to school," she said. She sat down to wait for the toast.

"I'll think about that," I said. And I did. Then I got to thinking about some other thing, and the next thing. My mind not really racing anymore, just going. And her mind, I thought, must be going too. We sat there with our minds going.

The toast sprang up and Danny and Clarissa came in, still buttoning their shirts.

"Hey, Mrs. Peretsky?" Danny said. "We're running real late. You have anything we could just grab?"

Martha looked at me.

"Not so fast, you two," I said. "I want the both of you to sit down and have a decent breakfast"—that's right, folks, Peter Jernigan saying *Not so fast* and talking about decent breakfasts—"and we'll have a little family conference."

"Dad, we're gonna miss the bus," said Danny. He picked up a tiny green tomato from the windowsill, examined it, put it back.

"Right you are," I said. Danny and Clarissa looked at each other. "Fortunately, old Dad happens to have some time on his hands this morning, and will be available to *drive* you to school. And I should warn our affiliates that we're going to be going a few minutes over this morning."

Clarissa's brow knit; Danny's head cocked. Not quick on the uptake, these kids.

"But. Old Dad will be happy to go into school with you and placate whoever needs to be placated."

What a way to talk. I didn't blame them for feeling contempt, assuming that's what those sullen expressions meant. In fact, I thought, that in itself might be a topic worth addressing.

"If you grow up and have kids of your own," I said, "I mean, *when* you grow up and *if* you have kids, and not necessarily even the two of you having kids with each *other*"—I was getting lost in all this—"if you ever have kids of your own, then you'll know what the hell I'm talking about," I said. "*And* you'll know what it is to behave in ways that are *contemptible*, and to read that contempt right there in the faces of your own children. And enough said about *that* aspect of things."

I was trying to talk about authority.

"Dad, are you okay?" said Danny.

"I am trying," I said, "to talk about authority."

Nobody said anything. Danny looked at Martha.

"Now I agree," I said, "that authority is probably arbitrary, okay? Ultimately probably arbitrary. That's not what we're talking about. But okay, let's even assume it *is* arbitrary. Simply contractual, okay? Not divinely fucking *ordained*. A simple agreement that I will play this role and you will play that role, for our mutual benefit and exploitation. Okay? Say that's the deal. The point I'm getting to is, that some of us in this room haven't been living up to the terms of that contract."

Clarissa was staring at the tabletop. She didn't seem to be aware that one leg was bouncing madly.

"Dad, I'm sorry we didn't help out last night," said Danny, probably thinking he was cutting right to the heart of the matter. "When I went to get Clarissa she was asleep and I didn't want to wake her up, and then *I* sort of fell asleep."

"Whatever," I said, graciously.

"Do you want more coffee?" said Martha. A pathetically transparent stratagem, and I came about *that close* to telling her so.

"Let's *all* have some coffee," I said. Mr. Genial. "You kids, now, you have some cereal or whatever, nice breakfast, and let's see if we can't agree on what the nature of our contract actually is."

I was about to begin asking Socratic questions.

Clarissa's leg had stopped bouncing. Now she was looking at her mother, lower lip trembling. "Mom?" she said, and couldn't go on. My heart went out to her: here was this horrible man in her house.

"It's all right, sweetie," she said, putting a hand on Clarissa's arm. "May I talk?" she said to me. "You're not making very much sense."

I pointed to her and called out, "Take it!" As if to a jazzman.

"This probably isn't a great time to make it official," she said, "but since we're all here and since everybody knows anyway that we're going to try to make a go of this together, you know, as a family, we thought it would be a good idea just to make clear what the rules were."

"Rule One," I said. "No hard drugs."

"Peter," said Martha, "I don't think—"

"No hard *drugs*," I said. "Going to be zero tolerance around this house. Simple as that. Rule One."

"What do you mean, hard drugs?" said Danny.

"White powder," I said. "Simple as that. Don't get Jesuitical with *me*."

He looked down at the tabletop.

"Two," I said.

"Peter," said Martha. "Enough. Really." Just in time, too: I had no idea what the fuck Two was going to be. "I'm sorry, kids," she said. "All I really wanted to say was that since we're all going to be living here together we've got to be as considerate as possible and each of us pitch in when something has to get done, okay?"

"Fairness," I said, "is the keynote."

"I'm putting him to bed," said Martha, getting to her feet. "Then I'll drive you to school, okay?"

"Christ," I said, "don't always be saying *okay*. It's like you're asking for their *approval*. You don't need their fucking approval, what *is* it with you?"

"Come on now," she said, trying to sound patient. I knew better.

"I know better," I said.

"It's all right," she said, getting me to my feet and leading me by the hand out of the kitchen. "Let's put you to bed now."

"No fucking, though," I said as we walked down the hall.

"Don't worry about it," she said. Not in a nice way.

V

1

The woman who'd sold us the house on Heritage Circle was so long gone from Century 21 that no one in the office even knew the name. A Mrs. Edmondson, which I remembered by thinking of Uncle Fred and the whole Edmund Wilson thing. So they turned me over to an Amy Somebody with a nice husky little phone voice.

When I'd been put to bed that morning after our family conference, Martha had gone out to one of her thrift stores and had found me a cowboy jacket. A garment for the lighthearted: white with black vines and blossoms embroidered all over and black arrowheads marking the ends of the pocket slits. Interesting who brought the peace offering to whom. *(Rusty sort of gave me a taste for that.)* "H-Bar-C Ranchwear," she said, holding it up by its shoulders and turning it from side to side in such a way that the arms made marching movements. "They obviously didn't know what they had."

I wore it to go meet this Amy, Martha waving approvingly from the open kitchen door, but as soon as I got to the stop sign I pulled over, wriggled out of the thing and draped it around the back of the passenger seat, as if dressing a mannequin. Felt nervous: me and a beautiful girl going alone to a deserted house in the middle of the day. I suppose I was picturing her like Amy Irving, that would have been true to form: hear a name, make an association. I must have thought it was okay to have this discrepancy between your thoughts and what was actually going on, that you could just keep the two going side by side, no problem.

When I got to Heritage Circle, a little Ford Escort or something was already parked in front of the house. And in the driveway, an old black Cadillac, maybe mid-'70s. Long after tail-fins, at any rate. One side of the rear end sagging, rocker panels rusted, vinyl roof peeling. What was this shitheap doing here? A woman in a tan trench coat—she must have thought it made her look dashing—got out of the Escort. (I'm just going to go ahead and call it an Escort.) Clearly Amy. Running shoes on. The kind of stern black horn-rims you only wear if you think you're so beautiful you can get away with it, except that she wasn't especially beautiful. She stuck out a hand, and just for an instant there I forgot why people did that. Then I remembered, and gave her my women's handshake, which wasn't really a shake. Handtake.

"Amy O'Connor Century 21," she said. "Sounds like you've got a party going on."

"I sure as hell better *not*," I said. But it sure as hell sounded like drums and shrieking guitar. "I imagine that's my son and his friends," I said. "I can't quite believe he would play hooky, but." I headed for the breezeway, Amy ducking into her car for a clipboard, then following. A dated expression like *playing hooky* wasn't going to cut much ice with this Amy, who wasn't really pretty enough for me to want to cut ice with anyway. I opened the kitchen door and music hit me,

physically, in the chest. A female voice howled off-key above everything else. The noise was obviously coming from the living room, but
even here in the kitchen it hurt my ears so much that I didn't dare
go nearer. Like a force-field on *Star Trek*. I held up a palm to Amy,
signifying Wait Here, and opened the door to the basement. I trotted
down the steps and crossed under whomping bass notes to the breaker
box. I pulled down the main switch and in about one second the
drums were playing alone. Then the drums stopped and some kid
called, "Hey! What the fuck *happened*?"

Back upstairs I found Danny flipping wall switches, and Clarissa
moaning "Bummer" as she sank into the couch. A wiry kid in a tank
top, with platinum hair like Clarissa's, sat behind an array of drums
and cymbals, lighting a cigarette. An overweight boy, his white Da-
cron shirt bulging over black suit pants, was still walking his fingers
over the neck of his silent bass guitar. He had glasses like Amy's, and
short hair neatly parted and combed. Did he use hair tonic? Did they
even *have* hair tonic anymore? A quarter of a century ago, he would
have looked like a normal, studious fat boy.

I whistled and four heads turned. Danny stared at me, then past
my shoulder at trench-coated Amy.

"This lady," I said, "is here to go through the house. I trust there
are no surprises for her in any of the bedrooms?"

Four blank looks.

"I'm going to go turn the power back on," I said, "so you'll kindly
turn the machinery off. And when I'm done showing her through, I
would like to have a little chat with the two of you." Pointing a two-
finger fork at Danny and Clarissa. *A little chat*, for Christ's sake: talking
like a high school principal. I imagined this Amy wasn't too impressed,
either. "Sorry about all this," I said, as I walked her down the echoing
hall, bare hardwood floors, bare eggshell walls, to point out the bath
over here, master bedroom right next door, linen closet.

"Day's work," she said, not that graciously.

Basement.

"Workbench stay?" she said, pen poised.

"Sure, why not. It was here when *I* got here," I said. "Tools I'm
taking, obviously." I'd truly intended to use this workshop. Bought
a yard-sale table saw, and a brand-new router after reading in some

handyman magazine that its uses were "nearly limitless." I liked the name of it: rout your enemies. I ended up using the thing only once, to make a little bookcase for Danny's room. Instead of the shelves resting on cleats or whatever, I routed grooves in the sides and back. Just slide the shelves in and there you were. After the first year or so here, I didn't do much more than sharpen the lawnmower blade on the bench grinder. Not that it needed sharpening, really: that lawn was a pretty well-tamed piece of nature.

"Washer and dryer?" she said.

"Come again?"

"Do the washer and dryer stay?"

"Well," I said, "let me think." Should I cart them over to Martha's or was she already equipped? My God, I'd been staying at her house how long now? Middle of July, say, to middle of October? Three months? Well, hell, she had to have a washing machine: she was always putting clean clothes away in drawers, right? But all I could remember in the basement were the cages and the haybales. "I don't know," I said. "Yeah. Yeah, leave 'em."

"You're saying they stay here."

"Yep," I said. She could be testy, I could be testy. "Ah, listen, screw it. Let the tools go too. I'm just going to take a couple of screwdrivers and wrenches and shit. Got a table saw here, bench grinder, the router I bought new, what else, good bench vise. . . ."

Now she was looking worried.

"If you really have no use for them," she said, "you'd be better advised to sell them privately. They're not really going to add to the value of the home. Generally buyers who want these things tend to already have them."

I saw what she was saying, though literally it made no sense: you can't *want* what you actually *have*, right? I mean, look at the old usage: *Thou art weighed in the balances, and found wanting.*

"I see what you're saying," I said. "But they sort of go with the house, you know? Whoever buys the house can do what they want with them. Same with the lawnmower, all the shit in the garage, string trimmer, whatever's out there. They're buying the whole life, okay?"

"Well—"

"Dishes," I said. "Dishes, silverware. All the"—the expression escaped me—"the linen. Household linen. Right? The Mr. Clean under the fucking sink." I had said fucking. "I'm sorry," I said. "You have to excuse me."

Silence.

"I understand this can be upsetting for people," she said. Finally. "Then, I take it, the kitchen appliances as well?"

"Poof," I said. "Gone. Like a cool breeze."

"I don't think I need to trouble you any further," she said. "If you'll come by the office this afternoon, we can get things moving for you right away. You'll be seeing our Mr. Pagliarulo."

Oh, she did it smoothly, all right, but I'll bet you one thing: the first old Pagliarulo heard about it was later on, when she got back to the office and said she'd owe him one if he'd take this asshole off her hands.

"Pagliarulo like the baseball player?" I said.

"I don't follow baseball," she said.

After seeing her to her car, I went back in and found the fat kid slipping his bass into a bass-shaped black vinyl bag, and the platinum-haired kid lifting a cymbal off a threaded rod. Danny and Clarissa were on the sofa, arms around each other's waists, the picture of persecuted young love.

"You two," I said, and nodded toward the kitchen. They looked at each other, got up and went in. I pulled out a chair for Clarissa. She sat. I gestured at another for Danny. He sat. I leaned against the refrigerator.

"So," I said.

They said nothing. Clarissa stared at the tabletop, her leg going.

"What am I supposed to say?" I said. "You know you should be in school."

Nothing. Crafty little bastards: if they could keep me talking, eventually I was bound to say something for which they had an answer. Well fuck that. All I had to do was keep the silence going, and one of them would sooner or later blurt out something for which *I* had an answer. I looked up at the clock high above the sink. It had been there when we bought the place, and I'd always hated the beige oblong son of a bitch. Beige: the oblong of colors. Oblong: the beige of shapes.

The second hand was now on the two. Now a hair after. Then I looked at the kids, who were looking at the roosters on the wallpaper. On one of the days when Judith's sense of camp was at its most manic, she'd gone to half a dozen places before she found wallpaper with roosters. You could hear the other kids packing up out in the living room. Sizzle of a cymbal, rrrip of a zipper.

After what seemed a long time I peeked again at the clock. Second hand was on the nine. They seemed willing to sit there for as long as I pleased. Probably because they didn't have much in the way of inner lives. Or maybe they had exceptionally absorbing ones. Or they could have been stoned. The second hand passed the twelve.

"The hell with it," I said. "You guys want to flunk out of school, it's your lookout, okay? I'm officially out of the cop business as of right now." I stood up straight, a free man. "Ta ta," I said.

"Does that mean it's okay if we stay here?" said Danny.

"Nice try," I said, "but I won't play. If you want to be told what's okay, go find a guru or something. I am *weary* of the job." I touched a farewell hand to my head and extended it palm up, Jimmy Durante saying *Good night, Mrs. Calabash, wherever you are*, and headed for the door. "See you when I see you," I said.

"Hey Dustin?" Danny called. "It's o-*kay*, we don't have to split. Mitchell?"

2

The next morning I filled out papers with their Mr. Pagliarulo— "Jim!" he cried (meaning himself), and shot out his hand—and by the following afternoon he had an offer of one thirty-five. "I'm obliged to bring this to you," he said on the phone. "But crash or no crash, I can virtually guarantee it's going to be no problem you getting at least your one sixty. Not out of these people necessarily. But sooner rather than later."

"You mean people have actually *heard* about that?" I said. I couldn't believe this. "And it freaks them out about buying the house?"

"What do you mean have people *heard* about it? What else is even on the news?"

Now I understood that it must be the stock market crash he was talking about.

"Fact is," he said, "nobody really knows how it's all going to shake down. My personal opinion, I don't think it's going to hurt real estate one iota. Interest rates look like they're going to stay low, and people who didn't totally get wiped are still going to need a place to live."

Three weeks later Jim Pagliarulo called to say the couple who had offered the one thirty-five had come back at one thirty-seven five.

"Do it," I said.

"I think you might be well advised," he said.

I pawed around under the sink and came out with an unopened jar of Tim's moonshine. Any excuse to celebrate, right? It was about two in the afternoon; Martha was out making a dumpster run, kids still at school supposedly. I poured a couple of inches into a jelly glass, topped off the jar with tapwater so Martha would be none the wiser, screwed the lid back on as tight as it would go, and put the jar back where I'd found it. I tried to compose a joke: You're not losing twenty-two thousand five hundred dollars, you're gaining whatever. But I couldn't think what I was gaining. Around three, Danny and Clarissa burst in, singing. "The way you make-a me feel," sang Danny. "You knock me offa my feet," she answered, in some other key. If it was a key. Then they saw me in the Morris chair, and that shut them up fast enough.

"Just be a sec," she said to Danny, and headed off to the bathroom.

Danny said "Hiya Dad" and went upstairs. Came back down with his guitar case. He stood looking out the window, as if he gave any more of a shit than I did about what was out a window. It was another astonishing fall day for those in the mood to be astonished by fall days. Sky such a pure blue that it bothered me. Because here I was, sulking and spurning yet another gift from the Creator.

"I'm going to give you forty thousand dollars," I announced.

"Yeah, what's the catch?" said Danny, still looking out.

"No catch," I said. "Somebody bought the house today. And I'm setting aside forty thousand dollars off the top for your college. Probably put it in CDs. But it's going to be in your name." This made him turn around, at least, though probably because he thought I was talking about forty thousand dollars' worth of compact discs. "Now ten thousand a year," I said, "is not going to buy you a hell of a lot anymore, but it'll buy you *something*. Basically what it will buy you is enough of a degree someplace so you won't have to work in a factory. Provided your grades are decent enough so you can get in somewhere, and then provided you work hard enough so you don't flunk out."

Not much of a pep talk for college, I suppose. Useless anyway. I couldn't imagine Danny ever being capable of even the modest effort it took to get through your average college these days. The guitar was the only thing I'd ever seen him buckle down to—*buckle down to*, now there was an old-fart expression—and what the hell was that, the guitar? This was stuff I didn't think much about, because it made me so afraid for him. Christ, these days he'd be *lucky* to end up in a factory. No factories anymore to end up in. And he wasn't what they used to call good with his hands, so plumbing or fixing cars was out. He would end up on the drug shitheap.

"Listen, Dad?" he said. "You mind if we talk about it later? We're late to practice."

"Sure, why not?" I said. "I know how intensely *boring* it all is." It was not true that I got mean when I drank.

The toilet flushed and Clarissa came down the hall, seeming to wander from one side to the other. She saw me looking and started walking straight, watching her feet.

"We don't have to stop using the house yet, do we?" said Danny.

"Use away," I said. "Closing probably isn't for another month."

"So when do we have to get our stuff out?"

I shrugged. "A lot of it we might just as well leave," I said. "The girls seem like they're pretty well equipped. Any of the furniture or anything that you're particularly attached to?"

"Nah," he said. "I might give a lot of my stuff away. Like to poor kids or something."

"It's your stuff," I said. Now, a mean drunk would have said, This so-called *stuff* is *stuff* I bought you.

Clarissa took Danny's hand. "Daniel?" she said.

"So you're off to practice," I said.

"Yeah," said Danny. "We better do it."

"Come up with a name yet for your band?" A mean drunk would've been keeping this up just to watch them chafe to be gone. What I was, was an interested father.

"I don't know, sort of," said Danny. "Dad, we have to get going, okay?"

"And what were you thinking of calling it?"

"I don't know. Dustin wants to call it Naked Movie Star."

"And what do *you* think about that?"

"I don't know. I guess it's pretty cool. Hey Dad? We're gonna be late."

Clarissa was looking at the floor.

"And what about you, Clarissa?" I said. "What do *you* think about Naked Movie Star?"

Her pale face got red. So after all these years, the word *naked* still had the old sockeroo.

And they made their escape, like Hansel and Gretel from the horrible gingerbread house. I sat there and tried to think why Naked Movie Star rang a bell. Then I got it. McMartin Preschool. The twistos who were making the videos of the little kids. At least according to the little kids. So one of Danny's friends must at least watch *60 Minutes* or something. Now which one was Dustin again?

3

I woke up on the sofa. From a "nap." Quarter to something, probably seven, according to the greenish hands of my watch, glowing feebly in the murk. Darkness at a quarter to seven, if that's what it was a quarter to, argued that it must be p.m. I padded to the kitchen in stocking feet. So apparently I'd gotten my shoes off before passing out. God takes care of drunks and whatever the other thing is He takes care of. Fools? Madmen? Children? Damn it was cold. *Rest of*

November, December, January, February and most of March, I said to myself, flicking out fingers: *five more months of this.* Five months was half the year, just about. Hey, one day at a time, right? Thing to do now was fire up the woodstove. Which involved: crumpling up the paper, sticking in the kindling, waiting for that to get going, and then and only then adding the first logs. Right, and *then* sitting right in front of the fucking thing for a half hour until the room warmed up. So the thing to do really was just reach up and crank the old Honeywell and get the oil burner going. Right, and then have Martha go on a fucking rant about the cost of heating oil.

Not much in the old refrigerator. Eggs. Skimmed milk, which everybody now seems to call skim. Back when Danny was learning to read, I used to take a magic marker sometimes and caret in MED on the cartons. Back when I gave a shit. (Speaking of which, shouldn't "stocking feet," see above, be *stockinged*?) A dumpster cantaloupe, just one moldy spot, which would have been the most appealing thing in there if you hadn't had to cut the son of a bitch open and scoop seeds. White box of generic bran flakes, kept in the refrigerator because of the mouse problem. Which Martha, mass murderess of bunnies, refused to solve with d-Con. D-Con: deconstructor of the innards of rodents. "Do you know how that stuff *works*?" she'd said when I proposed it. "Do I care?" I'd said. But she had carried the day, by dint of sheer moral earnestness. Huh, dint. Dint dint dint. Like you get in your shield, isn't that another meaning? Dint in your shield, from a truncheon or something.

So really the thing to do was to put your shoes back on and get your coat and go drive someplace in the car so you could run the heater. Go eat at McDonald's or something, to make it all seem purposeful. There was a McDonald's on Hamilton, someplace along that strip out past the mall. And another on Route 17. We're a two-McDonald's town, Jack.

Now, usually I don't trust the Drive-Thru at McDonald's. Not the Jernigan style, I know, doing business face-to-face, but too much can go wrong with the Drive-Thru: miscommunication through a scratchy squawkbox, holding up a line of cars while you complain. Tonight, though, it was so cold I stayed right in the car and just kept that heater pumping it out and the Drive-Thru worked like a well-oiled machine, just boom boom boom and you were out of there. Then I drove maybe another mile out Hamilton, to Seaman's Furniture, closed at this hour, and parked in front, facing the traffic. Thinking I guess of Wild Bill Hickok with his back to the door, which is where you get the expression Dead Man's Hand, unless I'm really off the beam here. I sat there with the lights off and the engine running, heater still blowing out warm, invisible clouds around my shins. Got startled for a second—thought somebody was suddenly sitting there in the passenger seat—but it was just the white cowboy jacket. I nursed the small fries to make them last two cheeseburgers, then stuck all the wrappings back in the bag, crumpled the bag and stuffed it into the empty milkshake thing, put the plastic lid back on to keep everything neat and put it on the floor in the back, among the Diet Coke cans and styrofoam coffee cups whose lids had little triangles torn out of them.

The usual bloat and disgust.

The only thing to do was to drink more. Not that drinking more was really going to do it either, but. I checked the old wallet: a five and three singles. Enough either to get a fifth of Gordon's at the discount liquor place, or to get a pint and enough gas to keep driving around, sneaking sips when headlights were far enough behind and listening to the Walkman. What I did for music these days was just keep a Walkman and a few tapes in the glove compartment; that way they might still break in, but they wouldn't know they had a reason to. So I checked to see what tapes were on hand, as if that would help me decide. Assorted Beach Boys, good for either cheap irony or actual enjoyment, or for some condition veering back and forth between the two. Assorted George Jones (a gift from Uncle Fred). The Webb Pierce tape Martha had made me. All white people's music today. So maybe that would give me a safe frisson, driving around some ghetto-y part of Newark listening to white people's music and sipping from a pint of white people's liquor.

On the other hand, wasn't a pint going to leave me just a smidgen short of where I wanted to be?

And then I remembered there was still a bottle of gin—and not some God damn crappy little fifth, either, but a whole big sturdy welcoming quart!—in the kitchen cabinet at Heritage Circle. At least half full, if the kids hadn't gotten into it. Which wasn't likely: I'd put it on the top shelf, behind a cylinder of Quaker Oats. Well all *right*.

Every light in the house was on, and the sagging Cadillac was back in the driveway. God damn shitheap parked there meant I had to walk an extra carlength in the cold. Well, I'd live. At least Danny wasn't just sitting in his room with guitar and Rockman, looping music back into his own head. I opened the car door to the expected shot of cold air but didn't hear the expected din. Taking a break? To do what? The screen door onto the breezeway was unlocked, kitchen door too. I stuck my head inside and yelled "Hello anybody *home?*" to give fair warning, then walked into where it was warm. And in strolled the fat kid, in stocking feet.

"So," I said. "How's it going tonight?"

"Pretty reasonably," he said. "I don't believe we were actually introduced." He stuck out a hand. "Dustin Sanders?"

"Pete Jernigan," I said, giving the man's handshake. God knows why Pete: I never went by Pete. Powerful Pete. Some compulsion to be hearty. By which I guess I mean not oppressively parental. "Gang all here?" I said.

"Nah," he said. "I think Danny's probably still over at Mitchell's. And I dropped Clarissa off at her place."

"You're the only one here, in other words?"

"Yeah," he said. "I don't know, we played for about half an hour, and it completely sounded like crap. So we just sort of got depressed and bagged it. I guess we should've tried to work through it or something. Did you use to be in a band, Mr. Jernigan?"

"Did I use to be in a band," I said. "No. No, of the many things I used to be—" Then I decided why give the kid shit. "So now what happened to Danny again?"

"Well, I *think* he's still at Mitchell's."

"Mitchell being?" I said.

"Kid who plays the drums? We went over to check out his new CD player."

"But you came back here," I said.

"I hate CDs," he said. "It's like you can't get *away* from it. And my dad thinks it's cold compared to vinyl. Of course he's into pretty much strictly classical. So anyhow, I decided I'd just go get some videos to watch."

"But what are you *doing* here?" I said. "I mean, if you don't mind my asking."

"You mean Danny didn't *say* anything? Jeez, what a space cadet." He bethought himself. "Sorry," he said. "I didn't mean he was really *spacey* or anything. So this must seem pretty weird to you, if he didn't say anything. See, he told me I could stay here for a couple days. I hope that was okay."

"What about your—" I was going to say parents plural, but these days. "Don't you have another place to go?" I said, meaning to be delicate. Instead it sounded inhospitable, I heard it as soon as it came out.

He laughed. "I'm not a homeless person or anything," he said. "It's just a thing where—" He shrugged. "Parents and kids, you know?"

"No, I *don't* know," I said. I did know.

"It was like it was going to go critical around there," he said. "Like when you get too many neutrons bouncing around and then, *balooey*." He slowly spread cupped hands as if to show an expanding fireball.

"Do people know where you are?"

He thought, then said, "They know I'm *okay*."

"You won't mind if I call them," I said. Not a question.

He took a pack of Camels out of the pocket of his white shirt. "Four three seven, seven seven three four," he said. "Same forwards and backwards. I'll write it down for you if you want. Or you can just look up under Martin Sanders." He tapped the end of the pack against a forefinger and the ends of three cigarettes appeared, each a different length, like the pipes of an organ. It made me want one. After, what, more than a year? "If you could try to not give him the address here," he said, "that would be good. But I guess if he asks you, you have to say, right? Is it okay to smoke in your house, by the way? I could go outside if you'd rather."

"It's just barely my house anymore, anyway," I said. If he didn't know the place was sold, he must have wondered what the hell *that* meant. "Enjoy. Wish it was me."

He lit a cigarette and looked around for where to put the spent match. He chose an empty can of Betty Crocker chocolate frosting on the counter. He'd laid in provisions, apparently.

"You're a quit smoker?" he said. "That's excellent. After tonight I'm not going to smoke anymore. *Or* eat junk."

"So you're having a last fling, huh?"

"A fling," he said. "Yeah, I guess. Were you going anyplace? Or can you stay and talk for a minute?"

"Sure," I said. "My time is your time. Go in where we can sit?"

I followed him into the living room. A VCR now sat on top of the television; on top of the VCR, three yellow plastic bags. I could make out BED in gothic type on the top one. I thought *bedlam*, and how that was actually a corruption of Bethlehem. Cheap Christian irony. "You *have* made yourself at home," I said.

"What, that?" he said, nodding at the VCR. "Don't worry, it's mine from my room. All I really *took* was one of my dad's porno tapes that he's got hidden in the basement, and he'd be way too embarrassed to bust my horns on *that*." He sat down in my recliner, facing the tv. I took a corner of the sofa. "I'm actually glad you came by," he said. "I'm kind of worried about Danny."

I looked at him.

"It's kind of hard to say this," he said. "Like have you noticed that he seems kind of down or something?"

"Like how?" I said. As a matter of fact, Danny had seemed as usual to me. But to say that was to reveal you'd been failing as a father.

"Well, like has he been saying stuff about death to you?"

"Not to me, no." I mean he hadn't, had he? "What has he been saying?"

"You're not going to tell Danny I told you this, right?"

"Dustin," I said.

"Okay, you know when those two kids killed themselves? The ones on the news, with the car in the garage?" Teen suicide pact, next town over. I remembered. Back in the summer. "When that happened he was saying stuff like that they were better off. And, you know, like that it was peaceful and they were with God and everything." This didn't sound like Danny. "But what's weird to me is, he's still talking about it."

"And saying what?"

"I don't know, a lot of stuff."

"Like *what*, Dustin? Has he said something about killing himself?"

"Well, not as such," he said. "But we had this thing at school, after it happened? Where they come in and talk about it and tell you things to look for. Like if a kid starts giving away all his stuff."

I might give a lot of my stuff away. Like to poor kids or something.

"Has Danny been giving stuff away?" I said.

"Not as such," he said. "But he said if anything happened to him he wanted me to have his guitar. And they also tell you that if a kid's even talking about it that it might be a cry for help."

"Jesus," I said. "What else should I know about, Dustin? What about drugs? How heavily is he into that?"

"I don't want to get Danny in trouble," he said. "You know, kids like to party. If I had a kid, I'd be a lot more worried about how the kid was feeling, inside himself, instead of did he do drugs or something."

"And you don't think Danny is feeling very well."

"Well, yeah, no. I think he's feeling really really bad. And other kids can't do anything to help, because they're just kids too."

"Dustin, thank you," I said. "You did the right thing to tell me."

"You were kind of my last chance," he said. "It was weird that you just came by."

"Tell me something," I said. "What are they really doing over at what's-his-name's? Is it all right him being there?"

"Mitchell's? Oh yeah. No problem. They're probably just listening to music and everything." He stubbed out his cigarette. "I don't think anything would happen as long as there was somebody around. It's when you're alone that things really get weird. You know—Mr. Jernigan, I know this sounds really heavy, but I would *not* trust Danny by himself right now."

I got up and went back into the kitchen. I opened the cabinet, reached up and took down the Quaker Oats. Sure enough: there was the gin, still about half full. But I couldn't. Not and live with myself. This had turned into a night where you stayed sober and did your best to handle something. Dustin had followed me in. What he must have seen was a grown man gazing up at a bottle of liquor.

"Mr. Jernigan?" he said. "I'm sure Danny's okay over there. You're welcome to stay around and watch a movie." I put the Quaker Oats back. "That sounds weird," he said. "Telling somebody they're welcome in their own house. Sorry about that."

"Look, it's fine that you're here, Dustin," I said. "But in light of what you've told me, I think I'd better get going and see if Danny's back yet."

"I understand," he said. "Absolutely. Anyhow, I'm glad we got to talk. I would have felt really bad if I hadn't tried everything, you know?"

"You've really helped," I said, "and I'm really grateful to you. I know it took a lot of nerve. And meanwhile, if there's anything I can do to help out your situation—you know, is there anything you'd like me to say to your dad when I talk to him?"

He shook his head. "It's no big deal," he said. "Everybody'll get over it okay."

"Well, I'm still going to call up and touch base with him," I said. The thought of that changed my mind about the gin. A little jolt couldn't hurt, might help. I took the Quaker Oats down again, got up on tiptoes for the bottle and brandished it yo-ho-ho style to show cheerful self-irony. "So what are you watching tonight?" I said, replacing the Quaker Oats once more. The old geezer on the box looked at me nonjudgmentally.

"I don't know yet," he said. "It seemed like I should make it like a special occasion, so I sort of pigged out at the video place. I got *Re-Animator* and *Texas Chain Saw*. I tried to get *Night of the Living Dead* but somebody already had it out. You ever see that?"

"Yow," I said. "You're a better man than I am."

"They're not actually that bad," he said. "They're pretty funny, actually. And I got a couple of operas too."

"A rock-and-roll guy like you?" I said. "Or is that the latest thing?"

"Nah," he said. "My dad got me into it when I was really little. Being a music teacher and everything."

"Be great if you could get Danny into it," I said. "Sake of a little variety." Whatever a little variety was worth. I was way overacting the concerned parent. Standing there trying to jam a fucking gin bottle into an overcoat pocket that was too small and talking about opera providing a little variety. "So what did you get for operas?" I said.

"I don't know if you know it," he said, "but *Les Troyens*? It's by Berlioz? It's really long. And I got *Madama Butterfly*."

"Madama, yet," I said.

"I hate when people say Madame," he said. "My dad taught me a lot of stuff, he really did. Oh, and then I got—I mean, it's really actually pretty stupid, but this old movie *It's a Wonderful Life*?"

"Great movie," I said, sounding like the old fuck on tv who says "great story" when he catches his grandson reading *Moby-Dick*. (Ad for these leatherbound Great Books.) "Sounds like you're in for quite an evening of it. Listen, I don't mean to sound like a parent, but don't stay up too late, okay?"

"No chance," he said. "Listen, thanks."

"*Por nada*," I said, opening the door to the breezeway. "Thank *you*. And don't worry about my blowing your cover with Danny."

"Oh, it's okay if you do," he said. "It's not going to make any difference now."

"Well," I said, "whatever."

"Whatever," he said, and gave me a mock salute. Good kid, this Dustin. I saluted back.

When I got to the car, I looked back at the house. At the left-hand side of the picture window, the drapery was being held aside just a crack. I saw white fingers against the dark fabric, half a face peeping. So despite what he wanted me to think, some sort of sneaky shit was probably going on.

4

Martha's Reliant was still gone when I got back to the house, but Clarissa's window glowed yellow. I called, "Hey, anybody home?" from the kitchen, which now felt as cold as out-of-doors. No answer. Holed up as always. Clarissa had one of those oil-filled electric radiators in her room; with plastic over the window and an old blanket over the door, she and Danny could just settle in and everybody else could go fuck themselves.

I put the gin in the refrigerator and went into the stone-cold living room. From in there I could hear the God damn music going. Meaning that Danny either had or hadn't rolled in. What pissed me off especially was that I couldn't let myself be pissed off. Instead I had to prepare to talk to my son about whether or not he might be thinking about killing himself. First thing to do was go back in the kitchen and have a couple good slugs of that gin right off the bat, then get that stove going while the gin was taking hold. That way you'd have someplace warm to have your talk in and you'd also be in a little steadier frame of mind. But it was a hell of a thing when you couldn't even go in your own house and just take your coat off and sit down. Though of course it *wasn't* your own house, so what did you expect.

I went in and had about three good belts, meaning five or six, then came back and opened the stove's clanky iron door. Ashes in there six inches deep for Christ's sake. So I went back to the kitchen one more time and got the Rubbermaid bucket Martha used for stuff that was going into the compost. I couldn't think what to use for a scoop. Finally I found a loaf pan. So I was down on my knees in the cold, scooping ashes out of a stove with a tin pan and dumping them in this stinking bucket. And I remembered coming in here the first time, on the Fourth of July, and thinking *Hey, nice, a woodstove*. When I got most of the ashes out, I packed the bottom of the firebox with crumpled pages of *The New York Times*, then snapped sticks over my knee, laid them crisscross on top of the paper, lit the corner of page C7, made sure it blazed up okay, and clanked the door shut. Took the bucket of ashes out the kitchen door and through the backyard to the compost pile, leaving dark footprints in the crisped, whitened grass. Not just some rotting heap for old Martha, boy, but a whole big deal fenced in with chicken wire. Stakes here and there in the pile that you were supposed to pull out at some point to let air in. I dumped the ashes on top of withered carrot tops and cantaloupe rinds. And I'd probably hear about that, too. You were probably supposed to put down a layer of grass clippings first. Grass clippings or blood meal, whatever the hell blood meal was. For the nitrogen. No ashes on top of cantaloupe rinds without an intervening layer of blood meal, that was probably the rule around here.

By the time I got back inside, the newspaper had burned away and left the sticks blazing. I thrust in some pieces of scavenged two-by-four, nails and all—hey, give her a little iron to go with her nitrogen when *these* ashes hit the compost—and dragged the Morris chair over close to the stove and sat down, still in my coat. What I would do was wait until the living room was entirely warm and welcoming: it would be easier explaining to Danny why it was a bad idea to kill himself if we weren't both sitting huddled in our coats and blowing on our hands. I would open by saying that he seemed down lately. If he admitted it, we were in business; if he denied it, then I'd say that sometimes you could be so down that you didn't even realize it. What was truly scary about being in that kind of shape, I would inform him, was that nothing was scary anymore. That what might ordinarily be unthinkable started to seem reasonable. Then, once I'd gotten him this far, we could get into why it was a bad idea to kill yourself. Except all I could think of was the usual worldly dog treats. Consent to live and you can fuck more. Listen to more records. He'd *already* fucked and listened to records; why should he be struck dumb and reverent at the prospect of doing it some more? Better girls! Better records! Oh yeah, and his Art. Forgot all about his Art. Kill yourself and the world will be short one guitar player. No, this was the wrong approach. The way to play this was just to stick to how bad he felt and why, assuming I could get it out of him. And then, probably, life would reassert itself without my feeble help. Assuming it really made people feel any better to talk about how bad they felt and why.

I got up and went into the kitchen again. One more good jolt and then back you go and see if it's warm enough to take off your coat, and then we get this thing rolling, okay? Assuming Danny was actually home. I opened the refrigerator, unscrewed the cap of the gin bottle and took a good mouthful. Just let my tongue marinate for a few seconds, then swallowed. Then one more, and a last one for good measure. I screwed the cap back on, closed the refrigerator and turned to see Clarissa in the doorway, watching.

"Hey," I said. That was my new breezy hello with the kids.

"Mr. Jernigan?" she said, though it had been agreed that I was Peter now. "I think I'm in trouble."

She looked it. I mean, more than usual. Staring. Hair every which way. And I noticed she was barefoot: what that must have felt like in this cold I couldn't imagine. Shit, I thought, here we go, barefoot and pregnant. So this was what was on Danny's mind. And here I'd been thinking it was *mal de siècle*.

"Come stand by the stove," I said. I put a hand on her arm, to guide and protect. You should've seen her jump.

"You're not my father," she said.

"Spared that much," I said, possibly not loud enough for her to hear. "Clarissa," I said, beckoning her to follow me into the living room. "Please, sit." She took the Morris chair; I chose the cold floor beside her. Once you got any distance from that stove, boy, it wasn't any fucking *Déjeuner sur l'herbe* in here. "Now, what's up with *you*?" I said. "Please tell me you're not pregnant."

She shook her head and said, "LSD monster babies."

"Say again?" I said.

"It makes people have monster babies," she said. "I think I took too much." She shook her head. "Whew. I don't think it's good to think about that," she said, then looked around the room. "Whew."

"Okay, easy," I said. "Clarissa, are you by any chance tripping?"

"Except I think I took too much," she said. "I took three because Dustin said it was going to be a real special occasion, but I think three was too much. Because I'm little." That set her off laughing. "I'm *little*."

"Oh Christ," I said. "Listen, Clarissa? Where's Danny? Did—" Better go one question at a time. "Okay. Now, where is Danny?"

"All *right*," she said. "I *heard* you."

"Is Danny here?" I said.

"No, he's still over Mitchell's," she said. "Do you know how *far* that is?"

"Clarissa. Now, did Danny take some too?"

"He was scared to," she said. "And then he got real mad at me, and so me and Dustin went to the mall but I didn't like it there. Could you take me to the hospital?"

"Poor Clarissa," I said, meaning it. "You're really having a tough time of it, aren't you?"

"I think they can give me a shot," she said. "Dustin said they can give you one. Could you take me?"

"Believe me, Clarissa, I know what you're going through. It *will* get better."

"How can you know?" she said.

She had a point there.

"What I mean is," I said, "I've had this same sort of thing happen to me, and . . ." And what—just look at me now? "And you do come down and you do feel better. Now listen, can you tell me who else took this stuff?"

"I told you already," she said. "Dustin. Dustin Dustin Dustin."

"Okay, easy," I said.

"Whew," she said.

"Now did Dustin actually take it with you?" I said. "Or did he just give it to you?" The kid had seemed rational enough to me. And we know how much *that* means.

"How come you want to know so much about Dustin?" she said. "I want to go to the hospital."

"Okay, okay," I said. "The hospital it is." Better, I supposed, than trying to deal with this by myself. Old Martha was going to owe me one when *this* was over. "We're going to go in just a sec," I said. "The reason I'm asking about Dustin is because I'm worried that he might be having a bad time too."

"Dustin can handle it," she said. "He was driving his car and everything. We went to the mall, but I didn't like it there."

"Terrific," I said. Little shit had probably swallowed a Pez and given her the real McCoy. Not unheard of back in Jernigan's day. "Okay, I guess we'll have to let Dustin worry about Dustin."

This struck her funny. She squirmed around in the chair giggling, then stopped. "My teeth feel too big in my mouth."

"Clarissa? Try to relax. This is not going to go on forever, and we'll get you to where they can help you out, okay? Now, why don't you go get some shoes on, get your coat on, and we'll go get you some help, okay?"

"Get some shoes on," she said. "Shoes on, get some shoes on. Whew. I think I'm still getting higher."

"I'd better give you a hand," I said, then realized that if *shoes on* had stopped her, giving her a hand might *really* sound grotesque. But it just slid by. I thought about being so high that nothing—not a word, not a visual image, not an idea—made any sense or was attached to anything else. In that kind of state, was even terror just one more *thing*? Clarissa seemed to be getting close enough to send back a report, but of course asking such a question would be a bad idea. And if she was close enough to know the answer, she wouldn't be able to understand the question. Wouldn't know what a *question* was. I stood up and held out my hand; she remembered enough about how things went to take it and get to her feet. It was one of the many processes that, luckily, she hadn't yet thought to examine. It was possible that Clarissa simply wasn't bright enough to get herself in serious trouble. No denying, on the other hand, that she was suffering.

I walked her upstairs to her room and sat her down on the bed. "Socks in here?" I said, opening the top dresser drawer. They were. "How about these?" I said, holding up a pink pair rolled together. She lifted her sweatshirt over her head. Nothing on underneath.

"Put it back on, Clarissa," I said. "Now." Pretty little white breasts, same size as the pink sock-roll in my hand. "I'm not kidding," I said.

I picked up the sweatshirt and thrust it at her. I was proud of myself for not being tempted, even fleetingly; apparently there was a point past which even Jernigan wouldn't go. She just sat staring at the sweatshirt, so I took it out of her hands and located the label inside the neckhole, showing which was front and which was back. Then I stretched open the bottom of the sweatshirt and commanded her to raise her arms. This worked. I got each hand through a sleeve, got her head into the neckhole and pulled the thing down. "Now *keep* it on," I said. "And hold still." I knelt and worked a pink sock on over each foot. One Reebok peeped out from under the bed; its mate was over by the dresser. "Here," I said, handing them to her. "You can do this. You're not an infant." She seemed to respond better to this stuff than to a bunch of *I know what you're going through.*

She sat with a shoe in each hand, looking enchanted. "Whew," she said. "Is this what a bad trip is?"

The emergency room doctor—when we were finally vouchsafed an audience—was a tall, horsey woman my age. Snaggle-toothed smile and wrinkles at the corners of her eyes. You couldn't help but think of the woman on *The Beverly Hillbillies*. Banker Drysdale's secretary or whatever she was.

"Clarissa?" she said. "I'm Dr. James. Would you like to come with me? Mr. Peretsky, it might be helpful if you came along too."

"Jernigan, actually," I said. "I'm her stepfather."

The eyes narrowed, the wrinkles deepened. Either because this was no time to be setting the record straight about what my name happened to be, or because a stepfather meant it was more likely something creepy was going on. Of course she might simply have smelled my breath.

The doctor sat her down on the paper-covered examining table; gently, just fingertips under the chin, she got Clarissa to look into her eyes. I felt suddenly unwelcome. Right, she's tall, has no wedding ring and, most damning of all, does something useful in this world, and right away you assume. Dear God, I thought, please let her keep her fucking mouth shut about the thing with the sweatshirt.

"Clarissa?" said the doctor. "Can you tell me what you took, and how long ago you took it?"

Clarissa burst into tears.

The doctor turned to me. "What has she told you?"

"She said three tabs of acid," I said. "Or actually all she really said was that she took three of *something*, but I'm *assuming* it was acid." Babble babble. "I don't know how long ago she got hold of it, but I don't think it was probably before three or four this afternoon." What I'd have liked to get hold of was that fat little fuck of a Dustin.

"Clarissa," she said, "do you have any more of what you took? So I could look at it?"

Clarissa shook her head.

"Can you tell me what they looked like?"

"Green," said Clarissa. "They were so *little*, you know?" She was staring down, now at one hand, now at the other, as they cupped her knees.

"About this big?" said the doctor, holding up thumb and forefinger.

Clarissa nodded.

"No," said the doctor. "Look at what I'm showing you. Were they this big? Or were they smaller than that?"

Clarissa looked. "That big," she said. She looked back down at her hand and wiggled the fingers. Each fingernail was painted black. "Whew," she said.

"Were they a *bright* green?" said the doctor. "Or kind of pale green? Did they have little specks?"

"Yeah," said Clarissa. "Wow, did you take some too?"

"No, honey," said the doctor. "Don't worry, you're going to be fine. We're just going to give you a shot and it's going to make you feel better."

She walked over to a tall gray metal cabinet. Clarissa, unbidden, began rolling up a sleeve of her sweatshirt. "At least we know what we're dealing with," the doctor said to me. "We've been seeing this green stuff since the summer. From what I'm told, three would be more than enough to take you to Disneyland. I'd love to know who thought it was a good idea to bring this stuff to town."

"You and me both," I said, hypocritical son of a bitch. Uncle Fred and I had once bought fifty caps of what the guy had said was purple Owsley, sold enough to break even and gave away the rest to people in the dorm. One kid, then pre-med, now lives in Maine, doing scrimshaw. Uncle Fred saw him when he was up there a few years ago. Makes a decent living at it, apparently.

The doctor was poking a needle through the rubber seal of a small bottle of clear liquid. Clarissa, meanwhile, had taken off her belt and wrapped it around her upper arm; she had the end of the belt in her teeth and she was pumping her fist. The doctor looked at me, then touched her fingers to Clarissa's shoulder. "That's not going to be necessary," she said. "This is an intramuscular injection."

Clarissa looked up at her, teeth still bared. Then over at me. Then she loosened the belt.

"Have that sleeve up a little bit more?" the doctor said. "Now this might pinch for just a second, but I'm not going to hurt you." She swabbed Clarissa's shoulder with a piece of cotton, and I turned away.

"Okey-doke," she said, after a few seconds. "Now Clarissa, I'd like you just to lie back on the table for a bit, you can hold that piece of cotton for me, and very soon you'll be feeling better."

"Okay," said Clarissa, her voice small.

"She's going to rest for a few minutes," said the doctor. "May I speak to you?" She nodded toward the doorway. I followed her into a small office.

"This child has problems," she said, seating herself behind her desk. "What are you doing about it?" There was a chair beside the desk, but she didn't invite me to sit. So I stood there like a bad boy. "Move a little to your left, please?" she said. "I need to keep an eye on her."

"To tell you the truth," I said, "this is all a bit of a revelation to me. See, I've only known her mother for a short time and . . ." And what?

"I thought you were her stepfather."

Careful.

"Well," I said. "Sort of de facto. We're not actually married, but her mother and I have been living together more or less since, oh, let me think, August. So at this point, stepfather is just sort of always, I don't know, the least confusing."

"And where is Clarissa's mother?"

"She's—I mean, she's *here*. She just happened to be out tonight when all this started happening."

"Mmm," she said. She had picked up a clipboard and one of those pens whose other end is a letter opener. She began tapping the clipboard with the letter-opener end, looking past my shoulder. In this small space, I tried to blow my boozy breath out the side of my mouth. It must've looked like I was making faces.

"Well," she said, "at the very least I should think Clarissa needs counseling of some sort. I can refer you to a couple of very good programs."

"Would you?" I said.

She looked at me. "Yes," she said, "I would."

Back in the car, Clarissa sat with her hands folded in her lap, as I cursed, quietly as I could, twisted the key and pumped the gas pedal. This was only November, for Christ's sake; what was I supposed to do in January?

"Could we have the radio?" she said when I finally got the God damn engine to turn over. "Oh yeah, and the heater?"

"Heater we can do in just a second," I said, backing out of the parking space. "Soon as the car warms up a little. Have this jacket over you if you want." I held up a sleeve of the cowboy jacket, still draped over the passenger seat. But she was looking at something out the window. "Now for music," I said, "if you'll check in the dashboard there, you should find a Walkman and all sorts of tapes." She shook her head, still looking out, as if despairing of being able to listen to any sort of tape I might have.

The hospital was on Division Street, and I realized that all you had to do was go all the way out Division, cut through the mall parking lot and, bingo, you were on Hamilton Avenue. We'd come here by way of JFK Boulevard and it had probably taken an extra five minutes with all the lights. So if you wanted to believe that something good always came out of everything, this was what you could point to tonight: a new shortcut.

"How you feeling?" I said.

"Really excellent," said Clarissa. "Have you been watching the *moon*?"

"No, I've been watching the road," I said. Now that the crisis seemed to be over, I could go back to being a prick and a put-upon.

"Look," she said, and pointed out her window.

I leaned forward, chin beyond the steering wheel, and looked up and to the right. White disk of moon hanging there with a face in it. "Yeah," I said, sitting back, "full moon."

"Could we just drive around or something?" she said. "I'm really not freaking out anymore, and it's just so excellent."

"I think we should get you home," I said. "Enough adventure for one night, *n'est-ce pas*?"

"That's cool," she said. "Whatever. I'm just kind of sorry for *you*. Like you're missing out."

5

Clarissa was humming a mad little tune when we pulled up in front
of the house again. Something like Schoenberg to the beat of "Do
You Know the Muffin Man?" The Reliant was back at last.

Martha opened the door for us. "So I'm all ears," she said. "Do
you know what *time* it is?"

"I'm sure you'll get around to telling us," I said. "I might ask where
the hell *you* were."

"Hey Ma?" said Clarissa. "Danny come home yet? I really have to
talk to him."

"Danny," said Martha, "came in two hours ago and went right up
to bed. Now what goes on here, young lady?"

"Look, Ma, I'm real tired all of a sudden, okay?" And she was off
down the hall.

"Peter, now what's all this about? It's almost two in the morning.
I've been *frantic*."

"I knew we'd get a time check sooner or later," I said. "Would you
mind very much if I take my coat off and sit down? And get myself
a drink? This has not been a pleasant evening." At least she'd gotten
it warm in here. I took off my coat and draped it over a chair. "I trust
you had a delightful time, whatever it was you saw fit to do." I got
the gin out of the refrigerator and—in deference to Martha's sensi-
bilities—a peanut butter jar out of the dish drainer.

"I saw *fit*," she said, "to go to work. As you know."

"What do you mean *as I know*?"

"We had this conversation yesterday morning, Peter. I can't believe
that you've forgotten."

I shrugged. "So refresh me."

"Peter," she said. "Yesterday morning. You were sitting right
here"—she pointed at what had become my chair at the kitchen table—
"and I told you that I was going to be gone nights because I was back

working at Alexander's. For the holidays. You've heard of holidays? You know, Christmas? Or is that just all beneath your notice? And as a *matter* of fact we talked about it again this morning, because I said I wasn't going to be home until really late because we're open till midnight and what were you going to do about supper? Right? You don't remember this?"

I went back over to the sink. A little water in with the gin might look less compulsive. More debonair. I stirred with my index finger. "Yeah, I don't know," I said. "I guess so."

"You honestly don't remember."

"Yeah, right, I do remember now," I said, sitting down at the table. I had no idea what the fuck she was talking about.

"Now what happened tonight?" she said.

"Where to begin," I said. "Okay, first of all I had one of Danny's little friends tell me he might be suicidal."

"That *Danny* is?" she said. "Or the friend is?"

"Please," I said, holding up my hand. "This is not the time. So first I find this out—no, actually, first I find out this friend of Danny's has taken up residence in my house. *Then* I find out Danny is suicidal."

"I wasn't making a joke, by the way, Peter. I was honestly confused. Sorry if I'm so *stupid*."

"Then," I said, ignoring this, "I get back here, where I find your daughter in the midst of having a bad acid trip and screaming to be taken to the emergency room. Where we have just finished spending an edifying several hours cooling our fucking heels and finally getting in to see a doctor and getting shot up with tranquilizers. Plus a little interrogation about the living arrangements around here. Just for good measure."

"Oh my God," said Martha, looking toward the hallway. "What happened? Is she all right?"

"How the fuck would I know?" I said. "I mean, you saw her. She walks and talks. Whatever they shot her up with put a stop to the screaming meemies at least. Which believe me is no small boon."

"Oh my God."

"But what I particularly wish you'd been around for was when they were giving her the shot and she tied herself off with her belt. That was really attractive. You know, to get a vein up? You should've seen the doctor taking *that* in." I stopped for a swallow of that gin. Pissed me off that I'd watered it down. "You told me Clarissa had once had a little drug problem," I said. "You never told me she was shooting *up*, for Christ's sake."

"What did you *think* I meant, that she was taking too many aspirin?"

I took another swallow. "You should have told me."

"Right," she said. "So you'd look at her like a freak. And me like some welfare mother. She needs to be treated like a normal child, Peter. It's part of her recovery."

"Right," I said. "Some recovery. She's recovered so well that all she does anymore is drop a little acid now and then and jump out of her fucking skin." What I didn't add was that it was a friend of Danny's who'd given it to her; this didn't really fit into a rant about Martha and her daughter. "Jesus," I said, "some fucking situation I got myself into *this* time."

"Well," she said, "you didn't *use* to mind it."

"I didn't use to know what it *was*," I said.

"The rate you put *that* stuff away," she said, "you're in a really great position to be making judgments on Clarissa."

"Whoa," I said. "*Touché*. Too fuckin' shay. *I'm* fucked up, right? *I'm* the fucked-up one." Jabbing a forefinger into my chest. Then I had to laugh. "God, I sound just like Ralph Kramden," I said. "Did you hear it?"

She stared. "Is there some particular time of the day," she said, "when you might be sober enough for us to actually talk? I think we could really use it."

"*I'm* ready to talk," I said. "What. Because I can stand *outside* myself for one second, I'm suddenly not in any shape to *deal* with anything? I was in enough shape to get your daughter to the hospital. You want to talk about shape?"

"I'm going to go check on Clarissa," she said. "You'll excuse me?"

"Thank you," I prompted her.

"For what?" she said. "What are you thanking *me* for?"

"Forget it," I said. "Go." I flopped a sloppy-wristed hand to dismiss her. "You might check on Danny while you're at it."

"Of course," she said.

I sat there at the table, in my accustomed chair, head of the family, and drank off the rest of that watered-down gin. Waste of good gin to water it down, though actually it wasn't because it was still the same quantity of gin. Well, at least Danny was safe in bed, presumably, so that much could wait. But this whole thing was unbelievable. I felt like just crashing on the couch tonight, but I couldn't even do *that* because then in the morning the kids would know there'd been a fight. Morning meaning when the alarm went off in a few hours. Some schoolday tomorrow was going to be.

I got up, went to the refrigerator, took a good belt of gin straight out of the bottle, then poured the rest of it into the peanut butter jar, and that was all she wrote for Old Mr. Gordon's. I sat down at the table again to drink this last inch and try to figure out where to sleep. Go back to my house? While it still *was* my house? Except the God damn fat kid was there. And doing what? Innocently revelling in videos and canned frosting to console himself for not getting into Clarissa's pants? Or playing a far deeper game? I mean, what if he *hadn't* simply popped a Pez or some such, and all the time he'd been talking to me he'd been sneakily tripping his brains out, holding himself together while he watched, say, my face disintegrate. Which was probably even more dangerous than manifestly freaking out, like Clarissa. I thought about it in terms of pressure: Clarissa's freakout had been an ultimately harmless outrush, whereas whatever was building up under that surface that Dustin was using so much counterpressure to maintain—no need to finish the thought. Then I wondered if thinking of the mind in this kind of Newtonian way made any sense. Which was as far as I'd managed to get with my thinking when Martha came back in.

"I guess they're both asleep," said Martha, sitting down in her accustomed chair, the one across from mine. "I kind of tapped on the door and all I heard was breathing."

"Hey, as long as they're breathing," I said. "Here." I fumbled in my pants pocket. "Doctor gave me a list of, I don't know, places you can call."

"Places," she said.

"Places you could get her into treatment," I said.

I held aloft the piece of paper, let it drop, and shot it across the tabletop at her with the flick of a fingertip. It came to rest against a plate smeared with dried egg yolk. Fucking thing had sat there since breakfast, and now it was getting on toward breakfast again.

Martha picked up the piece of paper and stared at it, then put it down. "Basically," she said, "what Clarissa needs is for the last ten or fifteen years not to have happened."

"So you just throw up your hands, right?"

"So what do *you* propose? Hand the problem back to the experts so you don't have to deal with it?"

"Wait a minute," I said. "Why is this *my* problem?"

"I meant anybody," she said. "So *one* doesn't have to deal with it, all right? But actually, yes: you, Peter. Because I actually was stupid enough to think you could've been some help. God, from her father to you . . . *I'm* the one who ought to be locked up."

I got to my feet. "Believe I'll put up on the couch for tonight," I said. "Fascinating as this all is."

"Uh uh," she said. "No. I believe you'll put up in your own house tonight. I don't want you here. You're welcome to call a taxi if you're not able to drive yourself. But I want you gone."

"I am fully well able," I said, "to drive myself." I was man enough, barely, not to plead that an LSD-maddened teenager might be waiting at my house. Behind the door with a knife, say, to cut out my heart to see how it worked. I raised the peanut butter jar, said "Here's how," drained the last half inch of gin and wiped my hand across my mouth. " 'Wipe your hand across your mouth and laugh,' " I said. " 'The something something something something. The words revolve—' I don't know, goes on from there." I raised an Uncle Fred forefinger. " 'Some infinitely gentle, infinitely suffering thing.' "

"And I can really do without the ironies," she said. "Whatever they're supposed to mean."

"*You*, maybe," I said. "But as for me."

I put on my coat and felt around in the right-hand pocket for keys. Good: two bunches; one car keys, one house keys. You could tell the house keys by feel. They were the ones with Powerful Pete on the key ring, unless that was the car keys. Probably not your finest hour, getting yourself kicked out of here before you were able to talk your son out of killing himself.

"Just remember," I said, hand on the doorknob. "If anything

happens to me"—I was thinking Manson murder, but she probably thought I just meant a car wreck—"you're going to have some
pret-ty tall explaining to do to old Danny."

"I'll risk it," she said.

"Famous last words," I said. Meaning from my point of view.

6

Late as it was, the lights were still on when I pulled into the driveway
behind what's-his-name's Cadillac. Dustin. And I noticed for the first
time—God knows how long it had been there—that the FOR SALE
sign had been replaced by a similar sign reading SOLD. A sign, in
other words, not to benefit me but to bring in new business. I was
giving the fuckers free advertising! I tugged and wrestled it out of the
frozen ground, took it onto the breezeway and threw it clattering on
the cement floor, a warning to all exploiters. And incidentally to put
young Dustin on notice, just in case he was thinking of trying to
Manson-murder me, that I was coming in angry and dangerous. The
kitchen door was still unlocked. I walked in and took off my coat—
the little bastard certainly hadn't stinted himself on the heat that I
was paying for—tossed it on the kitchen table and called "Anybody
home?" But he had the tv going. "Is this the place?" a tv voice was
saying.

"Of course it's the place." James Stewart, boy, you could tell that
braying voice. So Dustin had his movie on.

The other voice said, "Well, this house ain't been lived in for twenty
years."

I went into the living room. Dustin was on the sofa, lying on his
side facing the blaring tv. Bert pulled his police car up beside Ernie's
cab. "What's up, Ernie?" he said. I watched them watch James Stewart
approach the ruined house.

"I don't know," said Ernie, "but we better keep an eye on this guy.

He's bats." Bert was Ward Bond, who ended up on *Wagon Train*.

"Hey Dustin?" I said. Dead to the world, boy.

"Mary! Mary!" James Stewart called. "Tommy! Pete! Jamie! Zuzu! Where are you?"

I didn't want him finally rousing himself to get up and go into the bedroom and finding me there. Thought I'd better make sure, too, that he wasn't just lying there bug-eyed and catatonic.

"They're not here, George," said Henry Travers. "You have no children."

I touched his shoulder. "Dustin?"

"Where are you?" said James Stewart. "What have you done with them?"

Dustin didn't move.

"All right, put up your hands." I looked back at the screen. Ward Bond had pulled a gun on James Stewart. I didn't want to miss the scene that was coming up right after this, where his mother is all hard-faced and doesn't recognize him.

I gripped Dustin's shoulder lightly, just fingertips, and shook. Flesh felt loose, strangely heavy.

"Bert!" James Stewart brayed. "Thank heaven you're here." Then I looked down and saw the stilled trickle of what looked like bright red paint, down across his cheek to the corner of his half-open mouth. It came from a hole in his temple too small to stick a pencil into.

"Stand back," said Ward Bond.

This was probably a practical joke, right?

"Bert," said James Stewart, "what's happened to this house? Where's Mary? Where's my kids?"

Then I saw the little pistol on the floor, right beneath the hand drooping over the edge of the sofa: instantly knew it was Martha's, instantly imagined Danny slipping it to him for protection, instantly saw Danny led away to jail. (It *was* a .22, but of course not Martha's; they ended up pressing some kind of charges against the kid who'd sold it to him.) I put the back of my hand up to his nose and mouth, as a flirting lady would to a courtly gentleman. No breath coming out. Then I touched the hand. Never in my life touched anything like that flesh, boy. Soft and cold.

I ran to the kitchen for the phone. Though I might as well have walked. Might as well have let a year go by.

"Look," said Ward Bond, "now why don't you be a good kid and we'll take you in to a doctor. Everything's going to be all right."

I jabbed the O. Somebody better know what to do.

VI

1

The people here are getting sick of my bullshit.

What *is* this document you're writing? they want to know. Just a simple *list*, we told you: you write down the people you've harmed and what you did to them, period. Then you get started making your amends; that's how the program *works*. But up to now they haven't really been able to nail me. I'm still trying to sort this stuff *out*, I tell them. You know, what I *did* to people: is it really just this straight-forward deal where, pow, you do something shitty and, thud, some-body *feels* shitty? I mean, take Judith. Please. (Little joke.) On the one hand, this is someone who actually *died* because, bottom line, I made her miserable, right? But then there's all this stuff about how people are responsible for their own feelings—I mean, I'm responsible for *my* own feelings, right?—so therefore did I really *make* her miserable? They have a name for this kind of talk: the Retreat Into Confusion. Getting befuddled, they say, is one more strategy for avoiding the real issue. No, I tell them, it's just the *opposite*. What I'm after, I tell them, is a little clarity here, about what *happens* in this world: is that not a real issue? They say writing all this stuff down is only a strategy to gain time. (Or lose time, if you want to think of it that way.) And that makes them feel smart, to think they've really got old Jernigan's number. Which isn't to say they haven't. You have to bear with me a little on this, I tell them; I've got my own way of doing things. Right, they say, that's what got you here.

Though of course I almost *didn't* get here, which is a story outside this story really. More Uncle Fred's story than mine, anyway: he was the one who called the police; I was only the mumbling thing carried out of his trailer. (I do remember at some point looking down at the bandaged hand and thinking the shape of it looked wrong. But that must've been later, in the hospital.) I gather from what Uncle Fred tells me that the hospital and this place have eaten up all the money from selling Heritage Circle and then some. I'd thought a couple of times about health insurance after I got shit-canned, but. At any rate, Uncle Fred says I'm not to worry about any of that now. He says that handling all this stuff has only taken him a couple of vacation days; I know *that* has to be bullshit. And he says it was really Danny who saved my life: by calling him when he did, to say I was headed for New Hampshire in bad shape. He's the one you ought to be thanking, Uncle Fred says, not me. I tell him, Fuck it, let's talk about fucking *sports*, man. How about those Islanders? How about the Pittsburgh fucking *Penguins*? But he's lost his sense of irony or something.

All I remember of that story is what was supposed to be the end.

As the first stars came out over Studebaker Hill, I left the trailer and trudged back up to my car, taking the same roundabout way so as not to defile the open snow. I drove to the state store a couple of towns over—at New Hampshire prices, I had enough money left for a whole quart—and when I got back, I kept going on past the camp and parked by the frozen pond a mile farther up the road. I took the rubber hose out of the trunk, paid it out into the gas tank until it hit bottom, knelt and sucked until I got gasoline in the mouth, and then laid the end of the hose down so it would keep pissing into the snow. In fact, I thought about swallowing that mouthful of gasoline, but I didn't know enough about what would happen. Staggering around in the snow, blind and puking, that was no way to go out. So I spat, then picked up handfuls of snow and sloshed them around in my mouth. The walk back to the camp was mostly downhill, but it still takes it out of you to walk in that kind of cold. Only one car passed by, and I saw the lights coming from far enough away so that I had time to crash through the snowbank and hide behind a tree. From the place where you left the plowed road and went down to the trailer I broke new trail, even deeper in the woods and farther from the open field. I could have saved energy by walking in my old footprints, but that wasn't the idea. The idea was to get there on something like my last legs. Inside, in the dark, I didn't bother with the stove anymore. I lit a match long enough to locate what blankets there were, blew it out, pulled the blankets over me and got going on that bottle. One of the last things I remember is getting up to go outside and piss, and being pleased to find I couldn't walk straight. I'd been doubting that the gin was taking hold the way it should, half inclined to blame the bargain price. But now I was lurching in the heroic style, stumbling into one wall, bouncing off it and hitting something else, probably a different wall. I couldn't really feel the impact. When I finally did get to the door I no longer saw the sense of all this hoo-ha and figured Fuck it, might as well just let 'er go in your pants. It felt warm (though only briefly) and oh such release.

2

But. As I say. Whole other story.

My immediate response to the Dustin business wasn't to get pants-pissing drunk. Quite the reverse. I decided to consider it a sign, just as I had back when Danny was two and I woke up on somebody's floor among marble obelisks, and it turned out to be the studio of a man who hadn't had a drink in twenty years. But that was a self-generated sign, or so I assume: I must have wanted, deep down, to get to a place where I could be saved. Dustin's killing himself was a sign from outside. I mean, it wasn't anything *I'd* done. It told me I'd been making a loveless hell here, and that to stop drinking was only one of a bunch of things I had to do. Why wasn't I using my gifts, such as they were, to serve others? Okay, you're not a doctor. But you could damn well work in a soup kitchen. Or volunteer in a nursing home. Go to some hospital and hold unwanted babies before they died of not being held. Simply physically held: you could do it with an IQ of twenty. If you were lucky enough to be able-bodied, you dropped your self-absorbed bullshit and you went out and got any job you could get to keep yourself alive so you could help those who weren't able-bodied. I mean, *anybody* knows this.

But Jernigan is no life-changer. Though willing enough to lie back and let it happen. So I ended up simply resolving to limit things to maybe a beer once in a while but really just *a* beer, and to do better with the little daily stuff. A smile of greeting, a thank you after a meal—oh believe me, I know how *Reader's Digest*y this all sounds— and really listening to what loved ones are saying instead of finding ways to let them know that you wish they'd leave you the fuck alone. I thought: Martin Sanders's family is shot to shit, but *you* still have a family. Or what might yet be made to approximate a family. And you've been sinking down and down and down into yourself and taking no care of it. Now that was going to stop. I was going to be part of this household again: take my turn doing dishes and feeding the bunnies. Death-chamber duty too. Danny was going to have a mother and Clarissa was going to have a father and Martha and I were going to have a sex life again and we were going to get a set of friends and everybody was going to do things together. I was going to look into health insurance and so on, and sock away that money from the house in some kind of a good bank thing so it would be there for Danny. I was going to start wearing that fun cowboy jacket. Christmas was only two weeks away, and we were going to have a tree and people over and things in the windows.

I mean, I *say* Dustin's death was none of my doing, but I should have picked up the clues he'd taken such pains both to drop and to disguise. When he said kids who talked about suicide were crying for help. When he said he would have felt bad if he hadn't tried everything. When he said it was when you were alone that things got weird. On the other hand, he'd been a devious little fuck, and I wouldn't have put it past him to *know* how guilty everybody was going to feel afterwards. It wasn't just me, as I found out. He'd told Danny that the *other* kid in the band, the feral one with the tank top and the platinum hair, was talking suicide. Then there was the kid from the community college—some good police work on this, I have to say—who'd been selling him drugs and who had soaked him a hundred bucks for that twenty-dollar pistol. Dustin had foxed *him* by claiming he'd been getting threats from a gang of Vietnamese kids at the high school because he was giving drugs away to their paying customers. Except there *weren't* any Vietnamese kids at the high school.

And then there was the father.

I never found out just what the trouble there had been about. But I did sit with the father in their living room the day after the funeral to tell him what I could tell him, though he'd already heard it secondhand from the police. And to explain why I hadn't called him to say his son was staying in my house and was that okay. A medical emergency that evening, that was the way I put it. That the quote unquote medical emergency was *also* his son's doing—not that he'd had to twist Clarissa's arm, probably—didn't seem like anything the poor bastard needed to know at this point. Jernigan and his lonely burden.

When he went into the kitchen to get me a cup of coffee, I looked around at all the right angles of chrome, glass, stone, black leather. I was the only shapeless thing here. Martin Sanders was thin and looked like a mean son of a bitch. Glasses like Gloria Steinem's. He could never have had even the minimal flair required to name a kid Dustin. It must have been the wife. Hard, too, to imagine him with a secret collection of videos like the one they found at the house, which sure as hell hadn't come from Bedford Falls Video. No it wasn't.

He handed me a black stoneware cup and sat down empty-handed.

"This is my wife's idea," he said. "She's asked me to ask you about it, so that I can then tell it to her. She didn't seem to feel she could talk to you personally at this point." He wasn't doing too well himself. Off came the glasses and out came a white handkerchief from the pocket of the gray wool slacks. When he finished with the handkerchief you could see two little white ovals where the glasses dug into his bony nose.

"It's the first thing she's asked of me in God knows *how* long," he said. Then he said, "You don't need to hear this."

"Please," I said. "If you need to talk."

"Let me rephrase myself," he said. "What I mean is, it's none of your business. And I want you the hell out of my house as soon as I've heard what I need to hear. Is that a little clearer?"

3

It was right around this time, gearing up for the holiday season, that we had the closing on the house. Danny and I brought the last couple of carloads of stuff over the day before, and Clarissa came along on one trip to help him go through his clothes. Most of what we brought was boxes of my books, including the Britannica eleventh edition I'd never unpacked since Barrow Street. Another precious legacy to my son. (Little joke.) The rest of his records, some extra blankets (Martha's request), a few towels. And the color tv, which went straight up to the kids' room: in Clarissa's eyes, my high-water mark as stepfather. Hey, if the kids wanted to think that sticking to the old black-and-white was one more sign of my unselfishness, who was I to enlighten them? Though Danny must've known me better.

After signing the papers and handing over the keys, I took the whole family into the city for dinner and a movie. It was going to be dinner and a show but none of the shows sounded any good, big surprise. Martha picked the Russian Tea Room and I said fine. I mean, it could have been Mamma Leone's. (That was uncalled-for.) We brought a *Daily News* in with us so we could look at movie times, but there weren't even any movies anybody wanted to see all that much. So after dinner we just walked down to Rockefeller Center and looked at the tree and the skaters and it turned out to be a good family thing to do and then we went back to New Jersey like probably thousands of other New Jersey families that night.

"Dan, what do you say?" I asked him at breakfast the next morning. (Another thing: I was going to be making it to breakfast from now on. And not because I'd been up all night drinking, either. It would be because at bedtime I would have fucked Martha and then gone right off to sleep.) "You busy this weekend?"

He considered this, obviously wondering what a *no* would let him in for. "I don't know yet," he said.

"Well, here's what I was thinking. Why don't you and me hop in the car and drive up around where Grandpa Jernigan's old place was and get a tree."

"What do you mean get a tree?"

"Christmas tree," I said. "You know, ho ho ho?" Forgetting I wasn't going to be sarcastic anymore. Okay, so just breeze on past it. "I thought we'd cut our own this year," I said.

"Isn't it going to end up costing you just as much in gas anyway?" he said.

"Probably," I said. "Viewed purely in crass economic terms, it's undoubtedly a washout. But viewed as a father-son bonding ritual? This could be more precious than diamonds. More lasting than fucking bronze." I couldn't help it: he was being willfully stupid.

He stared down at the peanut butter melting into his toast. I wouldn't have known what to say, either.

"Anybody for more coffee?" said helpful Martha. Danny looked up at her. Clarissa, of course, just sat there twisting platinum hair around a black-nailed finger.

"I'm sorry," I said. "I don't mean to be such a prick, pardon my French." This for Clarissa's benefit. "I'd just like for us to spend some time together, and I thought this might be a nice way to do it. Go off on a little mission."

"Why?" he said. "So I won't kill myself like Dustin?"

"Good," I said. "You know, you're really beginning to show some promise there. Keep it up and by the time you're my age you might be just as big a prick as your old dad."

"Jesus Christ," said Martha. "*Both* of you. You make me want to cover my ears. Danny, why don't you give your father a chance? And Peter. Stop being so *ugly*. You might as well take a strap to him. At least that would be *clean*."

"Sorry," I said.

"Sorry, Mrs. Peretsky," he said.

"Listen," I said, "it *is* a long way up there and everything. We don't really have to have such a major expedition. It was just a thought."

"It's okay," he said. "I don't care."

You sullen little son of a bitch, I almost said.

"Well," I said, "how about Saturday, then? Leave good and early, get you back in time to do what you want Saturday night—what do you say?"

He stared extra hard at his toast, his brow crumpling with the smile of relief he was suppressing. "Yeah, if that's okay with you," he said, in a deep voice that wasn't quite his own yet. In that moment I loved him so.

And pitied him for what had been done to him, and for the long road ahead. Oh, not the road to Connecticut, I was just using a worn-out metaphor. Though not too worn-out, apparently, for the likes of Jernigan. Because I really did picture Danny, under a featureless sky, on a featureless road heading for a vanishing point, as in *Jon Nagy's Television Art Book*. Which Santa had brought me one year. My father's friends always used to come over for Christmas—most of them didn't have kids—and when I clawed the paper off and held it up they all laughed and cheered.

4

I laid Martha's ax on the floor in the back seat of the Datsun and got behind the wheel. Danny slumped in the passenger seat half asleep as I bustled, the cowboy jacket over his knees. "Guess we better take the scythe along too," I said, as if he gave a fuck.

"For what?" he said, then yawned. It was eight in the morning, bright blue sky, fierce sun, frost still on the grass.

"Case we have to clear any brush to get at the tree," I said. "Don't want to snag your ax when you're trying to swing it." I swung a hypothetical ax to show him. "You want to leave plenty of room around you." We were talking about things that mattered to men. I had already had three cups of coffee.

He stretched as best he could in a cramped car—more of a squirm really—and settled back down.

Well so of course no matter which way you turned it, the son-of-a-bitching scythe wouldn't go. God damn little shitbox foreign cars anyway. I ended up having to find a wrench and take off the blade; the snath had to go lengthwise, one end of it up between the front seats.

"How are we supposed to fit a tree in here?" said Danny.

"O ye of little faith," I said. "We're not going to try. Going to tie it to the roof. Like a deer." He didn't seem to understand what I meant about a deer. It got me thinking, though: if this went all right and we had a good time, why couldn't Danny and I start going hunting together? Couple of deer rifles, go upcountry and bring home some *real* meat instead of your God damn pissy little rabbits. Meat enough to last us.

When we finally got under way, he took the Walkman out of the dash first thing. I mean, he did ask if I minded, but of course he had you there: if you said you did mind and would rather talk, what the hell kind of a tone did that set for any conversation you were going to have? As we crossed the GW, I turned my head for a glance at the skyscrapers on such a clear day, and there he was, head resting on the window glass, eyes closed, mouth open. Fleeting thought about which hospital was closest (but not some Bronx one) before I saw his shoulder rise, then fall, then rise. I reached over and locked his door.

Just below Hartford, he suddenly sat up and took off the earphones. The thing had long since clicked off, but he'd slept on through the silence. "How much longer?" he said.

"Forty-five minutes?" I said. "Little more, maybe." I didn't want to say another hour.

"Mmmf," he said.

"You have a good sleep?"

"Had this weird dream," he said. "You and Mom were in it. It was like I really thought it was real, you know. Like even after I woke up I still thought some of it was true." He tossed the cowboy jacket into the back seat and did his squirming stretch.

"What did you think was true?" I said.

"I don't know. It's kind of hard to explain. Where are we anyway?"

"That's Hartford," I said, pointing.

"Are we gonna go past the Colt factory?"

"Right," I said. "You remember that?"

"Sure," he said. "I wasn't *that* little. The horse on top."

"So what was this dream?" I said, obliged to ask, dreading to hear. The last time I'd heard him mention Judith was the day we'd moved the last stuff out of Heritage Circle. I'd come out of the house with a box of books in time to catch him flipping a thumb at the driveway and saying to Clarissa, "Right there's the place where my mom bought it."

"I don't remember," he said, "except that you and Mom were both in it and we were doing something. Do they still make guns there?"

"Got me," I said. "For all I know, they made it into condos now. Colt Condominiums," I announced in a Don Pardo voice. "All the comforts of home, and none of the horseshit."

He laughed, probably not so much at the very small joke as at his father saying *shit* to him. Oh, we were doing fine now.

"So," I said. "You still think a lot about Mom?"

He shrugged. "Not a lot."

I waited.

"Sometimes I think it's sad that I don't think about her."

"Yeah, I know the feeling," I said. "You just have to remember that it's natural, and that it doesn't mean you love her any less. It's just that as you go along, your life fills up with new things, *and* people, that need your attention."

"It just seems like I'm going on and leaving her back there alone," he said. He began to cry. The first time I'd seen since the funeral. Not that I would have been likely to see. Maybe this was cathartic for him, if there was such a thing as catharsis.

"Danny," I said. "However it is, I don't think it's like that. That people are just left alone somewhere."

"Well how do *you* think it is?" he said, taking rough swipes at his cheeks with the back of a wrist. "How do *you* know so much?"

"I'm not claiming to know anything," I said. "I'm only telling you what I think."

"You think it because that's what you *want* to think."

"Could well be," I said. "This is stuff that to be honest I really can't help you with a lot. If this is something that's really troubling you, you could . . ." Yeah, he could what? "I mean, there are people, you know, priests and so forth, who really, you know, in all sincerity believe they have answers to some of these things. I guess what happened with me is that I just sort of indefinitely put off trying to decide about any of it."

"But how can you stand not knowing?" he said.

"I don't know," I said. "You know, most of the time it's just not what you're thinking about. Not that I'm recommending the unexamined life, mind you." I jerked my thumb at the window. "There's your Colt factory."

A fluted blue dome, elevated on a circle of white columns. Atop the dome, a golden ball. Atop the golden ball, a rearing golden horse. *Colt guns are better than anything in the world*: that much of the symbolism I understood. The rest of it suggested the thing where the turtle's resting on the back of whatever it is, back of an elephant. Or the other way around, elephant on the turtle. Some literalist had defaced the ideal blue of the dome with gold stars.

"Dustin used a Colt," said Danny. "Colt forty-five automatic."

"What are you talking about?" I said.

"That's what Mitchell says."

"Mitchell's talking through his hat," I said. I hit the brakes and shifted down to make the sharp right over the bridge. "It was just some crappy little twenty-two pistol, Danny. Little Mark David Chapman fat-boy special. What, are all the kids romanticizing this thing now?"

"You mean like what Mrs. Peretsky has for the rabbits?"

"So you know about that," I said.

"Clarissa showed me." He shrugged. "Pretty weird."

I pointed again. "Connecticut River, by the way."

"I *know*, Dad."

"So," I said, "have you and Mitchell been thinking about a replacement for Dustin?"

"You can't replace Dustin," he said.

"Well," I said. "You know what I mean."

"I'm not kidding," he said. "I mean, it was all his songs and everything. We just sort of tried to play what he told us. He could play guitar as good as me any day. He just played bass so he could sing. You know, nobody else could even *sing*."

"What about Clarissa?" I said. "Wasn't she singing that day I walked in on your practice?"

"Clarissa?" he said. "She's a joke."

I looked over at him.

"Dustin had her sing on a couple things because I think he sort of felt bad for her," he said. "But she was really just image. You know, we sort of started out with her and then we didn't know how to tell her it wasn't happening. I mean, in a way, if this had to happen . . ."

"Hold the phone," I said. "What I'm hearing is that you and Mitchell are using this as an excuse to close up shop because you're afraid to tell Clarissa she can't sing."

"Bull *shit*."

"Look. Danny. I realize these things aren't easy. Obviously Clarissa's going to get her feelings hurt. I don't blame her. There'll probably be a big scene. On the other hand, do you want to give up your music just to avoid a confrontation?" Me and fucking Robert Young, boy.

"I'm not giving it *up*," he said. "I'm going to still practice guitar and everything. All I have to do is just make it through the rest of this year and then senior year, and then I can do what I want to anyway."

"That's a long time," I said.

He looked at his watch. "Tell me about it," he said. *"Dad."*

"Am I also hearing," I said, "that things aren't going so well with you and Clarissa?"

"I think she might be a little crazy," he said. "Sometimes I wish I could just, like, get out of it, you know?"

"Can't say I'm surprised to hear it," I said. "Particularly after our little soirée at the emergency room."

"Except I really like Mrs. Peretsky, you know? Hey Dad?" he said. "Listen, I'm going bonkers without a cigarette, okay? I mean, you know I smoke, right? Do you mind if I have one? You can even lecture me about it if you want, but I'd really like to have one."

"What the hey," I said. "Haven't you figured out by now that I'm one of those permissive parents?"

You never saw cigarettes come out of anybody's jacket so fast. So he'd moved on to Camels.

"Thanks," he said, fumbling for matches.

"Just crack your window," I said, "so you don't hasten the old man's inevitable whatever with passive smoke, right?"

He opened his window a crack and blew a great cloud of smoke at it. It smelled wonderful.

"Well, I knew this whole deal was a mistake," I said. "I absolutely knew the minute we sold the God damn house we'd be sorry." (Don't you love the "we"?)

"I guess so," he said. "But it would've been weird anyway to go back there after Dustin, right? And, you know, what happened to Mom and everything."

"There's an argument to be made," I said, "that the thing with Dustin wouldn't have happened if we'd been in our own house where we belonged."

"Is that what Mr. Sanders said?"

"No," I said, "I thought of it all by myself."

He looked at his watch again. "So how much longer?"

"Half an hour?" I said. "Assuming you mean to Woodstock. So. I guess maybe we should start rethinking this whole arrangement, the two of us."

"I don't know," he said. "I should just shut up. I feel bad because you're like really into it. Getting a Christmas tree and everything. And before, you were sort of drinking a lot. I mean, I guess it's not all that bad."

"At my age," I said, "that would be a ringing testimonial. At *your* age it doesn't sound like something you should have to settle for."

"It's okay. Really."

"Exactly how crazy is crazy?" I said. He looked puzzled. "You said Clarissa was kind of crazy."

He inhaled so deeply I imagined I could feel it in my own chest. Then he let it out. "You're not going to get mad, right?"

"I hadn't planned on it," I said.

"Okay, this sounds pretty weird, all right? But you didn't, like, do anything to her, right? Like the night she was freaking out?"

"Say again?"

"I knew you'd get mad."

"I'm not *mad*," I said. "I'm just amazed. I mean, actually I'm not even amazed." Better tell the story. "She was pretty out of it, and at one point when I was trying to get her to the hospital, I had to stop her from taking her sweatshirt off. Now, what does *she* think was going on?"

He shook his head. "She's got stories about a lot of stuff," he said. "Like she says her father used to make her do stuff. At first I used to be really sorry for her."

"Do stuff," I said, meaning *Explain*.

"You know," he said. "But I mean Mrs. Peretsky wouldn't have ever let anything really happen."

"Ho, brother," I said.

The farther we got from Hartford and the river, the hillier the country and the fewer the houses. All the trees bare, and the last tinge of green draining out of the grass. You could see the different shapes of the different kinds of trees: some squat with branches like antlers, some straight and slender. It amounted to a moral failing not to have learned the names of trees. A moral failing, too, that this landscape looked dead and tattered to me, instead of sternly beautiful. In this part of the world, if you couldn't see a leafless tree as sternly beautiful you were in deep shit half the year. And probably pissing away the other half worrying that it was transient.

We got off the interstate at the familiar exit. I hadn't been back this way since my father's funeral. It still looked like the country, even though there was a new house here and there, if I was remembering correctly. Five years. The white colonial with the swayback roof was now chocolate brown, with staring modern windows in place of the old six-over-six, a red plastic three-wheeler overturned in the front yard. We took the shortcut, the back road from Westford into Eastford, coming out by the General Lyon Inn, then left on 198 up toward Woodstock Valley. The place across from the post office, I remembered, had been a hippie house. One summer day, years ago, I'd driven past and seen a little wedding party posing for pictures on the lawn. A pretty blond-haired bride, a long-haired groom, a capering mongrel dog. Where were they anymore, and what had happened to them in all this time? Not here, I imagined, and nothing good.

A new house now sat at the corner of my father's road, in what used to be an overgrown field. They'd left the stone wall up and put a blacktop drive through the barway. Not a house, actually, but a double-wide trailer with a Florida room. A lamppost beside the flagstone walk. They did seem to keep the place up. Crew-cut brown grass, suggesting they hadn't lost the old vim as fall came on. Me, I'd always skipped what should have been the last couple of mowings, and settled for having my eye affronted all winter by lank dead grass.

"Strike one," I said to Danny. "Used to be tons of little evergreens in that field."

"What field?"

I flipped my thumb at the trailer. "Used to be a field," I said.

"I don't remember it too much here," he said.

"I know," I said. "It's a shame. Your grandfather didn't really know how to deal with kids, I don't think. After I was grown up he and I finally got to be sort of buddies, but before that . . ." I took one hand off the wheel and wiggled my fingers to suggest iffiness.

I pulled over to the side of the road. This was where the house had been. Two noble old maples—a tree I did know—one at each side of the cellar hole. Some kind of shitty little saplings now growing up out of it. I turned off the engine: sudden, profound silence.

"Well, let's check it out," I said. Too loud, too hearty. "I seem to remember some little pine trees or something up behind the house."

We got out and Danny stretched, holding fists aloft on stiff arms. "Might as well leave the tools here for the time being," I said.

"Who owns this place now?" he said. My God it was silent up here.

"Got *me*," I said. "Bank still, for all I know. Be a nice spot for somebody."

We walked through tangled dead hay that had been the front lawn, and stood at the lip of the cellar hole. A jumbled heap of bricks down there, once the chimney, and the charred end of a beam sticking out from the carpeting of brown and yellow maple leaves. The tops of the saplings growing up out of the old dirt floor were level with my knees. I led the way to the right, around the right-hand maple tree and into the side yard, where the old lilac stood in a waste of brier and burdock. "That was the studio," I said, pointing to a rectangle of low brick wall, mostly tumbled down, adjoining the old stone foundation. Here, too, saplings grew out of rubble, and I could make out a half-eaten elbow of rusted stovepipe.

"See, originally the henhouse was over there," I said, pointing. "Cost him an arm and a leg to have 'em move it and lay that foundation for it. Now the doorway into the kitchen, see, was right there. He'd go down to the kitchen in the morning, get his coffee and go straight in to work. So of course when the studio caught fire, the whole place went up. Hey, only connect, right?"

"I guess so," Danny said. Doing his best to fake it. As old Dad was doing his best to shut him out by talking over his head. Christ.

"Well, don't worry, champ," I said. "Your dad's not going to get into a big thing here. Let's see if we can't sneak up on one of those trees, okay? I think this is the time of day they come out to graze on the side hill." Not much of a joke, but at least it didn't demand any fucking erudition.

We crashed through some brush and brambles behind the house, stepped over the little brook that had been the boundary between backyard and apple orchard, sank into mud for a few steps and then found ourselves on solid ground again. Bloated yellow apples lay rotting into the dead grass. We kept the apple trees on our right and eventually struck a path I remembered, leading behind the orchard and up the hill.

"Sure as shootin'," I said, and pointed at the steep side hill with its outcroppings of ledge and patches of juniper. "Christmas trees galore." Here and there stood a man-high pine tree, or whatever they were. "Let's double back and get our weapons, amigo."

"You're sure it's okay to do this?" he said.

"If they take us," I said, "we'll go together."

Back at the car, I got out the ax, scythe blade and snath. "I'll let you be the grim reaper once I get this thing back together," I said, feeling around in my jacket pockets for the damn adjustable wrench. "You ever use one of these?"

"I've seen guys using 'em," he said. He must have meant on television.

"Hell is the *wrench*?" I said. "Christ, I know I brought it."

Danny patted his own pockets helpfully, though he surely knew there was no chance he had it.

"*Scheiss*," I said. "For want of a wrench the scythe was lost, for want of a scythe—here, would you check in the dash?"

He opened the passenger door and sat down heavily on the seat, as I kept thrusting my hands in and out of my pockets like some baggypants comedian. "How about these?" he said, holding up a pair of pliers.

"Saved the day," I said. "Cannot *believe* I left the wrench behind. What would Freud say about this? *Ist das nicht ein wrenchenslip? Ja, das ist ein wrenchenslip.*" He watched me put the scythe back together, probably wondering what the fuck I was babbling about now. It was impossible that he could love me. Although he certainly had no one else left to hang on to. His only other living relative was his Uncle

Rick, who'd broken up with his friend Rich shortly after Judith died, and had moved to Eureka, California. I toyed with the idea of asking Danny point-blank did he love me, but why ruin a nice day. If that's what we were having.

"Okay, bud," I said, handing him the scythe and picking up the ax. "Over the top."

The path behind the orchard led into what was left of an old two-rut track that went around the base of the hill, cut through the woods and ended up in what used to be some dairy farmer's haylot. Shoulder-high brush had now taken over the track, and we kept having to detour around patches of brier.

"Mess," I said. "Let's try a little ways up the hill. Looks like better going."

We climbed up out of the brush into the dry grass of the hillside. "Hey Dad?" Danny called. I turned around. He was pointing to a pine tree just above us. "What about that one?"

"Possibility," I said. "I don't know, though. See? The top is kind of forked there. I don't know what you'd do about that."

"Yeah, I guess not," he said.

"Bottom of it's nice and full," I said.

"Forget it," he said.

"It's a candidate if we don't run across something better," I said. It was a lousy tree. Though lousy, I reminded myself, only from our narrow perspective: you couldn't be too careful what you thought. We trudged diagonally uphill, always making our detours around the junipers on the high side.

"That one?" I said.

Danny looked. "Isn't that one kind of weird at the top too?" he said. "There's all that space there where there's not any branches."

"So you cut all that top stuff off," I said. "Cut the top, like a foot of it, right off. And stick your star on there."

"Yeah, I guess."

"Doesn't pull your trigger, huh?"

"Nah, it's okay."

"Hey," I said. "Let's find one we can really throw our support behind." No answer. The political metaphor made me think of a joke. "Presidential timber," I said. But it might have been too obscure.

We climbed on. Chilly as it was, I was starting to sweat. I could feel my heart going, and I had to make a conscious effort to breathe slowly and through my nose so Danny wouldn't hear his old man panting. He was just striding along on those long, lean, sixteen-year-old legs.

"Want to take a breather?" I said.

"We're almost to the *top*, Dad." Said with maybe just the edge of an edge. Or was he simply offering me encouragement? I looked back. From up here you could see the ruined foundation clearly, and you could tell that the lawn had been a lawn. Ruins that made sense only from above, like Erich von Däniken's landing strips for spacemen.

I sat down. "Tell you what," I said. "Since the old man's out of shape anyhow, let me have one of those things."

"Have what?" he said.

"Cigarette," I said. "Bertie Wooster calls them gaspers. Isn't that a great expression, gaspers?"

"Dad," he said. "I don't think you want to do that."

"Shows how much *you* know," I said. I was surprised that it came out sounding so brutal. I'd been aiming for witty.

"How long have you been off them this time?"

"Too God damn long," I said, standing up and holding out my hand.

"Dad, I really don't think you should," he said. "You're going to be real sorry if you get hooked on them again."

"That's my lookout," I said.

"They're my cigarettes," he said.

I stared at him. A good-looking boy, holding a scythe awkwardly over his shoulder, blade pointing back at his calf. A little taller than me. Gnawing on his lower lip.

"Oh hell," I said, and sat down again, using the ax as an old man would use a cane. My ass on the cold earth. Danny didn't move. I looked down again on the place where my father had died.

"Sorry, amigo," I said, after a while. "I said I wasn't going to make a scene, and here I am making a scene."

"I guess it must be weird for you to be here," he said.

"I hadn't thought so," I said. "I guess I shouldn't underestimate my capacity for having a normal reaction, right? At any rate, thanks for the tough love. You bastard." I'd meant that to be jocular too. Everything was going off-key. "Ho, brother," I said.

"Think we should get going?" said Danny.

I looked up at him. "I don't even know why we're doing this," I said. "The whole thing is fucked, right? I mean, are we really going to go through a whole Christmas thing with them, *knowing*?"

"Dad, how come you're asking *me*?" he said.

"I'm thinking out loud, for Christ's sake," I said. "I'm not *asking* you." If I didn't know what to do, at least I could be pissy. "You done any Christmas shopping yet?" I said, staring back down at the cellar hole.

"Some," he said.

"Stuff for Clarissa?"

"Dad, I don't get why you're *asking* me this stuff. You mean if we already bought Christmas presents we shouldn't let them go to *waste* or something? I can't see what you're saying."

"I'm just trying to think," I said.

"Look, we might as well just stay, you know? You and Mrs. Peretsky are doing okay again, and I get along with *her* really good and I can handle Clarissa okay. I mean maybe she'll OD or something."

That got me to look up.

"I'm *kidding*," he said. "Dad? It was just a joke. You know. Joke?"

"Well," I said, "I guess we better get this done." I got to my feet, leaning again on the ax handle. "Here. What's the problem with this one right here?"

He looked. "Come *on*."

"Seriously," I said. "Take it down and just use like the top six feet of it. It's got a nice shape up there."

"You're going to cut the whole—look, sure, I don't care."

"Good," I said. "Decided. Now let's clear away some of the little brush over that side, okay? And then we'll be in business."

He started just whanging away with the scythe.

"Hold it, *hold* it," I said. "Let me show you." I took the scythe from his hands. "You want to keep the blade level, okay? And . . ." I demonstrated. "Like so. Short strokes. It shouldn't take a lot of effort." I showed him again.

"Okay, *okay*," he said. "Let me *try*." He tried. "Right," he said. "Works better."

"Thought it might," I said, with fatherly understatement. So this was the moment I thought we'd never have together. However I might eventually come to remember it, it wasn't much right now.

When he finished, I went in and hacked away the tree's bottommost limbs to give a clear shot at the trunk. "What do you say?" I said. "You want to do the dirty deed?"

"Yeah, I guess." I handed him the ax and he stood up to the tree as if at home plate.

"Okay, now—"

"I know," he said. "Cut it like you're cutting a thing out of it, right?"

"And don't chop off your foot in the process," I said.

Danny managed to get the tree down, then I took over the rest of it. Cutting off the top six feet was tricky, with the tree on its side and the trunk way up off the ground and springing back every time you hit it. I got it done, finally. The bottom half of the tree looked sickening lying there, like the body of a deer you'd killed to take the head and feet for a coat rack. We dragged the shapely treetop down the hill and left the rest behind. Not wholly without compunction, at least on my part. Just without compunction that did any good.

5

When we got back to Martha's house, there wasn't much left of the day but some orange-pink sky off in the direction of Hamilton Avenue. I had a headache from squinting into the sun. We'd stopped at a Lum's on the way back, and I was able to get a couple of beers (in other words, three), which took the edge off things a little. To avoid talking about the immediate future—not, I swear to God, to nag—I'd brought up college one more time. He said he'd been thinking about Berklee, as in Berklee College of Music, and of course I thought he was saying Berkeley, as in the University of California *at*. So there was a big go-around about that, where I was saying he didn't have the grades to get into Berkeley and he was saying what did Berklee care if he'd gotten a C-minus in Ancient and Medieval. Oh, I'd heard of his Berklee, just wasn't thinking. It sounded like Danny, all right: trade school for musicians. What, I wondered, was the aspiration: to be in the house band on David Letterman? He had my blessing, I told him. (For what that was worth.) As long as he was really being honest with himself about his ability, I told him, and as long as that was what he really wanted to do. So nonjudgmental. Though come to think of it the artist's life had got my father a lot more than the drudge's life had got me. I mean, at least you could still find an early Francis Jernigan—they usually chose *Arrangement 3*—poorly reproduced in a few books. *My* best shot at having made a contribution to humanity would be giving Danny a couple of unharassed years in which to play scales. But Christ, did he even remember how to read music? He'd stopped going to his guitar teacher after Judith died, claiming he wasn't learning what he wanted to learn; since then he'd been spending hours a day in there playing God knows what through the Rockman and back into his own head. Well, fine: that showed dedication. Though that's probably not all it showed. But wasn't a place like Berklee going to demand some sort of basic proficiency? And, horrible thought: wouldn't he need a recommendation from the music teacher at his high school, and wasn't that Martin Sanders?

I worried about these things while driving back to New Jersey, as Danny napped, or feigned to nap. Then I worried about other things. Apparently I hadn't imbibed much tranquillity from being up on a quiet hilltop. Imbibe. I wanted to fucking imbibe *something* all right.

Martha's Reliant, as usual, was gone. I turned off the engine, and Danny, a bit theatrically, opened his eyes. "We're back," I said. "Like Nixon."

He made no move to open his door.

"So Dad?" he said. "We're just going to stay here and go along like we were? Do Christmas and everything?"

"I guess so, Dan," I said. "For now at least. I can't think what else to do, can you? Unless you just feel like, I don't know, packing your stuff right now and just lighting out. I'd do it, if that's what you felt like."

"Okay, thanks," he said. "That's all I wanted to know." He opened his door and got out.

"Hey," I said. "Wait a sec."

"I'm going to go in and see if Clarissa's home," he said. "I'll help with the tree after if you want."

"Don't knock yourself out," I said when I was sure he was out of earshot. Then I just sat there until it got too cold to sit there. Whatever that means. I suppose it means until the discomfort from the cold seemed worse than the other discomfort.

I dragged the treetop around back to the toolshed, found a handsaw and cut the trunk off straight where I'd mangled it with the ax. I also found a galvanized bucket, which I brought into the kitchen and filled with water. I set it outside by the kitchen door and balanced the tree on it, bottom branches resting on the rim, lopped-off stub of trunk down in the water. Dead but drinking deep. Now what we needed was a Christmas tree stand and we'd be all squared away here. Probably be easier just to go buy one instead of poking through the whole damn house looking for where Martha kept Christmas stuff. What could a thing like that run you, five ten dollars?

Thing was, I suddenly didn't feel up to dealing with the mall and trying to find a Christmas tree stand in Caldor's or some God damn place, with the people and the Christmas music and lines at the registers snaking back so far you couldn't push a carriage around the front of the aisles. What I felt like doing was going to the liquor store and calling it a day.

I knew I should at least get something and clean the pine pitch off Martha's saw. Gasoline, maybe? I always kept a hose in my trunk for emergencies; I could siphon a little out of the tank. But.

That headache wasn't getting any better.

And I suppose, judging by what I found myself doing next, other stuff must have been bothering me that I wasn't quite coming to grips with.

I went into the bathroom and took the last two Advils in the bottle, that's how it began, and then two of Martha's Pamprins. I was afraid to take the Pamprins, but that head really hurt, and I reasoned it out as follows. Once, years ago, I'd taken one of Judith's birth control pills to stop *her* from taking it because I was sure they were killing her. This was back before people noticed that so many other things were also killing women. Nothing had happened to me from taking the birth control pill—I mean, I didn't grow tits and my dick didn't shrivel—so probably Pamprin was all right too. Then I went to the kitchen, feeling as if I were watching myself doing all this, to see what alcohol there was. Zilch, as I knew already. I would have to go out. I couldn't go out. In the refrigerator I found one beer. Drank it in four swallows, then went back to the bathroom and took six more Pamprins and drank what was left of a bottle of Nyquil.

Then down to the basement and into the death chamber. Not with the idea of trying to kill myself. What I wanted, I think, was just to do something extreme. Something that would be hard afterwards to pretend I hadn't done. I got the gun out of the toolbox, sat down on a haybale, put my left hand palm-down on the rough hay, stuck the muzzle into that little web of skin between your thumb and the rest of your hand and shot myself there more or less experimentally. To see what it would be like. Jesus *Christ* it hurt. Oh, not the worst I ever felt: nothing to compare with, say, bright pain in a tooth. This was like hitting yourself with a hammer, hard, and knowing you've done damage; but with a sort of raw stinging afterwards that just seemed to get worse and worse and worse. That's Jernigan all over: first you swallow a bunch of drugstore anodynes and then you want to *feel* something and then you bitch and moan because it hurts.

VII

1

"Good morning," said Martha, setting something on the night table. Then she sat down on the bed. "Brought you your coffee," she said. "And you got some mail." She reached over to the night table and tapped a finger on two envelopes, one red, one white, next to a steaming mug.

So I was in her bedroom, not in the place I'd apparently been dreaming about. Which dissolved as I tried to recall it. "Bizarre," I said.

"What's bizarre?"

I shook my head. "Dream," I said. "Time is it?"

"Ten?" she said. "I thought I should wake you up. It's a beautiful day." The two ideas seemed to have some connection in her mind. "You were out like a light when I came in last night. What did you do to your hand?"

There was a bandage on my hand.

Now I remembered.

"I don't know," I said. Well, that wouldn't do. "Cut it on something," I said. "You find the tree?" Now that she'd mentioned it, I was aware that my hand hurt.

"I saw it first thing," she said, "when I got up to feed the bunnies. It's beautiful." That made two things that were beautiful. "I was hoping maybe we could get it up today." Was the *double entendre* deliberate? I examined her face for signs of roguishness; didn't look like it. Shame, I thought, in a way, looking at that bulge of thigh under denim. On the other hand, that was no way to extricate yourself, if what you wanted was to extricate yourself. Great: awake for what, thirty seconds, and here you are right back in the problem.

"I cut myself evening it off," I said. "The end of it."

I can see, reading this back, why she looked puzzled.

"With the saw," I said. "The Christmas tree." This sounded plausible. Plausible, that is, until the bandage came off and you had to explain a round scar. Well, maybe it wouldn't end up being round exactly. Maybe you better go in the bathroom and find out what you did to yourself.

"Does it still hurt this morning?" she said.

I nodded. "Stupid," I said.

"Think you should let somebody look at it?"

I shook my head. "I've had it with the emergency room for a while, thanks."

That did it.

"Approximately when," she said, "am I going to be allowed to stop eating shit?"

"Not giving you shit," I said. "Simple observation."

She lifted her hands, as if calling God to witness. "I can*not* discuss this one more time," she said. "You know, this is not 1952, Peter. It could just as easily have been Danny, and me sitting home on *my* ass while *you* were out working."

"As you obviously think I should be doing."

I had now been awake for maybe a minute and a half.

"Well, it was never my vision that you would just sit in the *house* day after day, no."

"Right. It was your vision that I was going to be a poet. 'The Compost Heap as the Letter C'."

"I'm sure that's something clever," she said. "Peter, my only *vision* was that whatever you did you might get some enjoyment out of your life for a change. I should've—I mean, everything I knew was literally *screaming* that you were absolutely incapable of any sort of joy whatsoever."

Should I say *figuratively*? Better not. "A trenchant analysis," I said.

"Fuck you too."

"Trenchanter and trenchanter," I said. "Repartee City around here this morning."

"I'm going out," she said. "I hope you enjoy your coffee."

"Oof," I called after her. "Slam-*dunk*." As if punningly, she slammed the door behind her. I picked up the coffee. Just looking at it you could tell she'd made it too weak. Hey, work at it a little, I thought, and you could *really* get to be a monster.

She flounced back in, slammed the door again and stared at me, her back against the door and her arms folded. Shoulders rising and falling.

"Your contempt for me," she said, "is really boundless, isn't it?"

"Why?" I said, the hand hurting like a son of a bitch. "Is that an idea that turns you on?"

That made her eyes open so wide you could see white above the iris. "You incredible bastard," she said. Apparently she found the suggestion worth addressing. I'd just thrown it out there to be a prick.

"Get over here," I said.

"For what?"

"So I don't have to be raising my voice," I said. "Unless you want the kids to savor every nuance of this."

That got her over to the bed. She stood stubbornly.

"So what's on your mind?" I said.

"You tell *me*," she said. "I didn't do anything but be nice to you."

"It's *so* unjust," I said.

"You just know *so much*, Peter," she said. "What a *man*. Treat 'em bad and they come back for more, right? You're a true asshole."

"Why don't you sit down?" I said. "You're not in the principal's office."

She sat down.

I stared at her breasts and let the silence just go and go.

After a while she said, "This is too weird for me."

"Right," I said. "You didn't do anything but be nice. That husband of yours ever hit you?"

She began to sob. I watched it for a while, wondering what the hell I thought I was doing, then told her come here. She wouldn't and I grabbed her; she tried to twist away and I wrestled her down, which got me hard. I should add, not that it makes the whole thing any less sick, that I get hard over nothing when I first wake up. Oh no, not life reasserting itself or anything; it's just because I haven't pissed. Pressure of bladder on whatever it is, prostate? Or some explanation equally—what's the word? Opposite of mystical. I got the jeans and underpants down around her knees. Give her the old Norman Mailer.

"I'm really going to be sorry someday"—she inhaled, hissing through her teeth—"that I showed you so much."

Afterwards, we lay there not saying anything. That hand really starting to worry me. Finally she said, in a small voice, "Do you remember when I used to have my names?"

"I have to go to the bathroom," I said. You had to wonder sometimes: yesterday, talking to Danny, I'd been all set to get out, well almost all set, and now this. Sick and brutal? No question. But still, a way of drawing closer. Unless what I was doing was simply drawing closer in order to increase the tension for another recoil; this time, perhaps, a recoil strong enough to achieve escape velocity. Thinking about that *Star Trek* where they head straight into the sun so its gravitational force will help them spring away on the rebound—the slingshot effect, they call it—and back into their own time period. See, they'd been flung back into the past by getting too close to a black star and its gravitational forces. Another thing I was doing was watching too much *Star Trek*.

I pissed, then grabbed a towel down from the shower curtain rod, slung it over my shoulder and took a wad of it between my teeth. I bit down and tore off the bandage. Angry red hole, scab starting to form at the edges, a little thick blood still oozing. I would have the scar from doing this insane thing for the rest of my life. This time I made a better bandage than the drunk one the night before: a fold of gauze covering both entrance and exit wounds, and tape going all the way around the hand. Then I unbit the towel and took four Pamprins.

I went back in and lay down next to Martha. "You all done in there?" she said.

"For now," I said.

"Okay, I'll be right back."

"I'll count the moments," I said.

I was still staring at the ceiling when she came back and lay down next to me. Trying to imagine that the branching cracks made pictures, as the ancients found archers and shit in the random stars. The closest I could come to anything was sort of George Washington's profile.

"So how many moments?" she said.

"Seventeen hundred and seventy-six," I said.

"That's an awful lot of moments."

"You think *that's* a lot," I said, "try subdividing it into instants."

"I think I might try counting sheep," she said. "You mind if I nap a little? I've been up since five-thirty."

A nicer man would have asked why.

"Would you stay with me till I drop off?" she said.

"I'm not going anywhere," I said.

She rolled on her side, her back to me, and began the deep, slow breaths she used to relax herself. I picked up the cup and had a sip of cold, weak coffee. I stared back up at George Washington. Then I did that thing you do when you're a kid where you imagine the ceiling as the floor, stepping high to climb through a doorway, squatting by the light fixture as if at a campfire.

Martha's breathing got quieter and her shoulder rose and sank. I sat up and reached for the envelopes. My Christmas cards, apparently, judging by the squareness. Usual guilt over never sending any; usual

contempt for those who still bothered. The white envelope was post-
marked California: therefore from Rick, who had never blamed me
for his sister. Which I thought said something creepy about him. I
put it back, unopened. The red envelope said Warriner/Kaplan. (Now
I remembered: I'd been dreaming of Uncle Fred's funky old trailer.
That combined with my father's house in Woodstock sort of, because
the rooms had just gone on and on and on.) It was one of those kitschy
gilded cards: Mother and Child and Wise Men and the Star of Bethlehem and a gold-haloed angel looking down. Uncle Fred had doctored
it up with faces he'd cut out of somewhere. The Virgin was a lipsticked
Madonna, the Wise Men were Curly, Moe and Larry, the angel was
Liberace, the Christ Child, for some reason, Nixon. Must've taken
the son of a bitch hours to find all the pictures. And he'd cut them
out so carefully, with nail scissors or something. God I missed Uncle
Fred. He was the still point of the turning world. I mean, there was
Uncle Fred, right? Still thinking blasphemy was funny.

I opened the card. Below the printed Bible verse ("For God so loved
the world, that he gave his only begotten Son, that whosoever be-
lieveth in him should not perish, but have everlasting life. John 3:16"),
a handwritten message:

*How many more years do you think you can count on before the Lord
returns? And what bullshit excuse are you going to give Him for not
seeing your old friends when you still had time? Call me instantly. You
know the number. Now, schmuck.*

Love (not to mince words),
Your Uncle Fred

p.s. Now. Go to the phone.

I got up and went to the phone. What time was it? Would he be in
his office or out to lunch or what? Hell, what *day* was it? I recon-
structed. Yesterday we went for the tree. So that must have been
Saturday. So this was a Sunday. So he was home, if he was home.

Uncle Fred was 222 something. Somewhere along the way I'd lost
track of my address book, so I ended up having to get the number

from Information. His phone rang twice, then gave a click and Jim Reeves sang, "Put your sweet lips a little closer to the phone." Then Uncle Fred singing, in some other key, "And don't forget to leave a mess-age at the tone." I waited for the beep and said, "Uncle Fred. This is the wand'ring O'Jernigan. I got your card, and, uh, thank you for—essentially for doing what I should have done, except I didn't, and, what can I say here, let me just leave you a number here where—"

A click and Penny's voice. *"Peter?"* The phone began to howl. "Don't go 'way, Peter, just let me turn this stupid thing off." Another click and the howling stopped. "Hi," she said. "So good to hear your *voice.*"

"Hey," I said, right back in the old ways. "Ditto mutual, hon'. How you been keepin'?"

"Uh," she said. "Holidays."

"Busy, huh?"

"Busy?"

"Cooking?"

"Cooking? Peter, you were always a master of understatement."

"Can still understate any son of a bitch in the house," I said. "Listen, speaking of sons of bitches in the house, is that Uncle Fred around?"

"Sure is," she said. *"Mikey?* Peter, when are we going to *see* you? *Mikey, it's Peter Jernigan.*"

"Good question," I said. "Maybe we can reason it out."

"Here's the Fredster," she said.

"Jernigan." Uncle Fred's voice. "Stand and give the password."

"I can't go on I'll go on," I said.

"I know that's *something*," said Uncle Fred. "I'm just too God damn *illiterate* to know what. How the hell are you? *Where* the hell are you?"

"Jersey still," I said.

"Well either you're coming in here or I'm coming out there. What are you doing this afternoon?"

"I can't this afternoon."

"Bullshit."

"Seriously."

"Right," he said, "you're seriously bullshitting me. What's the big deal this afternoon? Cleaning up a toxic spill in the old backyard?"

"Truly," I said. "I've got stuff to take care of here. But let's do it after Christmas, all right?"

"No chance," he said. "Your Uncle Fred says today."

"You're a hard man," I said.

"That's what my—no, second thought, I'm not going to touch that one. My bride here gets chagrined when I talk dirty. Isn't that right, dear? So you're coming to our place, right? I hate fucking New Jersey."

"In your will, my peace," I said.

"Now you're talkin'. I might not know what you're *sayin'* . . . So you bringing your sweetie along for inspection?"

"*Pas de sweetie*," I said. "She's got to work today." This was probably even true; wouldn't she be going in every day now until Christmas?

"A likely story," he said. "Where does this alleged sweetie work that she's got to go in on a Sunday? Some top-secret chemical plant?"

"Department store," I said. "She's just working there over the holidays."

"What's her name? Glendora? Jernigan, how do I put this delicately? This sweetie isn't, like, *inflatable*? Wait a second, my bride is telling me I'm terrible. So listen, whenever you can get here. You remember about the buzzer, right? Top floor, bottom buzzer?"

"What can I bring?" I said. You offer to bring something.

"Just your long-absent self," he said. "Those shrieks of anguish you hear in the background is the fatted calf getting slain."

And when you're told you don't have to bring anything you bring something anyway.

2

First order of business was to get the old enthusiasm level up where it belonged. That one cup of shit coffee didn't have enough caffeine to lift me a psychic millimeter, let alone to fight off four Pamprins.

Christ, the way I talk you'd think these were real drugs I was taking, and not just Jernigan micro-managing his consciousness. So I went down to the kitchen, dick-swinging naked, and put on more water. (One thing I *will* say, Martha had managed to get it warm enough in there so the linoleum wasn't unkind to bare feet.) If the kids were in the house—which they must be, right? since Martha had in fact come nearer when I'd asked her if she wanted the kids to hear us—and they came in and caught an eyeful, that was their problem, not mine. For a long time I hadn't understood the story of Noah naked in his tent, probably because I was never sent to Sunday school, where somebody could have told me what to think about it. I didn't get why the son had to be punished: A, his father was drunk, and B, he did his best not to look at his father's quote unquote nakedness. I read about it, I must've been about twelve, in the Vulgate my father kept, ostentatiously, on a little decorative bookshelf in the front room on Barrow Street with *Grimms' Fairy Tales* and J. Edgar Hoover's *Masters of Deceit*. (His real books were floor-to-ceiling in the bedroom.) The story both outraged me and made me afraid my outrage was punishable, since God was so irrational about anything that had to do with sex or nakedness or authority. These days I could see it God's way.

I put three good big heaping teaspoons of instant coffee in a cup and poured in the boiling water. After Judith, I'd stopped buying the French roast Colombian beans she'd kept in the freezer and ground fresh for us every morning: Medaglia d'Oro would be good enough for the likes of me. Martha had started me out on Maxwell House with cinnamon; she had an old plastic filter basket kicking around, though instead of buying paper filters she kept washing out and re-using the same piece of cloth. But now we'd moved down to white-label generic instant. And you know something? It did you just the same. By trial and error I'd found that three spoons to the cup was the upper limit of drinkable, provided you put a little milk in. Although I suppose three spoons to the cup defeated the purpose of buying cheap coffee.

So of course I tried to drink the stuff right away and burned my tongue. Then I put in some cold water, which defeated the purpose of using three spoons, though it didn't really. I made that same mistake trying to think about gin a while back. I drank that cup, then drank another one, then went back to the bedroom and picked my clothes up off the floor. Penny and Uncle Fred weren't going to know they were the same clothes as yesterday—and the day before, come to think of it—and anybody else could go fuck themselves, meaning Martha. Save her some work, anyway. If you wore the same clothes for three days, it was the equivalent of having to wash a third as many clothes. In a way it cancelled out the coffee. I went into the bathroom and brushed my teeth, then blew against my palm to check my breath. Still not great. I'd have to stop off and pick up some Carefree peppermint gum. That was my brand. Chosen for its name—one more way to grind in some cheap irony—and its sugarlessness. Then I looked my face over. I'd probably gone without shaving long enough now so it looked as if I'd started a beard. Another week would have been better, but. I got my wallet and car keys off the dresser and forced myself to look at Martha. Still on her side, mouth pouting, lower lip fat. Probably asleep. I felt my dick stir; so much for sexual disgust. It was as if a body inside my body and coterminous, my astral body I guess is what I'm talking about, were calling me back to life. Or simply living its own life in spite of me. I mean, getting not one but two erections out of Jernigan in a single morning? Had to be some kind of hoodoo. Mystics describe the astral body as silvery; it was as if I'd wounded that silvery thing yesterday, shooting it in its silvery hand, and it was taking action in its own defense at the same time the grosser physical body was cranking up its production of, what, white blood cells. This was the sort of shit Martha actually *believed* in, though it had taken a while to find that out; she was no longer gung-ho about it, but she still had the books around. Said she'd tried a couple of times to travel in the astral plane, but it hadn't really worked. I told her, keep trying and maybe she could project herself right into the bughouse. Believe me, if I'd gotten a look at those books . . . Right, I'm sure that would've made all the difference.

I walked past Clarissa's door and heard her going *Ooh ooh ooh*. Something in the air this morning, boy. Maybe it was just that winter was coming on. Last chance for life.

I bought a Diet Coke and a can of Colt 45 at the E-Z Mart on Hamilton Avenue. Back out in the car I popped the Diet Coke, took a good long pull for just a trace of extra caffeine, then poured the rest out on the blacktop, refilled the can with Colt 45 and got rid of the Colt 45 can in the dumpster. This way I could drive and drink with absolute peace of mind. (Little joke.) Then off to New York! I felt so terrific what with the caffeine and the Colt 45 and about to see old friends and Martha not along that I dug out the Walkman. It still had the tape in it that Danny had been listening to. Something called Megadeth, and I figured why the fuck not. As the name promised, it was loud and destructive, and I was able to work it into my mood without thinking too much about what such music said about Danny. One way to think of it was just teenage hormones, so that's what I ended up thinking.

I got off the highway before the tunnel and stopped at a gas station. The guy pumped as the law required, but I checked the oil myself: manly Jernigan. Since the slovenly fuckers were out of paper towels, it was either wipe the dipstick on my pants or use the cowboy jacket, which had ended up on the floor in the back. Fuck it: I hated the thing anyway. They had a pay phone mounted on the corner of the building, so I called 212 Information and asked for a Miranda McCaslin somewhere in the West 90s. What would make this day even greater would be to have a brand-new woman with you that you weren't quite sure yet would go to bed with you. And bingo: an M. McCaslin on West 98th. I scratched the last four digits on the brickface with my ignition key—the 222 I could remember because of Uncle Fred—and dialed. Sixty cents, for Christ's sake, just because of the fucking Hudson River. What I got was a guarded answering-machine message, just her voice (but it *was* her voice) saying what number you'd reached and please leave a message. "Miranda," I said. "Peter Jernigan. Your fellow former—your former fellow Kelsey and Chittendener. Chittendenite. I was just in your neighborhood and I thought I'd give you a jingle to see if you were around. But I guess you're not and"—I waited a few seconds for her to pick up the phone in case she was there listening, trying to decide about me. "Oh well. Another time. Hope you're well, ta ta, whatever, I don't know. Well, enough of this. Before I descend into total incoherence. 'Bye now." I left the empty Diet Coke can on top of the metal cowl enshrining the phone, as an offering. The more I thought about it, the more I guessed I was actually glad her message was so unwelcoming: it would stiff-arm lesser men. I was bound and determined not to let this little setback ruin a really up mood. Let's hit it, I told myself, and no more fucking around.

Penny and Uncle Fred had the top floor of a brownstone on 102nd between Riverside and West End. Even though it was Sunday, when you'd think people would be out of town, I had to drive around and around and around looking for a parking place. Ended up on 105th or something. How I'd ever put up with this on a daily basis I couldn't imagine. Not just the parking but all of it. Although if I was so much better off now, what was I doing with a bullet hole in my hand? I certainly hadn't gone around shooting myself in the hand when I lived here, so therefore.

I pushed the bottom buzzer and Uncle Fred's electric voice barked, "Stand and give the password."

What was it I'd said before? It would be just like Uncle Fred to give me a bunch of shit before he got around to buzzing me in. Couldn't remember. "I don't know," I said. "Allen Ludden."

The thing buzzed and as I got the door open I heard him barking, "*I'm* sorry. Allen Ludden is dead."

I stopped on the second-floor landing to get my breath. In addition to everything else, I thought, you really better try to do something about the shape you're in physically. I patted my coat pocket to make sure I had car keys, and remembered I hadn't brought anything the way you were supposed to no matter what they said. Well, look, they said not to and you didn't, so really how wrong could that be?

Uncle Fred was waiting at the top of the murky stairs, standing in his open door, through which light was streaming. That corny effect where it slants through dustmotes. "Old Jernigan," he said, giving me a one-armed lateral hug. "Income." Uncle Fred had been saying "Income" for twenty years. From psychedelic sabotage of language to annoying mannerism to something you could count on.

3

Uncle Fred brandished a platter of tortillas backhanded, as you would a frisbee. "Better have some more eggs ranchers," he said.

I waved it away. "Please," I said, meaning *Please, no more.*

"Little more of the old *Maria sangriente*?" Uncle Fred was now a person whose wife served brunch.

I shrugged, and with my right hand twisted my left forearm.

"I thought as much," he said. "Penny, *ma chère*. Would you be so kind?"

"You *guys*," said Penny, getting up. "I'm going to go hide the lampshades."

"Hell, better hide your dresses too," he said. "No telling *how* merry this is gonna get. But first." He snapped his fingers twice.

She curtsied, holding out an imaginary skirt, then opening her fingers to let it fall back against her blue jeans. "He's actually pussy-whipped," she said, screening her mouth with the back of her hand. "I just do this so I won't look like a castrating bitch in front of company."

"Enough girlish prattle, dear," said Uncle Fred. "You'll charm us another time."

She went into the kitchen and came back agitating a cocktail shaker full of something red, but using only her wrists so as not to drop the bottle of Absolut under her arm. The shaker was decorated with tilted martini glasses and modernistic boomerangs. "Here," she said. "I'm just going to leave you boys the wherewithal. I've got to work for a couple of hours or I'm going to be in terrible shape tomorrow. You can talk about broads while I'm in there. Mikey, you'll clean up, won't you?"

"Don' worr'," he said. "Zio Federico take care ev'ryt'ing."

"Thanks, Penny," I said. "It was delicious."

"You know you're welcome to stay for dinner."

"Thank you," I said. "Let me think about that. Right now, the very idea." I patted my stomach.

"It's taken us so long to get you here," she said, "that we're not going to let you go without a struggle. Mikey, why don't you just get him too drunk to drive?"

"*There's* a thought," he said.

"*Ciao* for now," she said, wiggling her fingers goodbye.

When she was gone, I said, "*You're* a lucky son of a bitch."

Uncle Fred thought about that. "Yes," he said.

"You know, I actually *like* the dining table in here," I said. "Cozier." Since the last time I'd been here, Penny had taken the dining room for workspace. Now they ate in a corner of the living room.

"Yeah, I think so too," he said. He mashed his last few crumbs of scrambled egg into the tines of his fork and ate them. "So what did you *really* do to your hand?"

"I told you," I said. "It's a gunshot wound."

"Christ, it probably is," he said. "Fucking crazy bastard." He lifted the vodka in one hand and the shaker in the other. Those proportions seemed about right.

"Half and half," I said. He mixed one for me and a weaker one for himself.

"Ice?"

I shook my head. "I try to stay away from that shit," I said. "Turns to water on you."

"Hear hear," he said. He tasted his. "Hmm," he said. "Not too shabby. So tell me about this Glendora. Did *you* get lucky?"

"Not particularly," I said.

We both waited.

"Tell Uncle Fred," he said. "That is, if you're in the mood for it."

"It's not all that interesting," I said.

"Fuck a bunch of interesting," he said. "Is this thing ongoing? Offgoing? On-and-offgoing?"

"As of today," I said, "I guess it's ongoing."

"Although you're not too happy about it."

"How does he know these things?" I asked the ceiling.

We waited again.

"So," he said. "Who do you like for the Super Bowl?"

"It's a real mess," I said.

"Who *is* this person, anyway?"

"Well, see," I said, "originally Danny was going out with her daughter and he was spending a lot of time over at their house. And they decided, I guess, the kids did, to introduce us. Because she was divorced, and I was, you know, whatever I was." Widowed. "Which was actually pretty irresponsible, that she and I hadn't even talked on the phone when the two kids were spending so much time, but I guess you get busy and stuff. At any rate, long story short I ended up with the mother, and now we're all, like, *there*."

"Hmm," he said.

"Sounds a little weird to you?"

"No," he said. "No, I'm just sitting here being nonjudgmental."

"Funny," I said, "I could've sworn you thought it was a little weird."

"So *is* it?"

"It's getting there," I said.

"Hmm," he said. "Can you get out? Is that an option? That is, it's obviously an *option*, but is it something you're seriously thinking about?"

"Problems with that too," I said.

"Danny and the girl."

"Among others," I said.

"Do you *like* this woman?" he said. "She have a name, by the way?"

"Martha," I said. I thought a little and said, "I guess not really. I mean, I *should*."

"Well, then it's simple, no? Rule One: Don't be with somebody you don't want to be with. Bad for you and bad for them. Right? Fuck a bunch of *should*."

"Right," I said.

"Do you think she loves you?"

"Don't know," I said. "She's, I don't know . . . Anxious to please."

"Except you're not pleased."

"When did you ever know me to be pleased?" I said.

"There's that," he said. He took a sip of his Bloody Mary. Then he set it down and said, "Nevertheless."

"Look, Danny's only got another two years of school," I said. "Year and a half. Then he'll be off to college or something, and then who knows. In the meantime—"

"In the meantime you're going to rot yourself," he said. "Or is that too harsh?"

I took a good gulp of Bloody Mary.

"I'm not trying to be Mr. Work Ethic here," said Uncle Fred, "but what do you *do* all day?"

I shook my head. "Think and get into trouble," I said.

"*You?*" he said.

"I do watch some television," I said.

"I'll bet," said Uncle Fred. "You have the *money* to move someplace else, right?"

"I don't know," I said. "Sort of. Not really."

"Like to clarify that a little for the folks back home?"

"Well, see, there's the money from the house," I said. "But a lot of that is for Danny's college, and the rest of it, if I just stick it in a checking account or something, it's going to get eaten up in taxes."

"So where do you have it now?"

"Well, right now it *is* in checking, but—"

"I'm beginning to lose my stolid patience," he said.

"Believe me," I said, "I don't blame you. It's not a very edifying spectacle."

"And don't glamorize this crash-and-burn shit," he said. "Not that I don't know the temptation, but this is your *life* here."

"No, you're absolutely right," I said. I drank the rest of my Bloody Mary and reached for the vodka. "May I?"

"Be my guest," he said. "In fact, you *are* my guest. I might add, though, since we're—"

"Let's not even get started on that," I said.

"Fair enough," he said. "To tell you the absolute truth, I may actually not have all that much of a right to preach to you on that score." He waited for me to mix mine, then poured enough vodka into his to raise the level an inch. "Boys will be boys, right?"

"To boys being boys," I said, and we clinked glasses. I stared at the row of Christmas cards on the mantel. "No tree?" I said, to let him know that his marriage wasn't so fucking perfect.

"You know it's funny," he said. "We actually went to the Koreans' on Broadway and looked at their trees, and we both got really depressed because they shape the God damn things with hedge clippers or something. They're all like *that*." He drew an isosceles triangle in air with his two forefingers. "They look like they came out of a fucking *barbershop*. Next year maybe we'll have time to drive up somewhere and get a tree looks like a fucking *tree*."

"*We* got a tree," I said.

Uncle Fred looked at me. "You're really in piss-poor shape, aren't you?"

I raised my glass and drank to that.

"Peter," he said. "If you need to get away and think about things, you're welcome to come here. You and Danny both. I know Penny will second me on this. Of course, we're talking floor space here, but it *is* at your disposal. Any time. Middle of the night, makes no difference."

"Shit," I said. "Thanks."

"Or listen," he said. "Another idea. If you want to be someplace and not have *us* underfoot, think about the camp. Since you're starting to get that mountain man look anyhow." He pinched his chin between thumb and forefinger. "Looks good on you, actually. At any rate, my neighbor up there tells me they got a foot of snow already, but if you didn't mind braving the cold a little, that stove heats up the whole trailer in nothing flat, and there must be two three cords of wood sitting there. Unless somebody made off with it. Now, I drained the pipes last time I went up, but I can tell you how to get the water going again. Hell, you could cart your stuff up there and move *in* if you felt like it. The place just sits."

"Sounds like a good fit," I said. "You know, I mean I probably won't end up doing anything that extreme, but I do appreciate it."

"Listen, you'd be doing me a favor by making it look like somebody lived there," he said. "They've broken in five or six times now. You know, local thug kids. One time they stole all the light bulbs out of the lamps. Everything but the God damn books: those they don't touch. You know when I went up there last time, to close the place up? I found a rubber stuck to the floor. Had to take it up with a putty knife."

"Thanks for sharing that," I said.

"Sorry," he said. "I'm just telling you this so you'll know I'm not operating purely out of the goodness of my heart. We never go up there in the winter because we neither of us ski or any of that shit. And now it's getting so we have less and less time in the summer. *Or* inclination, I guess. The drive eats up half your weekend right there, and then there's all the stuff you feel like you have to do or it's all going to fall down around your ears. Did I tell you Penny and I were talking for a while about actually building up there? Not down where the trailer is, but like halfway up the hill there's this outrageous spot where you can see off for like miles. But—by the way, Penny does *not* know about finding the rubber."

"We reach," I said, and made a diamond with thumbtips and fingertips.

"Good God," he said. "Don't tell me you've become a Trekkie on top of everything else."

"Nah," I said. "I just watch."

"So anyway," he said, "I don't know what to do. I have all these great memories, you know, going up there with my dad. But the place just seems violated. And the winters are really for shit." He drank off a little more Bloody Mary, poured in more vodka and stirred with his index finger, which he sucked clean and wiped on his pants. So okay, there was always that about Uncle Fred and me, deep down. I mean, what's male bonding ultimately about? On the other hand, what *wasn't* vile, deep down? Although you didn't want to think of that as vile but simply as another way of being. The thing was not to look deep down.

4

I woke up on a couch. In Uncle Fred's apartment. Almost dark in here. Right: I could remember asking if he minded if I just lay down for a few minutes. All that stuff still cluttering the table, glasses and plates and food every which way, and that bottle sticking up like a lighthouse above a stormy sea. I was alone in here and you could see the room darkening by the second, although that probably wasn't true. From where I lay you could raise your head and look down the hall all the way to their bedroom door. Closed. Except my head hurt when I raised the son of a bitch. I listened for sounds of fucking. The hand hurt too; I had accepted that it was just going to hurt from now on. I kept listening. I heard a car horn down in the street.

I got up and went down the hall to the bathroom. Apparently I hadn't taken my shoes off; hoped I hadn't put dirty shoe bottoms on the nice cushions. Bathroom door was open, but the bedroom door was definitely closed, not just almost. So either fucking or napping. Or first one then the other. I shut the bathroom door to piss. It turned the whole water yellow, so I'd have to flush: if it made noise it made noise. But first I went through the medicine cabinet. Penny had a thing of Pamprin in there, so I popped that open and took four. Washed them down with cupped handfuls of water, drinking like a frontiersman.

I went back and lay down on the couch again to wait for my head to stop hurting. It was as silent as before. Christ, what if they were in there like what's-his-name? If they'd put on this show of being oh so happy and had actually chosen today to carry out their suicide pact. And my fingerprints all over. Oh, I wasn't serious. Just one more thought; it doesn't pay off anyplace later in the story. I got up again and went to the table and had a good old belt of that Absolut right out of the bottle. Then I went back to the sofa and picked up a copy of *Vogue* lying there on the floor. That's what there was to read, unless I wanted to get up again and get one of the pieces of the *Times*. In the "Mind Health" section I found an item headed INSPIRED BY PLEASURE.

The creative muse is a surly mistress, demanding a hefty fee in anguish before she grants an artist's plea for inspiration. Well, here's some good news: Alice M. Isen, Ph.D., Kimberly Daubman, and Gary Nowicki of the University of Maryland find that what creativity really requires is . . . feeling good.

I tried to understand why this was good news. Then I looked through for ads with pictures of naked bodies. I found some, most notably an endearingly swollen breast with nipple, and tried to get excited. Finally I put the magazine back as I'd found it—at an angle from the sofa a bit sharper than forty-five degrees—then got up and had a last swallow of vodka and looked around for something to write a note with. Best I could do was a felt-tip pen I found on the kitchen counter. I tore a paper towel off the roll that hung from the underside of the cabinets and wrote HAD TO GET BACK. THANKS AGAIN FOR EVERY-THING.—J. A job just writing that much, since the ink seeped and spread into the soft paper, and the tip of the pen dug in and ripped it if you bore down at all. Now, where do you put it so they'll see it? I unscrewed the cap of the vodka bottle (took one last swallow), placed a corner of the paper towel over the mouth and screwed the cap back on. There: looked like somebody wearing a cape. Absolut Man, I thought: Dump ta dum!

When I got out on the street I couldn't remember where I'd left the car. Right, 105th. Which was actually easy to remember because a five was like a two: Penny and Fred lived on 102nd, therefore the car was on 105th. What do you mean, a five is like a two? Like a two reflected upside down.

Boy, did I not want to go home. I drove a few blocks down West End, intending to go to 96th and get on the West Side Highway the opposite way from all the happy weekenders coming back bumper-to-bumper from their happy weekends at fucking two miles an hour. Then I just pulled over and double-parked by a pay phone. I couldn't leave the city without giving old Miranda one last shot. Stupid, I grant you: You see Miranda and then what? You see Miranda and, one chance in a million, spend the *night* with Miranda and then what? I tried to make up a joke in my head with the name Miranda. Everything worked: Miranda decision, Miranda warning. Miranda rights, there was another one, something about how every man should have his Miranda rights. Oh, not in order to use such a joke on Miranda herself. It was just something I was doing in my head. If your name was Miranda, that stuff was probably like the old *Are you Upjohn?* to somebody named Upjohn. If there was really such a name as

Upjohn, which sounded improbable to me just then. Well, Upjohn Laboratories.

I got the number from Information again, and this time she picked up the phone herself. "Are you Upjohn?" I said, giving the whole thing probably one twist too many.

"What number are you calling?" she said.

"Miranda," I said. "Just joking. Peter Jernigan again. God, Jernigan again—sounds like Irish time here. Listen, how are you? I left you a kind of confused message before."

"Right," she said. "I was sort of half asleep when you called. How are you?"

"Oh, I'm, you know—" Get it together, I thought. When somebody says *How are you?* it's not a real question. "Couldn't be better," I said. "Listen, I happen to be in your, well, I was visiting friends right in your neighborhood, and I was wondering if, I mean this is very spur-of-the-moment stuff, but if you weren't doing anything I thought I'd invite you out for a quick drink or whatever. If there's, you know, someplace in the neighborhood."

"Well, that's nice of you," she said. "The thing is, I'm supposed to do something later on."

"Oh, well, look," I said.

"It was really sweet of you to call," she said. "I hope you're doing well."

"Yeah, relaxing, little of this, little of that," I said. "I actually find that if things are going well, that you're actually more creative rather than—"

The telephone went clunk. My quarter dropping from somewhere inside to somewhere else inside.

"Hello?" I said.

"Are you calling from a pay phone?" she said. She made it sound disreputable.

"Yeah," I said. "Well, listen, I shouldn't keep you. Why don't I, the next time I get to town, call you at work or something and maybe we can get together for lunch or whatnot."

"Well, the thing is," she said, "I'm not going to be there much longer because I decided to go to business school."

"You're kidding," I said. "I think that's splendid. We'll have to get together and hoist one to your success."

Silence.

"Well," she said, "the thing is that once classes get going I'm not sure I'm going to have an awful lot of time."

"Listen," I said, "I know exactly how it is. The important thing is to get your work done. So anyway, I should be getting along. It was good to talk to you, and—good luck, right?"

"I'm glad you understand," she said.

I got back in the car and went right into the dash after that Walkman. Megadeth, Webb Pierce, any fucking thing, whatever was in there, just get it going. I put the ear things on and turned the music up so loud it hurt. Then I turned it up louder, until I couldn't tell what it was.

VIII

1

When I came in, the house was dark. And cold. Again. Always. I pulled the string and the kitchen light came on. On the counter next to the toaster sat a Christmas tree stand. Like a big spider: red metal bowl up on green metal legs. Under one foot, a note: IF YOU CARE. I tried to think back. Hadn't we left things in reasonably decent shape? So what was the new offense? I wasn't crazy enough to think Martha could have known by spooky mind power about my calling what's-her-name, which I just wasn't going to think about. (Miranda.) One of those disgraces best dealt with by putting off thinking about it.

Once you'd moved on in time a little bit—making an analogy here between time and distance, though I'm not sure you can—it would be back in the past and therefore smaller. The law of perspective, as in *Jon Nagy's Television Art Book*. Like an A-bomb blast, which seared you less the farther away you stood, in a featureless Jon Nagy landscape. I'm not explaining this right.

What I was supposed to do now, to show I *cared*, was get the tree set up. So I dragged it into the kitchen, laid it on its side and unscrewed the thumbscrews on the Christmas tree stand so I could slip the collar over the sawed-off end. Then I tightened them again, going around and around, three turns each screw, so as to keep the trunk dead center. The screws bit into the soft wood and I clenched my teeth. When it hurt my fingers to turn the screws anymore, I stood the tree up. Son of a bitch was cockeyed anyway. So fuck it. I carried it standfirst into the living room, as if it were a battering ram, and set it in the corner, between the end of the sofa and the window. My idea was to keep it away from the woodstove. If that wasn't where she wanted the thing, she could move it. I filled a saucepan and poured water into the metal bowl so the tree could drink. Then I got the woodstove going and huddled on the sofa in my overcoat. What was it, Sunday? So *60 Minutes* was on, unless it was over.

I tried to think when Christmas must be. Late in the week, wasn't it? Friday? Saturday? Not enough information to think with: you'd need today's date and then you could go on from there. I hadn't bought anybody anything, assuming that we were exchanging gifts, as on a normal Christmas, and in what sense was this Christmas not normal? Technically speaking. There were grownups, kids and a tree: nothing to suggest an exemption. I thought, You could drive over to the mall right now and get that old Christmas shopping *done*, boy. Tomorrow the crowds would only be worse, and worse still the next day and even worse than that the day after.

But Christ, I just got the God damn stove going.

True, but you've still got your coat on. And now that the sun is over the yardarm you could work the old Diet Coke can trick with some gin, make the drive to the mall into a little adventure. All that old sun-over-the-yardarm shit, that's the way your real drunks talk.

I was proud to have remembered how to talk like that. I mean, it was all just an impersonation.

So let's hit it.

The vast lots around the mall had parking places galore. Even the video game arcade just inside South Entrance was deserted except for a black teenager wearing a turned-around Mets cap, his nose to the screen, and a girl sitting on the floor beside him, hugging her knees. Sunday before Christmas. Either I'd hit it just right or the stock market thing really *had* hurt business.

Now, the thing to do was keep it simple. Obviously you had to spend more on Danny than on Clarissa, though Clarissa's gift must still be substantial, because. So: fifty-dollar gift certificate at Record Town for Danny, fifty-dollar gift certificate at something like Benetton or The Gap for Clarissa, and maybe a hundred-dollar gift certificate at Sam Ash Music for Danny, assuming Sam Ash Music did that and why wouldn't they. And then maybe a few little crappo things so they'd have stuff to open, though I couldn't think what. Hickory Farms might have some kind of food. Well obviously. What I mean is, maybe the kids would like sausage and cheese and shit to eat in their room. Or some kind of silly toys from someplace. Puzzles where you had to roll BBs into holes, or one of those water-filled things where you had to spear drifting rings with a swordfish's nose. I mean, since they were in there getting stoned anyway, right?

Which left Martha. What might she like? A box of .22 shells? That was ugly, scratch that. I thought she'd said something once about Margaret Drabble, unless it was Margaret Atwood. Or Iris Murdoch. So maybe Waldenbooks was the best idea, except wasn't giving her books a way of saying, Keep your face in these and leave me the fuck alone? Although when things were in this kind of shape, any gift short of crotchless panties pretty much said the same thing.

It wasn't really much of a stand against disorder, I know, but I did do a good job of organizing my stops: getting the gift certificates first and saving the heaviest things to lug around, the books and all, for last. I found the perfect place for Clarissa, better even than The Gap: this place Mandee. You see their ads sometimes, where slutty girls talk in rhyme. Probably all her girlfriends went to Mandee, if she had any girlfriends, and she felt left out because there was never any money. The thought of it made me sorry enough for her to kick her gift certificate up to seventy-five. With Danny's hundred at Sam Ash Music plus fifty at Record Town, that was saying she was half to me what Danny was. Hey, Christmas, right? After I got the gift certificates squared away I went looking for the little toys. Couldn't find one of those swordfish deals, but they did have an underwater penguin standing before a sylvan backdrop. (Why a penguin among green trees? Why, for that matter, green trees under water?) Five little plastic rings that you had to get over the penguin by tilting the thing just right. Also a sliding-squares puzzle that, when slid together correctly, showed Superman in flight. And two decks of Bicycle playing cards and a paperback Hoyle. Oh, not that I really pictured our little family learning canasta together, but at least the stuff would be on hand if things should ever get straightened out. Hey, if nothing else, it would be evidence that everything had been tried. Then on to Hickory Farms. I might as well admit that, due to the disposition of the stores, this rational and orderly scheme of going from lighter burdens to heavier in fact required going back and forth and back and forth. So again and again I walked past Bedford Falls Video, with old Entrepreneurial Steve probably in there radiating disapproval of me, and past the exhibit of snowblowers out in the center of the mall, where a salesman in a maroon blazer sat behind stacks of brochures. Through a bullhorn he prophesied an early winter.

At Hickory Farms I bought a shrink-wrapped box the size of a Monopoly set, with summer sausage and assorted cheeses. Cheshire and I forget what else. It was probably all the same Wisconsin cheddar with different food dyes. Right, the kids were really fucking likely to know the difference. Then back all the way in the other direction to Waldenbooks. By that time I was about ready to bag it. There wasn't any Iris Murdoch, and there really *was* a difference between Margaret Drabble and Margaret Atwood, though I couldn't have told you what, and I would probably pick the wrong one. When the only Jane Austen I could find was fucking *Pride and Prejudice*, I figured, Hey, end of expedition. Get Martha a gift certificate too, and you're out of here. Hundred dollars, bringing her main gift up even with Danny's, though his fifty at Record Town still put him ahead. So: Danny one fifty,

Martha a hundred, Clarissa seventy-five. Plus the small stuff. I hoped this all made the right statements. Though of course the overarching statement was that I didn't know these people. As I walked back to South Entrance the snowblower man was putting his brochures away in a cardboard box and stores were shutting off overhead lights. At The Gap a salesgirl ducked in under the half-lowered metal-link gate.

Back at the house, I hid the toys and the Hickory Farms box under the bed, then filled a water glass halfway up with gin and worked away on that until I "fell asleep" on the sofa, I think sometime during *Star Trek*. Before Martha rolled in, at any rate. The *Star Trek* was the Joan Collins one, where Joan Collins is the pacifist back during the Depression who has to be hit by a car and die so that all subsequent history won't be changed. See, if Joan Collins lives, America doesn't enter World War II and so forth and so on. It's the one where Bones is on some drug that makes him crazed, which is how the whole problem gets started in the first place, and they all jump through the time portal.

I woke up with a nightmare. Robert Stack was in it, and when the terror let up enough I tried to think why Robert Stack. It actually took me a couple of minutes to get *The Untouchables*. Oh for Christ's sake, I thought, tell me something I don't already know. The tv had been turned off, and the tablecloth draped back over it. I had a wicked headache, of course, and my hand was throbbing like a bastard. I went into the bathroom, pissed and took five Advils from a brand-new bottle—she'd noticed we were out—then went to the kitchen and drank some cold water out of the refrigerator. Mouth dry. Of course. I swore I wasn't going to drink tomorrow, tomorrow meaning whenever I woke up again. I went into the bedroom and found Martha there asleep, or pretending to be. And then I was asleep again too, though I can't imagine how. What with the hand and the head and, always, the thoughts going.

2

I woke up at noon or whatever the hell it was and she was gone again. On the way back from the kitchen, where I'd put water on for coffee, I looked over and saw the tree had been trimmed. Cruddy bunch of ornaments: metallic plastic with a line down the middle where the molded halves had been joined. Although it was cruel to judge her taste harshly just because she couldn't afford better. Or maybe it *was* just lousy taste. Certainly she'd used too God damn much tinsel. Unless one of the kids had done it. (Little joke.) I picked off maybe a third of it—any more than that would've been obvious—and hid it in a generic cornflakes box I found in the garbage. Another thing I didn't like was grocery bags on the kitchen floor for garbage, although because it wasn't *your* kitchen you couldn't say so. Then I rearranged the garbage to get a dripping can on top of the generic cornflakes box. By this time the water was boiling. Say, what a day *this* promised to be: everything just going snap snap snap. I chose the blue cup instead of the white one and spooned in my three spoonfuls. Blue suggested the sky and, therefore, transcendence. Though white also suggested transcendence, so there you were.

I brought the coffee into the living room and sat in the Morris chair to get the old day mapped out. One thing, I definitely wasn't going to get drunk. Hand still hurt, but it was only the third day, could that be possible? Saturday Sunday Monday—so yes, third day. So I guess you had to expect. Now. As to the day. First: go out to a drugstore or something and get the wrapping paper and Scotch tape and to-from tags that you forgot last night. Then: back here and get those sons of bitches wrapped. And then: try to arrange them under the tree so it looked bountiful. And then? Despite the coffee, I suddenly *could* not stay awake. Bedroom too far. I just set the cup down, boy, and got up, lurched across the room and pow, dived down into that couch.

The next thing I knew, the kids had come in. "Sorry," said Danny, in some context. I guess they'd been loud. Done something.

"No no," I said. "Time I was waking up anyway." A lowdown shame, really, for him to have to see this shit again and again. Well, maybe it would be a warning to him.

"What?" he said, putting hand to ear.

I shook my head and waved him away—*dis*missed—and off they went to their room or something. I must have looked pissed off. So let him think so. It was all too much even to begin to try to clear up.

I did finally get the stuff wrapped and under the tree and the rest of everything taken care of—meaning mostly that I washed out the blue coffee cup and turned on the tv. The one thing I really had to be sure and do was stay awake until Martha got in. Not a word exchanged since Sunday morning; even old Jernigan knew *that* wasn't the way to get the holidays rolling.

I decided that the problem wasn't having a drink or two per se. It was that I'd been drinking gin, which was no good for you. Vodka, on the other hand, probably didn't leave you feeling so vile the next day, and it gave you a completely different head. Not so alienated. This is the kind of shit you tell yourself. So after the news I went out to the discount liquor place and got a quart of that Absolut vodka. Some expensive shit, boy; made you realize what a high roller Uncle Fred was getting to be. But hey. Also stopped and picked up a big thing of V-8 juice and a cellophane package of bran. Not getting enough fiber in my diet, that was another thing. So I mixed the vodka and V-8 half and half, stirred in a good big heaping teaspoon of bran, shook a bunch of black pepper on top to make it festive, and hunkered down in the Morris chair with the old *Nothing but Wodehouse*, for all the world like a man settling in with a Bloody Mary and some light reading. Kids were all snug up there in their room; that was the way I wanted to think about the kids up in their room. First I read Ogden Nash's foreword, which told how hard it was to decide what to put in the book because P. G. Wodehouse was so good.

There are horrid omissions even in this monumental tome, and to you who mourn them, I can only say that this heart breaks with yours, and to ask you to consider for a moment the difficulties of the editor who is delegated to select the best from an author who seems always to be at his best.

Say what? I read this again, trying to figure out what the fuck tone he was trying to strike, and whether times had changed or this had been stupid even back then. (Not to mention that superfluous *to*: shouldn't it be just "and ask you"?) See, what complicated the whole thing was that you weren't supposed to think Ogden Nash was stupid just because he wrote light verse. You were supposed to think he might actually be smarter than somebody pretentious like Allen Tate or something. Some revisionist thing. Maybe I'm making this up. Well, anyhow, this was what reading was: not just going along with the words but thinking about things at the same time.

Now, after the foreword I would go on to maybe a couple of the Mr. Mulliner stories, then start on *Leave It to Psmith*, which I'd be in no danger of finishing tonight. I'd go until eleven, then put on the Independent News, with what's his name, Jerry Girard Very Independent Sports. Jerry Girard was the best local sports guy because he said what he thought. Then *The Honeymooners* at eleven-thirty and at midnight *Star Trek*. And probably at some point during *Star Trek* (I hoped it would be when a commercial was on) Martha would roll in and we could get this latest thing smoothed over and then we'd just see from there.

But Martha threw this whole scheme out of whack. I thought I had her schedule figured out and then pow, in she waltzes during the first commercial break in the Independent News! "Hey," I said, "just what the hell time *do* you get off work?"

I could hear, as I was saying it, that it sounded like real peevishness instead of parody peevishness. Really losing my sense of pitch here.

"It's *freezing* in this house," she said. So maybe she hadn't even heard me. People seemed to be having trouble with that lately. She bent down prettily, her coat still on, and opened the stove. "How can you stand to *sit* there?" she said. Stand to sit, I thought. Huh.

"I've got my love to keep me warm," I said.

Now, this I'd meant to be a sort of courtly compliment, I think, and not the cruel irony it must have sounded like. Though who knows *what* the hell I meant. Just Jernigan running his endless mouth. And a beep and a bop and a beep.

She started putting things in the stove. "You know," she said, "I really can't figure out what is *in* this for me anymore." She clanked the stove shut. She fetched a sigh. "Did you remember to feed the bunnies?" she said.

"I was just about to go down there," I said. "I thought you did a beautiful job with the tree." All I could do, though, not to say something about the tinsel.

"Thank you," she said. You couldn't tell exactly how she meant it. Coldly correct was my guess.

"Beautiful," I said. "Beautiful job." This was not moving the conversation forward.

She headed for the door to the basement.

"I was just about to do that," I said.

"Then I guess you got lucky, didn't you?" she said, and closed the door behind her. Not quite slammed.

When she came back up she closed it with almost exactly the same degree of force, if I was judging accurately. You'd measure it in foot-pounds per square inch or something.

"I had wanted to talk to you," I said, "regarding Christmas. I mean, what's the usual drill here? Like do you have your Christmas Christmas *Eve* or Christmas *Day?* You know, like for opening stuff."

She sat down on the couch, the end away from the tree. "You're obviously so unhappy, Peter," she said. "Why do you even care?"

"I can't imagine what you're talking about," I said. "You know, who thought up the whole God damn tree in the first place? I mean, check the *packages.*" I pointed to the tree. It would have made a feeble show without that box from Hickory Farms. But the point was, there *was* a box from Hickory Farms. A God damn good-sized box, for smaller boxes to sit on. And there were three white envelopes, heavy with promise.

"I got the tree," I said, "got my shopping done, got shit *wrapped* days in advance, so I don't frankly see what you're *basing* anything on."

"Oh all right, fine," she said. "I'll play, Peter. We used to open our presents Christmas Eve. Now what?"

"Now we're getting somewhere," I said.

"I wasn't even going to tell you," she said, "but Tim has invited us over to his place Christmas Eve. It didn't seem like you'd be very into it."

"You made that assumption," I said.

To her credit, she didn't even nod.

"Call him up," I said. "Tell him we will *be* there. Kids too."

"They won't want to go," she said.

"Well fuck that, they're going," I said. "Call him up."

"It's eleven o'clock at *night*, Peter."

"So tell me something else," I said. "How did this mysterious invitation get issued, exactly?" Now I was getting mean and crazy. "Two of you talk on the phone or what? What do you do, go see him when you're supposedly at this alleged *job* of yours?"

"As a matter of fact," she said, "he sent us a written invite. He believes in using the mail."

"Just like you," I said. I meant like m-a-l-e; it didn't seem to register. "You believe in the same thing," I said. Shit. "Skip it," I said.

She wiggled out of her coat and sat back on it. So I guessed it must be warming up in here.

"We make love," she said, "and then when I wake up you're gone, and that's all the contact we have for two days. And then I come home to this. You know, what's it *for*, Peter?"

"The holidays," I said, "can be a very difficult time."

"What do the holidays have to do with anything?"

"If we can just get through the holidays," I said. Maybe she thought I was suffering from memories of Judith. I was surprised I still had enough taste not to say so directly. At any rate, something made her decide to get up and pat me on the shoulder. That couldn't have been easy.

"It's getting late," she said. "Are you going to stay up and watch your program?"

"Fool about my program," I said.

"I think it relaxes you," she said. Based on what, I couldn't imagine. "Don't stay up too late, okay? Maybe you could get back on a better schedule."

I watched her walk toward the bedroom, getting smaller and smaller. I measured her with my right hand. After seven steps she fit between my thumb and middle finger as they made a C backwards.

3

He'd asked us for six, but Danny and Clarissa fiddle-fucked around until Martha yelled at them through their closed door, and we didn't roll in until a quarter to seven. Which I told Martha probably didn't matter because people counted on you to be a little late. (Mr. Reasonable.) That might be true of some people, Martha said, but Tim was "very direct." So excuse *me*.

When he opened the door I remembered him: sharp nose and timber wolf grin.

"Tim, you remember Peter," said Martha, getting both names in there; his for my benefit, mine for his. Was I right to admire such adeptness, or was this just an ordinary social thing?

"Peter, yes." He stuck out a hand. Full of shit, of course. "You didn't have the beard," he said. Okay, so he wasn't. "Merry Christmas," he said. "Noël Noël and all that good stuff. Clarissa? How you doin', sweetie? You look good." Kiss on the cheek. "And this is Danny?" Handshake. "And as for *you*—" He spread his arms and Martha came to him. The hug went on until I shut the door behind us, more loudly than I'd expected. It got his face out of her God damn hair at least. "Come on in the living room where it's warm," he said. "They're calling for snow tonight."

"Right, we heard the news," said Martha. "Wouldn't it be *great*?" Which sure as shit wasn't the line she'd been taking when we left the house. She'd gone on this rant about how the roads were going to be treacherous and the cops would be stopping drunk drivers.

"Nice," I said, looking around, though I might as well have kept my mouth shut since he was following up with Martha about how *great* a snowstorm would be. The outside was this dreary flat-roofed cement-block bunker-style thing. But inside it was all fresh and severe: white walls, stained pine doorframes and baseboards. Stained but stained discreetly: Golden Oak, say, rather than English Walnut. Track lighting along a couple of the exposed rafters, just old two-by-sixes but stained to match the trim. Worn Oriental rug on the gleaming hardwood floor (gleaming *too* much: polyurethane), Navajo rug on one wall. Red-enamelled woodstove going, stained pine bookshelves with a Bang & Olufsen turntable, all very Svenska-benska. He took our coats into another room, and we stood looking: Danny at that turntable, Martha at the Navajo rug, Clarissa at a white wall apparently. I stared at the coffee table, inside the L of burgundy-colored sectional. Not a table, really, but a giant glass box—big aquarium probably—with chrome-plated metal edges and a thick glass top overlapping a few inches on each side. Inside, for rusticity I supposed, a bale of hay.

"Sit," he called. Martha and I sat on one side of the right angle of sofa, Danny and Clarissa on the other. This Tim came and stood over us. I stole a glance at the front of his jeans, as if that was going to tell me anything.

"This wasn't here," said Martha, pointing at the Navajo rug.

"No?" he said. "Let me think, when *did* that come into my life?" Even he seemed to lose interest in the question. "Anyhow, who's for some Christmas cheer?"

"In for a dime, in for a dollar," I said.

"Sure," said Martha. "Clarissa? Danny?" The two of them were already whispering together. "You guys are old enough, don't you think, Peter?"

I just stared at her.

"Good," said this Tim, showing those timber wolf teeth. "Now. I don't know if Martha forewarned you, but I don't buy commercial liquor. What I *can* offer you is stuff I distill myself, which I guarantee won't blind you or anything."

"No need to sell *me*," I said. "I'm not mistaken, Martha had some of your stuff around when we first, how you say? Got together. The memory lingers."

"Well," she said. "I like *that*. The booze he *remembers*." She gave a laugh to let this Tim know it was all in fun. Boy did I want to get the fuck out of there.

"Good," he said. "People have been known to freak out a little. Now. I've whipped up some eggnog to put it in, or you're welcome to drink it straight. Or with water. Or I think I've got some Diet Coke and maybe tonic."

"Real eggnog?" said Martha. "From scratch?"

"Cross my heart," he said.

"Well, I've got to try *that*," she said. "I'll probably weigh two tons." "Peter?"

"Straight up," I said. "You know, not to knock your eggnog."

"Good man," he said. "One eggnog, one straight up. Clarissa?"

She just looked at him.

"Anything to drink?" he said.

She shook her head.

"This younger generation," he said. "Danny? You'll partake, I know."

"Can I have a Diet Coke?"

"Nothing in it?" he said.

Danny shook his head.

"*I* get it," he said. "These are your designated drivers. You sly doggies." He wagged a finger and trotted off to the kitchen. What an asshole.

We all just sat.

Finally I spoke up. "We're not being *difficile*, I hope."

"*Peter*," said Martha. "Don't push drinks on them. Jesus."

"It's the tone," I said. Out in the kitchen, a refrigerator door opened and shut. Then some electric thing went on for a few seconds. Martha jabbed a thumb over her shoulder and mouthed *He can hear us*.

"I could *give* a fuck," I said out loud.

We all sat there some more.

Then old Timber Wolf Tim came back out with a tray. He set it down on the glass tabletop and handed drinks around. He raised his glass (eggnog) and we raised our glasses back, Danny too. Poor Clarissa just had to sit there.

"So," he said.

Stuff of his was some smooth, boy.

"So how have you *been*," said Martha.

"Good," he said. "Things are good. Except for the fact that we may get our asses sued by the Grant Wood estate."

"You said," said Martha. (And when might that have been?)

"You seen January yet?" he said.

Martha shook her head. "It's good?" she said.

"Give you one before you go," he said. "Yeah. *I* think so. *Very* good piece on dealing with zoning boards. Thing on new ways to cook the stuff you canned. I figured it's the time of year people are starting to get bored. And, let's see. More stuff on keeping warm."

"God," said Martha. "Part five thousand."

"Hey," he said, "burning issue number one, no pun intended. Premise is that what you thought would work back in October may not be cutting it now that the real cold weather's here."

"Wow, is *that* ever true," she said. "So what kind of ideas?"

Out came the wolf teeth. "Read the *piece*," he said. "Then we've got one called 'Cutting the Cord,' which is about rethinking electricity. The idea being that you really can go all the way with this thing. It's like they say the *power's* cut off, right? We don't have any *power*. Which doesn't have to be true. It's like, *you* can cut *them* off. And then of course what the implications are in terms of stuff like food preservation, running water, et cetera, et cetera. Places you can still buy hand pumps. Smart research in that piece."

"By anyone we know?" said Martha.

"Ah," he said, "you know me too well."

"And people are really interested in this stuff anymore?" I said. "I mean, not to knock what you do." I looked over and the kids were whispering again. "I just sort of think, you know, 1970s."

"They buy the magazine, what can I tell you," he said. "Off the record, I have my doubts that very many of them actually *do* much of this stuff, but they sure as hell read about it. If you're *really* doing the whole program, you don't lay out three-fifty a month on some magazine: you go to the library. Though of course all the library ladies think we're *Soldier of Fortune* or something. I suppose we're dangerous in our *own* way, but still."

Danny set his glass on the tabletop. "Clarissa said to ask you," he said to this Tim, "if we can go in and watch videos. Do you mind, Mrs. Peretsky?"

I minded, but there didn't seem to be any way to get that into the record.

"I'm sorry, sweetie," he said, baring the old canines at Clarissa. "We were being boring, and it's probably not going to get any better. You know how to work the thing, right? I forget what-all is in there that you might like. Just rewind it after, okay?"

Clarissa got up and just about pulled Danny through the door where the coats had gone.

"You know I counted them up the other day?" said this Tim. "In that room, I have got: seventy-*three* movies. It is *unbelievable*. Samuel *Goldwyn* didn't have seventy-three movies in his bedroom. Or maybe he did, but Jesus. The changes."

"Doesn't sound like *you're* in any hurry to rethink electricity," I said.

Martha gave me a look.

"*Hell* no," he said. "Total pleasure pig. I just try and be efficient about it. You know, don't pay for stuff with your life."

"But you don't mind telling other people to give up electricity."

"Read the piece," he said. "I'm not telling people to do *anything*. All I'm saying is: here's what you can do if you want to do it. If it's worth it to you. To *you*. Obviously if watching videos is a priority to you, you don't cut off your electricity. Or making eggnog in a blender. Or cooking in a microwave—speaking of which, let me know if you're getting hungry. Dinner's not for a while, but there's cheese and all sorts of stuff. So anyhow, where was I, gadgets. If you're into gadgets, which I definitely am, then maybe you cut out something else, right? Not that electricity's all that expensive *now*, but hang on to your hats when they start decommissioning the nukes *and* having to shut down the coal burners at the same time. So maybe that's the point at which you want to think about getting a generator that'll run on methanol. Or some kind of solar setup. Windmill, maybe, provided you've got the proper location. And that way you'll have a little juice on hand when you want it and still be able to say fuck the power company. Or *don't*, you know? Keep your job, keep your retirement package—if you believe it's still going to be around. But I guess I *do* assume that anybody who picks up the magazine at all is probably a little discontented."

"Hey," I said. "If *that's* your target market, you're going to be a wealthy man."

"I'm keeping my head above water," he said. "Course I do have to cook the books some."

"Hey Tim?" said Martha, holding up her glass. "This is so yummy. Could you get me a little, little more?"

"I can get you *more*," he said. "Don't know about a *little*."

"Speaking of more," I said. I was beginning to like this Tim. I drank off the last of mine and held up my glass too. He took them out to the kitchen. "Weird place," I said to Martha.

"It used to be a drive-in theater," she said.

I didn't get it. "How so?" I said.

"See, he bought the whole land," she said, "and sold off the part where they had all the posts sticking up. You know, with the speakers? And the screen and everything. This right here was like the refreshment stand and the bathrooms and the office. And I guess where they had the projector and everything. Rusty said he used to remember coming here on dates."

"Hey Marty?" this Tim called. (*Marty?*) He came out of the kitchen. "This is sort of embarrassing. I just remembered there's a couple of, like, adult things in there along with everything else. I don't know if you worry about that stuff, but I thought I'd better tell you."

"Oh," she said, looking around at the closed bedroom door. "Gee." She got to her feet.

"Oh for Christ's sake," I said. "Sit the fuck down." I patted the sofa cushion as if I'd meant it to sound comradely.

She sat. "I guess it *is* kind of like closing the barn door," she said. "I mean, they aren't like S-and-M ones or anything, are they?"

"Please," Tim said, and went back to the kitchen.

"God, *listen* to me," she said, shaking her head. "Hey Tim?" she called. "How much are you *putting* in those things anyway?"

"No comment," he called back. I heard the blender go on.

"Christmas," I said.

"You're having an okay time, aren't you?" she said. "Anyhow, we'll go home after and open our presents, okay? Or we could wait till tomorrow morning if you rather. The only reason I like doing it Christmas Eve is 'cause that's when we always used to open stuff."

"Who, you and your sainted husband?" I said.

"My mom and dad," she said. "Rusty was like you. He liked Christmas morning."

"I just think it hangs together better," I said. "I mean, Santa's supposed to come while everybody's asleep, no? How did your folks finesse that one?"

She smiled, closed her eyes and put her head back against the cushion, her face turned up as if she were sunbathing. "What my dad used to do," she said, "at some point on Christmas Eve he'd go out to the kitchen for a drink, he *said*, and all of a sudden we'd hear—"

Tim clanked glasses down on the glass tabletop and her eyes flew open.

"Sorry," he said.

"No prob," she said. "I was just running off at the mouth, as per usual."

"No no, go on with what you're saying," said Tim.

"I was just telling about Christmas. See, my dad used to have this leather, like, belt, with sleigh bells on it? And Christmas Eve he'd fool us kids. It was like part of an old harness or something." She closed her eyes and smiled again.

"And?" said Tim.

"We'd hear these sleigh bells outside and we'd get all excited and then he'd come running in and tell he thought he heard Santa Claus, and of course *we'd* heard him too. I guess he snuck out the back door and went around front and shook the sleigh bells and then ran back around to the kitchen again. And then he'd come into the living room and ask if we'd heard Santa out there. Well, you can imagine: *pandemonium*. So then he'd make us go upstairs and hide, and when he gave the all clear we would come back down and there would be all the presents under the tree."

"Now don't tell me," said Tim, "that *you* of all people never sneaked down to check what was going on." (He was alluding to something about Martha that I was damned if I recognized. He was saying she was what?)

"Come on, he was too smart for *that*," she said. "He'd always send my mother up with us, to stand guard like. I remember he used to say, 'It's fo' yo' own protection, dollin'.'"

"Jesus," I said. "That's sinister enough. What the hell did he mean by that?"

"All he meant was if Santa saw you, you might not get any presents. It wasn't *sinister*, Peter."

"I withdraw the remark," I said. "So what was his excuse for being downstairs in this highly, what shall we say, *fraught* situation, while the rest of you were upstairs hiding from Santa Claus?"

She laughed. "It was so funny," she said. "He used to say he had to fix Santa a drink."

I shook my head. "Not good enough," I said. "Obviously he was down there at the same time as Santa, no? I thought no man could see Santa's face and live."

"Sue me," she said. "We were little kids, Peter. I'm sure if we'd had *you* there you could've gotten to the bottom of it in nothing flat." She took a slug of eggnog.

"You know, speaking of presents," said Tim, "I just happen to have a couple of little things here with you guys' names on 'em. Should we open them now or wait for Cindy?"

Martha sat up straight. "Is somebody coming?" she said. She put her glass down on the tabletop too hard.

"I didn't tell you?" he said. "Jesus. Good thing my head is screwed on. The woman I've been seeing. She's the one, in fact, who gave me that rug." He looked at the Navajo rug on the wall. Martha kept looking at him. "Her sister couldn't come until eight-thirty. What'd I say? Her *sitter*. Sister, Jesus. She doesn't even *have* a sister. I think you're right, Marty. I *am* putting too much rocket fuel in these babies."

"I didn't know you'd been seeing somebody," said Martha.

"Oh yeah," he said. "Three four months now. She's divorced, four-year-old son, uh, what else? We're pretty happy."

"She's leaving her child with a sitter on Christmas?" said Martha.

"Oh, he'll be asleep," he said. "She holds the line pretty well on bedtime. She's got a whole thing planned for tomorrow morning. But it's sad for her, you know?"

"I'm sorry," she said. "I didn't mean that the way it sounded. Like she was a bad mother or anything." Though she didn't specify how she *had* meant it.

"You'll like her," said Tim.

"Oh I'm sure," she said.

Silence. You could hear the tv going behind the bedroom door.

"Anybody getting peckish?" said Tim.

"No, I'm okay," I said. "I'll hold out until we've got a quorum."

Martha said nothing.

"Sure?" he said. "I've got some *primo* local goat cheese. I mean, not *local* local. Place they make it in Hunterdon County. Plus some real cheese. For real people. And I've got this huge mother-humping can of almonds my Aunt Jeannie sends me every year."

"No, I'll wait," I said.

Martha said nothing.

Silence.

"Jesus," he said, "you're practically running on empty there. How about another one of those bad boys?"

I lifted up my glass and took a sighting. "Nah, I'm fine for a while."

"Martha?" he said. "Hair more for you?"

She shook her head.

"Oh well," I said. "What the hell, right?"

"Good man," he said. "Why don't I just bring the jar in here and let you, ah, access it directly. No sense standing on ceremony."

When he went out to the kitchen, Martha turned to me. "I'd sort of like to get out of here," she said. "I don't feel very well."

"What's the trouble?" I said, putting as much kind concern into it as I could. But it was fucking typical.

She shook her head. "I don't know," she said, "too much to drink. Something. I just want to get home if you don't mind."

Back came Tim with a Mason jar. One more affectation. But forgivable. He set it down in front of me and said, "Go for it."

"Listen, Tim?" I said. "I don't think Martha's feeling terrifically well all of a sudden, and I think maybe I'd better get her home. I mean, I feel like a real shit, you made dinner and everything, but."

"I'm really sorry," said Martha, her voice small. "I'm ruining everybody's good time."

"Listen, don't worry about *that*," he said. "What's the trouble?"

"Just sort of sick," she said. "Might've drunk too much. I was just getting over something."

"You want to go in lie down?" he said.

"I think I probably better just go," she said. "I'm really really sorry. Honey, would you be a doll and collect the kids?" She *never* called me honey. I mean, thank God.

I knocked on the bedroom door, called "Hey Danny" to give fair warning, and counted five before opening it. They were propped side by side on a platform bed covered with what looked to be quite a good quilt. Baskets I think that design was supposed to be, though you had to know quilts to know they were baskets. Judith could've told you. They were watching what must have been one of the *Star Trek* movies, because the costumes were weird and everybody was old. They weren't even touching, the two of them. I mean touching each other.

"Sorry, guys," I said. "I'm afraid we gotta roll. Martha's not feeling too well."

"What happened?" said Danny, sitting up. "She okay?"

Clarissa looked at me as if I were something mildly interesting on tv.

"Probably just a stomach thing," I said. "I don't think it's any big deal, but I think we ought to get her home to bed, okay?"

Danny zapped the picture with the remote control and got to his feet. "Can I do anything?" he said.

Clarissa sat there. "Is my mother all right?" she said, talking slow.

"It's not anything to worry about," I said. "We'll just get her home."

"Daniel?" she said. "Don't forget to rewind it like he said."

"I've got it under *control*, Clarissa," he said. "You don't have to tell me fifty times."

When we got outside, snow was coming down. "Hey, a white Christmas," I said. I'd like to say I was being ironic; in fact, with all that moonshine in me, I could have been honestly trying to get some valedictory heartiness going. At any rate, nobody said anything back.

The ground wasn't absolutely white yet, but white enough that our passing left dark footprints.

We bundled into the car like a family. Kids in back, parents up front, Dad driving. Family friend waving from an open door.

4

Out on the main drag, tires had made black ribbons on the white pavement and snowflakes boiled in the headlight beams. When we'd left to come over here, I'd given Martha an argument about taking her Reliant: a vote of no confidence, I thought, in my ability to drive home, whereas in fact I was a *better* driver when drunk, my concentration more nearly absolute. But now I was glad she'd insisted; her tires were a little less bald.

"How are you doing?" I said.

"Let's just get home," she said.

"I'm still not clear," I said. "Is it stomach or what?"

"I just want to get *home*," she said. "Is that a big crime?"

I checked the rearview mirror. Danny was whispering to Clarissa, who was staring at her fingernails.

"Maybe somebody," I said, lowering my voice, "will kindly tell me what the hell is going on. Stud there announces he's got a girlfriend, and you suddenly have to go home. Maybe you'd like to tell me what it is, exactly, with the two of you?"

"Not what I'm sure you think."

"How do *you* know what I think?" I said. Shifting ground on her.

"Oh, don't worry, Peter," she said. "I don't *really* know what you think. You're still as *inscrutable* as you want to be. You're not in any danger of anybody getting *close*."

She clearly thought this was a home thrust.

"Hey, can we have the radio on?" said Danny. The other thing about the Reliant was that it had an actual radio.

"Not going to be much on but Christmas music, I don't think," I said.

"Right," he said, "that's what we want."

I put the radio on, but it was just an AM one and damned if I could find any Christmas music on the whole thing. News Radio 88, Latin music, a bunch of call-in shows. "Big night for the lonely souls," I said, and snapped the thing back off.

Martha started weeping.

"Fuck," I said. At least this shut everybody up the rest of the way. After a few miles Martha's shoulders even stopped heaving.

I pulled up in front of the house and turned the car off. They all just sat there. Without the engine going, it was as silent as it got in New Jersey. Snow hitting the windshield and melting. Finally Danny said, "We're going to go in, okay?"

I just gave a good big shrug, meaning What the fuck difference did it make what anybody did. This was called not helping matters any.

"Are you all right, Mrs. Peretsky?" he said.

"I'm fine," she said. "You guys run ahead in."

That left the two of us.

Martha said, "He was Rusty's best friend."

So apparently we were now going to get the story of Tim.

"Like before high school," she said. "And they both ended up back here after the army. I mean they weren't like in Vietnam or anything. Tim actually was in the Air Force, and Rusty was in Morocco most of his time. Anyhow, they were sharing this house, and Rusty and I started going out. I was done college and I had my first real job, you know, that wasn't like waiting tables, and now I had this cool boyfriend. And so eventually I moved in. I was the only one that had a job or anything. Once in a while Rusty would get like a package from Morocco, or he and Tim would go in on a key together and sell enough lids out of it to get their money back, but that was about as far as it went. The whole rent was like a hundred dollars. So Rusty and Tim would just kind of go around scrounging things, like I remember a lot of the wood we used to burn in the wintertime they got following these guys around from a tree service. I think Tim's dad got him into raising rabbits. At any rate, that stuff gave him the idea to start the magazine, which Rusty thought was crazy. Like Rusty used to call him the PM? Because he was going to be the Publishing Mogul. But I used to do typing for him sometimes after I got done work and kind of generally help out. And I used to do like little drawings to go at the bottom of the pages and stuff."

I suppose that was my cue to say *Oh really, I'd love to see some.* Didn't know she ever did drawings. At this late date it was kind of a so-what.

Snow was starting to stick to the windshield.

"So then when I got pregnant with Clarissa," she said, "Rusty and I were going to get married and everything, but we were going to all just keep living in the house like before. And then like a month before she was born Rusty sold some weed to an undercover cop and he got sent away for a year. This was, you know, '72. So anyhow, Tim just stayed and looked after me and Clarissa for that whole year. 'Cause I'd quit my job and everything. For a while he was even pumping gas at night at this service area on the Garden State so there'd be money coming in. And the whole time nothing ever happened, and you can believe that or not."

"Why shouldn't I believe it?" I said.

"I don't know," she said. "Rusty sure didn't. After he got out and everything, the three of us just kept living there, but he wouldn't talk to Tim very much. *Or* me much, either. It like really changed him. I always wondered if guys maybe did something to him there. Though the really weird stuff didn't start till we moved here and Tim got his own place."

"The really weird stuff," I said.

"Well he sort of hit me and stuff," she said.

Figured.

"At any rate," she said. "So after Rusty and I split up I started seeing Tim again. I mean, not *seeing* him seeing him, but we'd get together and talk and stuff, have dinner. So I'm sorry, I don't know why I suddenly got so weird tonight. I think I'm premenstrual."

"Oh for Christ's sake," I said. "Don't put yourself down."

"Is that putting myself down?" she said.

The whole windshield was white by this time. You couldn't see out.

"I don't know," I said. "I'm just talking." Truest thing I'd said in weeks. "It's cold," I said. "You want to go in?"

"It's cold in there too," she said.

"Unless the kids started the stove," I said. "Little joke."

We sat there with my little joke echoing.

"Well, look," I said. "I'm going in."

"Would you do me a big favor?" she said. "Could you just leave me the key and go in and start the stove and let me run the heater until it warms up in there? Just this one time? I really don't think I can stand it tonight going in there and having it be cold."

"What do you mean can you have the key?" I said. "It's your car, right?"

"I really appreciate it," she said. "I'm not going to make a habit of this."

"Hey," I said, and opened the door. "Christmas comes but once a year." Mr. Gracious.

Snow was really coming down. The walkway was completely white, and just a few blades of grass were sticking up out of the white lawn. It was a little warmer inside than out, but the stove had cooled enough to put your hand on. You could hear the tv going in the kids' room.

I got the stove started and sat there in my coat. First the heat hit my shins. Then I felt it on my face. Then I went out to fetch Martha. The car was throbbing away with the windows fogged up, and one of those impossible things crossed my mind: that she'd got a vacuum cleaner hose from somewhere and hooked it to the tailpipe. So did that mean that I wished her dead, or was it just one more thought?

I helped her up the steps so she wouldn't slip. She went in and sat down on the floor by the stove, hugging her knees like the woman in that Edward Hopper painting. My father used to have a print of it hanging in the living room, back when I was a kid. Woman sitting on her bed, window open, face full of sun. He'd done such a convincing job of painting harlequin sunglasses on her that I'd grown up thinking that was what the thing looked like. I tried to give myself a gratuitous feeling of awe by thinking about the comparative pinprick of fire in the stove versus the unimaginably vast fire of the sun. But of course your mind can't really leap magnitudes that way.

"So I guess the presents can wait until tomorrow," I said.

"Oh shit," she said. "I forgot to take the *presents*. He's going to think I'm terrible."

"Though it makes Him sad to see the way we live," I said, "He'll always say, 'I forgive.' You want anything to drink?"

She shook her head.

"Well that makes one of us," I said, and went into the kitchen. "How about to eat?" I called, pouring out a good big glassful of gin. No answer. I'd finished up that bottle of Absolut—waste not, want not—but it didn't touch the heart the way the old gin-ereeno did.

I stood in the kitchen doorway and looked at her. She'd worn her denim skirt tonight, probably as a message to Tim that in her heart the 1970s would never be over. She had the buttons undone to mid-thigh. The front of the skirt covered her knees as she hugged them; the back fell away, revealing white thigh down to the underpants. So I had finally gotten there: no desire at all.

She looked up and saw me looking. "You have my permission to get as fucked up as you want," she said. "If that's what you're worried about."

"What, me worry?" I said. I considered following this up with a *hugh-hugh-hugh* goofy moron laugh. But that would have taken things to too crazy a place.

You could hear stuff snapping in the woodstove.

"In case you're feeling guilty, Peter," she said, "this actually is not the worst Christmas I ever had. Or in case you're flattering yourself." She got to her feet and started for the bedroom.

"I thought you wanted to get warm," I said.

"I won't say the obvious," she said. I got her drift, but how, exactly, would she have phrased it?

I heard the bedroom door close. Just close, not slam. Which made me think about how everything went in circles, just like the Beatles used to say. You started out closing the door, then things got so bad you were slamming the door, and then things got really *really* bad and all you did was just close the fucking door. Why the Beatles, though? Probably thinking of that song. The one that goes *Of the beginning of the beginning of the beginning*.

IX

1

Me waking up, Martha gone, same old beginning again. What was different was, I really couldn't remember how I'd gotten to bed. I mean, it was obvious *how* I'd gotten to bed: leaning on Danny's strong young shoulder, right? (Little joke.) But I couldn't remember actually stumbling to the bedroom. Yet here I was. The old *res ipsa loquitur*. Odd that *loquor* should be a passive verb. Though in Latin, stuff like active/passive or masculine/feminine didn't really mean anything. Bully for Latin. Take *agricola*, famous example. According to Danny— who wasn't one of them—a few kids in his school wanted to take

Latin, probably because they thought it would help them get into better colleges, but there wasn't anybody left in the school system who could teach it. One more way you could have made yourself useful if back years ago you'd done everything differently. Funny shit to end up thinking about first thing on Christmas morning. If it was in fact morning. Though what the appropriate thoughts might have been I still can't imagine. What, you're supposed to lie there wondering why the Word *had* to be made flesh?

Clearly nobody in the house, whatever time it was. You could tell by the feel of things, not that I really believe in the feel of things. (And if things *did* have a feel, who less apt to feel that feel than Jernigan?) I mean, for all I know the kids were up in their room lying spent after the noisy fuck that I hadn't realized was what had awakened me. Cold as hell in here, maybe *that's* what I meant by the feel of things. Rick's card still unopened on the night table. What could he possibly have written that I'd want to read? (How about a ream of typed pages—some in prose paragraphs, some in verse, like Jack Nicholson's *opus magnum* in *The Shining*—saying over and over again *I forgive you I forgive you I forgive you?*) Most likely all it said was what last year's said: *Thinking of you.* Fuck a bunch of being thought of. I took it with me down to the kitchen and threw it in the garbage, still unopened. Let the good wishes go biodegrade themselves.

On the kitchen table I found a note, on a sheet torn from a spiral notebook, with ragged perforations along one side.

> *Peter and kids,*
> *I went over to Tim's to pick up our presents. If you wake up, there's o.j. all made in the fridge and some English muffins and REAL BUT-TER!!! Merry Xmas.*
>
> *—M*

The clock said like twenty-five of one. Wasn't she afraid of interrupting Tim and the girlfriend as they lolled? Though I was forgetting the girlfriend had a child to get back to, there's something I remembered, so no lolling probably for old Tim this Christmas morning. Wasn't there a pitcher named Tim Lollar?

I polished off the last little bit of gin in the old quart—must've been a hell of a rest of the night, boy—and opened a new one. More economical to buy half gallons, I know, but that was too alcoholic. (It was also alcoholic to worry about whether things were too alcoholic.) So I'd kept buying quarts, but two at a time so as not to have to go back so often. And another day began. I reminded myself to look out the window. Out of touch with nature: hell, that was probably, what, a good two percent of the problem right there. Bright outside. Sun seemed to have melted most of the snow—now there was another thing I remembered, snowstorm last night—except for what lay in the shadows of the tree trunks. I thought Hey, white shadows, how about that.

Well, so now we knew where Martha was, but what about the kids? What the hell kind of kids, more to the point, would absent themselves on Christmas morning? True, they couldn't have had high hopes, but. Maybe everybody'd simply gotten tired of waiting for old Dad to roll out, and decided to go ahead and have their Christmas just the three of them. I went into the living room and looked: all the shit was still under the tree. So. Big mystery. And of course so very interesting to think about.

I seemed to have burned up everything in the woodbox last night, so the first thing to do was put on shoes and a coat and go out and get some logs in. Et cetera. Upstairs I heard the tv go on. Maybe they'd just been waiting to hear me moving around so they wouldn't disturb my sleep. (Little joke.) It was probably more like, We know you're up now so this is just to let you know we're in here and you can go fuck yourself. Maybe old Martha had the right idea, sit in the car and run the heater—one more thing I remembered from last night. (Shit, it was all going to come back if I just relaxed and didn't think about it. The old Zen archery.) So I went and got dressed, put on overcoat and gloves, jammed the big new gin bottle into the big side pocket and went out to the car. Took another good belt and slipped the bottle under the seat, figuring fuck all this soda-can bullshit: if you can't even tell whether there's a cop car around or not, you're not in any shape to be driving anyway.

So I cruised around town for a while with the heater blowing, that and the gin warming me up nicely. The sky was already starting to cloud over again. And I just didn't want to go back to that God damn house. So I ended up driving all the way up to Paterson, and then east to the GW and down into Manhattan. Got off the West Side Highway at 96th Street and drove up to 102nd. I double-parked and looked up at Uncle Fred's windows. Nothing to see. Then down to 72nd and Broadway, to Gray's Papaya. It was illogical—fuck, it was *hypocritical*—to find it depressing that Gray's Papaya was open on Christmas. Had a hot dog and a piña colada, which I fucked up by dumping a bunch of gin in it. Cleaned out the car while I was parked there, got rid of all the Diet Coke cans and McDonald's bags and shit in a trash basket. That fucking cowboy jacket too. Laying it on top where some shivering derelict might see it. So that was about all she wrote for the world's greatest city.

By then the sky had darkened except for a fissure in the west where the sun was going down. Couple flakes of snow. On the GW again, pretty adequately fuzzed by this time, driving into that sunset, the golden glare ahead inviting me just to close my eyes and be absorbed. Thinking about Judith again. There must have been a nanosecond there when she went *Oh my God* and then *Oh all right, fuck it*. I had another headache. Or more of the same headache. From squinting. From that God damn hand hurting. From worrying about how bad I was being, disappearing for hours on Christmas Day, drunk, the presents still unopened.

Parked in front of the house was a red Suzuki Samurai. Shiny. Probably some snot-nosed little friend of Danny and Clarissa's. Well, fuck 'em, maybe they'd all go off drunk driving, or whatever kind of driving, and leave me in peace. This was, in effect, wishing your son dead.

In the kitchen, a black leather shoulderbag hung from one of the chairs. It stunk: that new-leather stink. I looked through the doorway into the living room. Danny and Clarissa were on the couch, at least a foot of cushion between them. Clarissa staring, as usual, at her black Reeboks. Danny smoking. Nobody talking. The visitor was in the Morris chair. From the doorway you could see an acute angle of leg: a cowboy boot, heel worn down, sticking up into acid-washed denim. Danny looked up at me and gave his head a little side-to-side shake. I gave him back a jaunty salute, meaning *Fuck you too*, and went to the dish drainer for a jelly glass. You don't just put the bottle to your mouth in front of company.

When I turned around, a man in the kitchen was saying, "You Jernigan?"

Taller than me by the worn boot heel. Thick hair like some politician trying to look Kennedyesque. One of those mask faces, skin way too tight. The face might have passed for younger than mine if not for those breastlike bags under the eyes. Smiling, or at least showing teeth. Black cable-knit sweater. Jeans tight on him. Daylight between his thighs.

"Rusty Ronson," he said.

Rusty sort of gave me a taste for that.

"Ronson?" I said.

"Hey, change my luck," he said, "you know what I'm saying? Let *her* have Peretsky, she's such a victim anyway. Fuck a lot of good it did *me*. Pah-RET-sky." He began to sing his name to the tune of "The Bowery":

> *Pah-ret-sky, Pah-RET-sky*
> *He says such things and he does such things oh Pah*
> *RET-sky, Pah-RET-sky*
> *I'll never be him anymore.*

I held up the bottle and the jelly glass level with his eyes. "Drink?" I said, figuring it would either smooth him out or not.

"I think we need to get to know each other first," he said. He worked his wallet out of his hip pocket and handed me a business card: on it, a Rolls Royce radiator with the RR emblem, and beneath it, in gothic typeface, RUSTY RONSON ENTERPRISES.

"You in the car business now?" I said, being oh so casual. Not scared.

"*Car* business?" he said. "That's what she told you? Shit." He shook his head. "Promotion business," he said. "Independent promoter. So tell me one thing. What kind of freak show you got going in my house here? We know you're fucking my wife. That's been established. You touch my daughter?"

Behind him, in the doorway, I saw Danny.

"Hey Dan?" I said. "Why don't you take Clarissa out for a walk, okay?"

"I asked you something."

"What is this about?" I said. *Pulling sweatshirt over head.* "Of course I didn't touch your daughter." *White breasts.*

"She says different."

I looked at Clarissa. She looked at me.

"I didn't," she said. "Mr. Jernigan, honest. Daddy's playing one of his weird-shit games."

"Kayokayo*kay*," he said, waving his hand back and forth as if erasing a blackboard. "I'm allowed to test you, right? My responsibility, right? As a parent. As a motherfucking *parent*, man. I am now fully satisfied that Danny Boy here and Danny Boy alone is putting the boots to my daughter. And I believe I *will* have that drink."

"I think we're out of tonic," I said. "Water do you okay?"

"Out of tonic," he said, shaking his head. "Old place *has* fallen to shit. Half a mind to come back and get things straightened out a little around here. Kick a little *ass*."

I filled the jelly glass a third of the way with gin. "How much water?" I said.

"Whatever *you* think," he said. "You're the man of the house now." I went to the sink, topped off the glass with water and stirred with a knife out of the dish drainer.

"You're a gentleman and a scholar," he said. "And a pussy," he stage-whispered. I got another jelly glass out of the dish drainer and filled it with gin. About all I could think of by way of rebuttal.

"So Danny *Boy*," he said. "How is she, hot and tight?"

"Danny," I said, looking at Rusty Ronson, "will you please take Clarissa the hell *out* of here now? *And* yourself?" My eyes still on Rusty Ronson, I saw their blurry shapes flit and vanish from the doorway. The gin bottle was in easy reach. Another point in favor of quart bottles: they had a neck you could grab and smash to make a jagged weapon, though I could picture a lot of things going wrong if this was the first time you tried it. Maybe just take and bonk the fucker with it.

Rusty Ronson looked over his shoulder at the empty doorway.

"Good," he said. "Now we can talk." He drank the gin-and-water down in a single swallow and set the glass on the counter.

"Let's talk about what you're doing here," I said.

"Hey, holiday visit," he said, putting up both hands. "When I come, I bring good cheer. Face it."

"You know," I said, "I'm sure Clarissa wants to see her father and everything. It's just that it doesn't seem to be very, sort of, favorable circumstances, you know?"

"Is that smoke I feel," he said, "being blown ever so gently up my ass? You're a fucking *cartoon*. Little cartoon man. Where the fuck do you get off telling *me* I can't come in my own house? Who the fuck *are* you?"

I shook my head. "I really don't think this is your house anymore."

"Bull *shit*. You show me on a piece of *paper*, babe, where it's not my house. I sell this place tomorrow, man. Out from under *your* ass, *her* ass, everybody's ass in the fuckin' *place*, man. Which I don't do because I am a *nice person*. I'm doing the best I can," he said in whiny-voice, "for my family. Listen, man to man: you want to get high?"

"On what?" I said. Thinking this might give me a clue.

"On what," he said. "I love it." He shook his head. "If you have to ask," he said, raising a forefinger, "you don't want to get high. That's what you teach the kids? Just Say On What? Ah, listen, don't pay any attention to my bullshit. You're doing a really really first-class job with them, man. Really. I was fuckin' impressed. Now me, I don't *give* a shit on what."

He fished around in the leather shoulderbag and brought out a small white canister. "Heads up," he said, and flipped it to me. Somehow I didn't fumble it. It was a plastic screwtop jar: Dr. Daniels' Summit Brand catnip. Picture on it of a crazed cat perched on a rocky summit with Andean-looking peaks all around. The cat had an outsized bow around its neck, perhaps suggesting it was still a harmless pet even though it was high on catnip. I unscrewed the lid. A delicate spoon half-buried in white powder. "Ronson's Own Blend," he said.

"Of?"

He shrugged. I screwed the lid back on, tightly, and handed it back.

"Don't mind me," he said, unscrewing the lid again. "I'm sure you've seen this on television." He put a heaping spoonful up each nostril. Then he did each nostril again. He kept snuffling and rubbing at the underside of his nose with his forefinger. "Rrrighty-o," he said. "Okay, for ten points, who said that? Rrrighty-o. Famous cartoon."

I knew it was Felix the Cat, but you couldn't say anything. Not and keep your dignity.

"As seen on television," he said. "I *know* you know. And you *know* I know you know. You just don't want to say because this is serious, right? An intruder right in your *home*, man. Which you just found out *isn't* your home."

"It's a little hard to believe," I said, "that somewhere in the divorce—"

"The divorce? *The* divorce? Oh now *don't* tell me that my little Martha is going around saying . . . Listen. Man to man, here: this is a sick bitch."

"You're telling me that you and Martha are not divorced," I said.

"C'mere," he said. "C'mere c'mere, I'm not going to do anything to you. You want to see it on paper? *C'mere.*"

He went right to the drawer where Martha kept the phone books, thumbed around and found the *P*'s. "Now," he said, flipping two pages forward, then one back, then running his finger down the column. "Peretsky R," he said. "Not Peretsky R *Mrs.*, not Peretsky M. Fuckin' *R*, babe." He tapped his chest. "See, I know Martha, Martha's great. But she's always had this problem, man. Like she doesn't tell the *truth*, you know what I'm saying?"

"Oh come on," I said. "So she didn't change the name."

"Danny *don't*!" cried Clarissa.

I turned and there was Danny pointing the little pistol and Clarissa reaching for him.

"Clarissa get the hell *away* from him," I said. She moved. "Danny. What do you think you're doing?"

"I want him to get out of here," said Danny.

"He was just about to leave," I said, giving Rusty Ronson a look. A steelier look, I must say, than I'd dared give him before. "Now put that thing up." Danny didn't move.

"Hey," said Rusty Ronson, "I like this Danny Boy."

"I don't like *you*," said Danny.

"Danny *enough*," I said. "He's on his way. Now put it down now." I took a step toward him and he moved the gun so it was pointed, wavering, at the space between Rusty Ronson and me.

"Dad," he said. "I'm really serious."

Rusty Ronson laughed. "Okay," he said. "Beautiful. I'm outta here. Okay, partner," he said to Danny, "now all's I'm doing, I'm just going in the other room get my coat—"

"Clarissa," said Danny, not looking at her, "go in get him his coat, all right?" He moved the gun so it was pointing back at Rusty Ronson, who put his hands up cowboy-style.

Clarissa brought in a stinking leather Eisenhower jacket.

"Okay, I'm just putting on the jacket," said Rusty Ronson. He put on the jacket. Then he moved toward his bag. "What I'm doing now, I'm just getting my bag off the chair, right?" he said. He slung it over his shoulder. "Danny?" he said. "Been a pleasure. Clarissa? Don't forget your old man now."

He saluted, wrist limp, fingers straight across the eyebrows, and then he was out the door. Clarissa ran into the living room and up the stairs.

"*You*, boy," I said to Danny, "are fucking crazy." I heard Clarissa's door slam. "You give me that thing immediately."

"He knows he's not supposed to come here," said Danny, heading for the door. "He was watching the house until Mrs. Peretsky left. She's got papers on him."

All news to me.

"Now, enough," I said. I stood with my back against the door. "You don't know what you're getting into. He's on *drugs*, this man, he could have a *gun* for all you know, he might be *waiting* out there. I'm calling the police."

Outside, a car engine started.

"That's *not* a real great idea, Dad," said Danny. "All he's going to do is say I was pointing a gun at him." I turned around and, with my index finger, parted the calico curtain that hid the panes of glass in the top half of the door. I peered through and watched red taillights recede. They winked and vanished over the crest of the hill.

"He leave?" said Danny.

"Sure," I said, letting the curtain drop, "for *now*." I went over and grabbed the receiver off the wall: dial tone in my ear. Danny sprang at me and clawed the cradle down: dial tone stopped.

"Please, Dad, just *forget* it, okay? He's not going to come back. All the cops are going to do, they're going to come here, they're going to probably find the gun, then they're going to search me and Clarissa's room, and—you know."

Well, now I did.

Danny opened the door and walked outside, long-legged cowboy swagger, as far as the street. I watched him standing there, his head sweeping slowly, all the way left, all the way right, all the way left again. His skinny neck. A couple of snowflakes came down. Then a few more. The way he stood there reminded me of his first day of real school. 1977. And him, six years old, standing at the end of the driveway, lunch bag in hand. Even then he knew lunch boxes were strictly for kids. Judith and I watched him from the living room window: he never turned around.

He came back in and laid the gun on the kitchen table. "Dad," he said, "could you do something with that, put it somewhere? I don't think it's that great of an idea for Clarissa to know where it is tonight." Then he went upstairs. Neither of them came down again.

2

I sat and drank more gin. Got out Martha's Rand McNally Road Atlas and looked at New Hampshire–Vermont. Oh, I knew the way to Uncle Fred's camp: I just wanted to look at the lone dot and at the red and blue roads like veins and arteries. Then turned on the tv and watched the Channel 9 news. At least we weren't on it: there was that to be said for the Channel 9 news. I preferred the Channel 7 news because I was hotter for Kaity Tong than I was for this one on Channel 9, whatever her name was, but the Channel 7 news wasn't on yet. I mean not hot, exactly; just something. Commercial came on and I got up to piss. It was "I'm Not Gonna Pay a Lot for This

Muffler." In the bathroom you could hear the same commercial going up in the kids' room. Water pipes maybe carried the sound. Tried to construct a joke around the idea of piped-in music, but I couldn't see how to set the son of a bitch up.

Martha came in just when they were getting to the sports, except there wasn't much sports because it was Christmas, although they still had to have the sports guy, who was nowhere near as good as Jerry Girard on Channel 11, Very Independent Sports. So which to confront her with: the Rusty Ronson thing, or where the hell she'd been all day? Ended up going with the Rusty Ronson thing, largely because I really didn't give a fuck about the other anymore. I mean, I was out of here anyway.

"Had a little holiday visit today," I said, being oh so sardonic.

"Did you," she said. Really interested, boy. Well she *would* be, in about one second.

"Do you want to know who from?" I said.

"Do I?" she said.

"Your husband," I said. "Who is going around saying he still *is* your husband. Which I found pretty disconcerting. Don't *you* find that pretty disconcerting?" She had enough dignity left not to say anything. "Imagine my surprise," I said.

She shook her head. Didn't look at me. "Weird beyond belief," she said. "I was just—I don't know, you probably won't believe this, I mean why should you, but I actually today did get the name of this lawyer that Tim's sister used. When she got her divorce."

"Did you," I said.

"I had a really long talk with Tim today," she said. "He really helped me."

"I can imagine," I said.

"But so now there's this," she said.

The stove grumbled: something inside shifting and settling. Me in the Morris chair; Martha, feet tucked under her, in the corner of the couch farthest from me. Each of us sitting still, yet voyaging through deep space, as if aboard the Starship Enterprise, where there was no north or south or even up or down, really. On the one hand, I wanted to see this whole deal blow into a million pieces right now, as in the Big Bang theory, and to get in the car and head for New Hampshire.

But on the other hand, I hoped this would be just one more dustup, and over by the time *Star Trek* came on. Maybe tonight, in tribute to Christmas, they'd have the one about the space people Captain Kirk thinks are sun-worshippers but actually turn out to be space Christians who worship the capital-S Son (i.e., of God). Though probably, if they were going to run it, they would have run it last night. Martha and I were really out there, boy. This whole thing was making me remember when Judith and I got married. Most of our friends were there (no family except Rick: she had vetoed her mother, forcing me to veto my father as compensation) and the minister had charged them to "support and defend" our marriage. *Defend*, yet: a minister in touch with his times. What he meant, I imagine, was that when one of us wanted to bag it, one of them was supposed to talk us out of it. Or that Uncle Fred wasn't supposed to introduce me to women he worked with anymore. But with me and Martha it had been just the two of us: no supporters, no defenders. Not that the supporters and defenders had done me and Judith much good in the long run. But me and Martha: even the kids had cut us loose as soon as they'd managed to get us together. And of course we didn't even know each other. I looked out the window. Snow really coming down now, boy.

"So this is actually true," I said.

"I'm sorry," she said. "It was so wrong not to tell you."

"Amazing," I said. "I thought—I mean, you *led* me to think—that I was walking into one situation, whereas I was actually walking into a whole other situation. Which if I had known about—"

"So in other words I was right," she said. "It *would* have made a difference to you."

"How can I say from hindsight?"

"Oh Peter, don't bullshit me. Not at this late date."

"Well? You've been bullshitting *me*, right? You were presenting this thing as this nice regular little American family that just somehow happened to run into a teensy weensy leetle speck of trouble." I pinched thumb and forefinger to show the dishonesty of it all. "Only later do I find out"—I started flipping fingers up to keep count—"A, that your daughter knows how to shoot up drugs; B, that your husband has been in the slammer; and C, that you're not even *divorced* from this character. And D, whatever creepy shit went on with him and your daughter. Plus him hitting you and God knows what-all else that you're *still* not telling me."

"You believed exactly what you wanted to believe, Peter," she said. "Did you actually think there were all these nice wholesome families just ready and waiting for *you* to come along? You're a drunk whose drunk wife killed herself. And you want to know something really pathetic? You looked good to me."

"So maybe we're even," I said. "You're disabused, I'm disabused."

"So I guess I should've known," she said. "That you couldn't actually be a friend to me without knowing what you were being a friend to. Except I was afraid to tell you because then you wouldn't want to be my friend. Catch-22."

"Something happened," I said. Right over her head.

She nodded. "Danny told you?"

Huh, I thought, so something did happen. Here it comes. "Sketchy version," I said.

She fetched a sigh. "I really didn't know," she said. "I mean, maybe I subconsciously knew, but I really didn't until I kind of walked in one day and he was—" She hung down her head and cried, like Tom Dooley. Fucking Tom Dooley anyway: years since we thought of *that*, probably.

I must have gone off onto Tom Dooley in order to distance myself.

"And this is the person you're still married to," I said. Not often that I found myself in a superior moral position; I wanted to see what it felt like to push it a little.

"You don't understand," she said, once she'd pulled herself together enough. "It's probably, you know, not very understandable. But I did kick him out of the house, and I told the police he'd hit me and been threatening us, which was true as far as it went, and I got a court order for him to keep away from us. And I also got Clarissa right into therapy after."

"So why is she not *still* in therapy?"

"Peter," she said. "You see how we live. And Rusty's always going to send money and then he doesn't, and then a bunch of other stuff was supposed to have worked out and it didn't, and it's just been really really hard. Ever since, really, when they sent him away. Like before Clarissa was even born."

I shook my head. "There are free places you can go," I said, based on nothing whatsoever. "There's the school shrink, for Christ's sake." This I did know. Danny had gone a couple of times when his grades dropped so badly. The shrink thought it had something to do with his mother dying. Hey, not for nothing was this guy pulling down twenty-five big ones or whatever it was.

"Right," she said. "And do you know how many kids he sees in the course of one day?"

This was all getting boring and technical. Plus my hand hurt.

"Why the hell didn't you divorce him?" I said. "You certainly had grounds. If you'd divorced him, he'd *have* to send you money, or else they'd throw him back in the jug."

"I was afraid what he might do," she said. "Really, just going through the thing itself would have been bad enough, plus putting Clarissa through it all again when she was really starting to get past it. But Rusty's a crazy person."

"And it didn't occur to you," I said, "to tell me any of this?"

"Yes, it *occurred* to me, Peter," she said. "I don't know, it's so stupid. I was afraid you'd run away. Which I guess is what's ended up happening anyhow. You're really not going to forgive this one, are you?"

That made me think of the old We forgive those who trespass against us. Like a sign they'd have up, say at the cleaner's: IN GOD WE TRUST, ALL OTHERS PAY CASH. All this stuff was so long ago: hanging down your head Tom Dooley and forgiving those who trespass against us. As if it had been someone else and not me who had known all that stuff and where it fit into anything. About all I could come up with right now was: If you could just get out of here tonight your hand would stop throbbing, maybe. But this was magical thinking. Magical thinking was wrong.

"As a matter of fact," I said, "Danny and I have been talking for a while now about how we should maybe be thinking about a place of our own." Well, we did talk about it once. "All this does really is just sort of—" Another thing I was sick of was searching all the time for the words for things. "Like, consolidate it." *Consolidate* was a word, almost certainly, but was it the *right* word? What about *reinforce*? What about *exacerbate*?

"Oh," she said. "See I didn't have any idea. I mean I don't know what I have the right to say at this point. You know, if I say you kept *me* in the dark, all you have to do is turn around and say I kept *you* in the dark, and . . ." She stretched out her palm and blew at it, as if blowing away all her claims to be dealt with squarely.

I stood up.

"Where do you think you're going?" she said.

"Speak to Danny," I said. "If it's all the same to you."

"No, what I mean is, where are you going to *go*? When you leave. I mean that's what this *is*, right?"

"That's what this is," I said. "We've been offered a place to stay. Up in New Hampshire."

"Offered," she said.

"A friend of mine," I said.

"Oh, there's always a friend, isn't there?" she said. "New Hampshire, though. Very cold in the winter. But nothing lasts forever, right?"

"Spare me," I said.

It was weird being on my feet. You know, after sitting. But I walked okay.

"I," I said, very dignified, hand resting on the newel post as in *It's a Wonderful Life* except the newel post didn't come off in my hand, "am going to speak to my son. You might want to take the opportunity to do the same." What I meant was, speak to her daughter. I must have thought I sounded Johnsonian or something.

She got up and followed. We were like a couple of parents going up to talk to the kids.

Star Trek or no *Star Trek*, I couldn't do one more night of this.

I knocked. No answer. Just the tv going. Then Danny called, "What?"

"Hey Dan? I hope I'm not interrupting, but I badly need to talk to you."

I heard the bolt snap, then the tv got louder as the door opened the width of a face. Danny's face: his eyes level with mine. The stink of reefer. "Badly?" he said. "Super bad?"

"Are you in any shape to talk?" I said.

"Are *you*?" he said.

"If you're together enough to be impertinent," I said, "you're together enough to talk. Would you get your things on, please, so we can take a walk?"

Impertinent, yet. Really increasing the old word power tonight, boy.

"A walk?" he said. "Dad, it's *snowing* out there."

"For Christ's sake," I said. "You're sixteen years old. It's *fun* to walk in the snow. You know: trippy."

Big teen-martyr sigh. "Okay," he said. "Give me a minute, all right?"

I went down and had a couple more slugs of gin, and stuck the bottle in my overcoat pocket. Outside, it had gotten so cold that dry snow squeaked under our feet. Danny trudged along, the hood of his parka thrown back, ungloved hands in his pockets. Christ, it was winter: did he even own a pair of gloves? Sixteen years old, what was he going to do, buy them for himself out of his allowance? Snowflakes alighting on his hair.

"I'm sorry to drag you out here," I said. "I just didn't feel like we could talk about this in the house. I didn't think it was"—it took me a second—"proper."

"That what was?" he said.

"Well," I said, "I remember your saying that time we drove up to get the tree, that your situation, you know, vis-à-vis Clarissa, was getting weird."

He said nothing.

"I mean, it's not—if you remember—that I disagreed. It was just . . . I don't know. But after this thing today—I mean, I just think you and I need to maybe, you know, step back. I think we rushed into this whole situation very very precipitously."

"So?" he said. "We're here now, right?"

"We're *not*," I said. "I mean, we *are*. But we do have options."

"Yeah, like what?" he said. "You don't even have a *job* anymore."

"We just sold a whole house for a hundred thirty-seven thousand dollars," I said. "We're not exactly helpless."

"So what happens when you go through that?"

"We'll worry about that when it happens," I said.

He stopped walking. The streetlights here were making the snow look pinkish. On the pink snow, black specks swam past us: the shadows of snowflakes.

"I *knew* you were going to just spend it all," he said. "Bye-bye Berklee, right?" Where had he ever heard of *Bye Bye Birdie*? Maybe they'd had it on tv. Assuming the pun was intentional.

"Look," I said. "We've been offered a place to live rent-free. I can easily get some little bullshit job and we'll never even have to dip into the money."

"What place?"

"Uncle Fred's place up in the country."

"You mean we're supposed to live in a trailer in New Hampshire?" he said. "*Da*-ad. That's crazy. Where would I even go to school?"

"They do have schools in New Hampshire," I said. "It's still the United States, you know?"

"Yeah, sure," he said, "schools for farmers. We don't even know any people up there."

"So you make new friends," I said. "We didn't know anybody here either, when we came from the city."

"How am I supposed to make friends with farmers?"

"Sell drugs," I said. "You'll make friends."

He bent down, formed a snowball with his bare hands and threw it at the stop sign. The snow was so dry it disintegrated in flight.

"Assuming you're so totally lacking in social graces that you can't make friends any *other* way," I said, "you've got your music, right? Some band up there is probably going to fall all over themselves to get somebody like you for a guitar player."

"Yeah, sure," he said. "Playing Willie Nelson farmer music."

"Anyhow," I said, "I'm not talking about moving up there forever. I just meant until we could get things figured out a little bit." I was totally winging it on this part. "We go up there where it's quiet, we cool out a little, and sort of go from there. I mean, basically we have the wherewithal to move pretty much anywhere we want. I mean, if you can think of a place you want to be, let's do it. Or at least let's talk about it."

"I *am* where I want to be," he said. He bent down and tried another snowball. "Stuff won't hold together," he said. He stuck his hands back in his pockets.

"Want to walk over to Oakdale?" I said.

"If you do," he said.

"Dad?" he said, when we'd walked another block. "Was there some-place *you* wanted to be?"

You don't tell your son *Dead and in heaven*.

"Trying to figure that out," I said. "That was one of the reasons Uncle Fred's place kind of appealed to me. You know, nature, quiet—all that Wordsworth kind of shit. Very nineteenth-century of me, I'm sure." I can't imagine who I thought I was talking to. He probably thought the nineteenth century was the 1900s. "You know," I said, "Thoreau or something." Silence. "Huck Finn," I said.

"So why don't just *you* go?" he said.

"Well, I'm certainly not going to leave *you* here."

"Why not?" he said. "I'm okay."

"You're *not*," I said. "I mean, even before all this shit today you were telling me how it was too weird around here. Today you have to run your girlfriend's father out of the house with a *gun*. This is not the way I'm going to have you growing up."

"He's just crazy," said Danny. "It's not that big of a deal." Up ahead, a branch crested with snow hung low over the sidewalk. Danny made a run at it—I took the opportunity to get the bottle out quick and have a good big gulp that made me cough and gag—and leaped, right arm high, as if going in for a lay-up. Snow showered his bare head. He waited for me to catch up, hand moving backward and forward across his hair, stirring up snowflakes that sparkled in the streetlight. Judith and I had made this beautiful boy.

"Danny," I said. "Nobody has to live that way. I mean unless they live in fucking Beirut."

"I don't know," he said. "I guess what I mean is, things come with stuff attached, you know?"

I hadn't thought Danny capable of discerning, let alone enunciating, a general truth. Even in so inchoate a form.

"That's very linear of you," I said. Oh, it didn't matter: he never knew what the fuck I was talking about anyway. I mean, if he could sit still for fucking Megadeth, for Christ's sake, he could sit still for me.

"Clarissa says he did this before a couple of times," he said. "One time she like tried to stab him with a pair of scissors and everything. He was grabbing at her or something and she just—yah!" He came at me like Mother in *Psycho*, mouth wide open, eyes bugging, imaginary knife raised.

"And you think this man isn't dangerous," I said.

"I don't know," he said. "Coming from Clarissa, it might not even be true."

"Either way," I said, "this is a freak show, and *we* are getting the hell out of it."

"It's okay most of the time, it really is," he said. "It's better than living in some trailer."

"Well, fortunately or unfortunately," I said, "it's not your decision to make."

"How come?" he said. "I thought we were having this big democracy."

"To put it at the very crudest level," I said, "you are a minor, and you will do what I say."

"Dad," he said. "Don't push it. You can't back it up."

"You just try me, sonny," I said. Knowing he was right.

We trudged another block, to absolutely no point. Danny stopped at the curb: obviously the place he'd told himself he was going to turn and make his stand. "Dad," he said. "My feet are getting cold. I'm going back."

"Mine too," I said. They probably were. We turned back and walked into our footprints as they filled with snow. The farther we went, the fuller they got. Hey, I thought, just like life.

"What are you laughing for?" said Danny. Damned if he wasn't right, too. Little joke must have really struck me funny.

"Nothing," I said. "I'm overtired."

"I guess you're pretty smashed," he said. Not disapprovingly: just a simple explanation for why his father might be walking along in the snow tittering away to himself.

"Look," I said. "Got another thought. How would it be if I went up there first, checked it all out, got settled in there, check out the schools, so forth, whole place squared away and everything, and then you come up? 'Cause right now, not going to lie to you, probably sort of a mess up there. You know, it hasn't been lived in or anything. Don't you think that's a much much better plan?"

"What is?"

"Danny. What I just *said*. I went up first, took care of some things."
No answer.

"You know something," I said, "for that matter you could probably
finish out the school year, you know? And come up weekends." Still
nothing. "Mrs. Peretsky, I mean, whatever she thinks of *me* at this
point, I'm sure she'd be glad to have *you* stay. You know, during the
school week. And then on the weekends you could sort of come up
and check it out. Sort of do it gradually."

Nothing.

"That actually might be the way to work it," I said.

We kept walking and the snow kept coming down. Really starting
to pile up, boy, really making me wonder how good an idea this
actually was, taking off in all this shit for New Hampshire. Though
they did say on the news that the snow, the worst part of it, was only
supposed to go as far up as Westchester and Rockland.

Danny said, "When would you go up there?"

"Actually," I said, "I was thinking of driving up part way tonight.
You know, I get too tired, just lay over someplace, do the rest in the
morning. Or if the snow gets too bad."

"You have a fight with Mrs. Peretsky or something?" he said.

"Or something," I said. "Doesn't affect *you*, really."

He thought about that. Or about something.

"What does it take you?" he said. "To get up there."

I shrugged. "Six hours?" I said. "Little more? Listen: what do you
say? You want to come along? We'll be a couple of old beatniks, you
know? Play the radio loud all the way up. You pick out the stations
for us."

"You don't have a radio," he said.

"Hell with it, I got the Walkman," I said. "You bring your tapes
and the headphones from your Rockman. You got one of those little
Y things we can plug 'em both in?"

"Dad."

"Okay, so *bag* the Walkman. Bring your guitar along. The ole git-
tar. Or I mean we could always talk. Like sort of a last resort? You
know, like the pioneers, man. In the old Conestoga wagon, you know?
Like one of 'em would be reading the new, I don't know, John Stuart

Mill book or something. So they'd have this big talk about Util-
itarianism."

"Hey Dad? Maybe we should talk about this tomorrow?"

"Tomorrow?" I said. "*What* tomorrow? *Today*, am I right?" I
scrunched down and pretended to be playing a guitar, jerking my
head. "Wock and *woll*," I said. He just looked. "Hell," I said.
"Thought you were supposed to be a free spirit."

"Dad," he said. "It's snowing like a bastard, and it's already like
midnight. And you're drunk and everything and I don't even want
to *be* up there, you know?"

We were back at the corner. You could just about make out our
footprints coming up the hill from Martha's house.

"Okay," I said. "Fine. No problem. Get you home here, then we
do whatever we end up doing."

We walked down the hill. I was fanatical by now about keeping
right in my old footprints—which I could distinguish from Danny's
because he had running shoes on—like a careful child coloring only
within the lines. Danny just walked.

"You know," I said as we passed the next-door neighbors, "I never
even knew these people's names. But they sure do have one ugly
fucking house." And all those Christmas lights didn't help any.

"The Molloys," said Danny.

"Jaysus," I said, "there goes the neighborhood."

No response. It occurred to me that Danny probably didn't even
know he was Irish. I sure as hell didn't remember the subject ever
coming up. Well, if he ever got curious, which I doubted, there was
probably someplace you could look a thing like that up. Looking stuff
up, whew. That was way back with John Stuart Mill and hang down
your head Tom Dooley. All these things you didn't think about anymore. Dooley: huh. Tom Dooley must have been Irish too.

Danny held the gate open for me. Snow was burying the lid of the
garbage can, which was lying there on the ground because somebody
hadn't cared.

3

Being in this place, among all these drunks, hearing their family histories, always the same family history pretty much, it just makes you think, No escape for old Danny. I mean, not just me and Judith, but going way the hell back. My father. Judith's father, who'd died the year before I met her. (Sixty-two years old, heart attack, heavy smoker, heavy drinker.) Judith's *grandfather*, for Christ's sake, her father's father. (I forget anymore what the story was with her mother's father.) I saw the grandfather once. We were on the way to Boston for Rick's graduation—which the family had agreed just not to tell Gramp about—and stopped off at his bungalow in Westerly. An empty Four Roses bottle lay among empty Broadcast Corned Beef Hash cans in the grocery bag he used for garbage; another Four Roses bottle, half full, stood beside his recliner chair. He just sat there, not reclining, a tartan blanket over his knees. Unshaven, cheekbones sticking out to here, false teeth in a peanut butter jar on the end table. Watching a western on a snowy black-and-white tv. Said he was sorry the place stunk so bad: the government was putting something in the water to make him piss his pants. This is not a moral failing, I told myself, but an affliction.

To keep transmitting such an affliction, though: was *that* not a moral failing? I used to wonder—I still wonder, Danny or no Danny—if Judith ought not to have had an abortion and just let the God damn thing end right there. But at the time—bear in mind how young we were—there seemed something mystical in the way this child was coming to us past diaphragm and spermicide, as if determined to win through to life. Although now I'm talking about him as if he'd come shooting out of my dick, a Danny-shaped homunculus, and become implanted in her, which is wrong.

He was born in 1971. August 14. Which is V-J Day, I found out. No particular meaning to that, just a thing to remember. Judith and

I were living in the rent-controlled apartment I'd grown up in. My father had moved to his place in Connecticut for good, and had given us the keys to Barrow Street and a box of checks and deposit slips from his New York bank. We tore each month's rent check out of a different checkbook, on the off chance the landlord, who'd wanted to get him out for years, might be keeping track of the check numbers. And we just let the faucets drip, afraid the super would tell the landlord a young couple had moved into the old man's apartment.

I remember it had rained all morning. Then, around noon, the clouds broke apart, fled to the horizons, and out from behind one old gray-black brute burst the sun. I was watching it all from a bench by the fountain in Washington Square Park, sitting on a *New York Times* to keep the seat of my pants dry, drinking from a can of Bud in a paper bag. "I'm in a vile mood," Judith had said. (I'd noticed.) "You'd be doing yourself a favor and me a favor if you just went out for a walk or something."

"Me a favor," I said. "Is that like Mia Farrow?" I was twenty-three years old.

"I am going to scream," she said.

As I was going out the door she said, "I understand that you mean well."

I finished the beer and got up to walk back to Barrow Street. The pretty girls had begun to come out, and I decided to go home in part because I was ashamed to be looking at them instead of keeping my mind on my poor pregnant cow of a wife. At this time I had never been unfaithful—we'd been married what, all of a year?—and neither, I'm sure, had Judith. It was so hot walking back I unbuttoned my shirt. Hotter than Tophet, Grandpa Jernigan used to say. I used to imagine Tophet as something hot, wet and sticky: taffy, I guess I was thinking of. Christ I hated the city that day. Every day. The puddles already gray and stinking. Filthy, dying men with their palms out God-blessing you. One thing for sure: I would never raise a child in this. Never be able to afford to anyway. Even if the landlord never found us out, a safe private school that might actually educate a kid was going to bleed us white. I had never meant to end up with a kid, but now that it was happening I was by God going to do it right.

When I came back in, Judith's face looked softer. "My thing broke," she said. I thought she was talking about the string of African trade beads her brother Rick had given her as consolation for feeling fat and hideous. "Can we go?" she said. "We better go, I think. Am I going to need a jacket?"

"A jacket?" I said, not as nicely as I might have. "It's ninety *degrees* out there." I suppose I was terrified. Though I was also just being a prick because now I wouldn't even get to sit for a second in front of the God damn fan.

"I don't know," she said. "You find out you just don't know anything."

The rest I remember only in patches. The point is, we got to St. Vincent's okay and our son, Daniel, was born at about eleven-thirty that night. In the waiting room—that was how long ago this was—I tried to concentrate on making sense of "The Comedian as the Letter C," figuring I might as well use the time intelligently. That was how young I was. I kept staring at this one line—"The ruses that were shattered by the large"—and wondering how personally I should take it.

They brought me in when it was all over and Judith was lying exhausted and at peace. Stoned, the nurse told me later, on Demerol and whatever else. The baby bundled at her side.

"Oh Peter," she said. "Isn't it amazing? But I really really thought I was going to die."

I sat down on the tight sheets and put a hand over her hand.

"They told me you had a tough time of it," I said.

"You have no conception," she said. "Little joke."

"I love your little jokes," I said, relieved that she was still Judith.

"You better, pal," she said. "You're stuck with this one for life. You want to hold him?"

"Can I?"

"*Can* you?" she said, and laughed. "He's *yours*, Peter. Sure you know how?"

"You just be careful, right? Support the head and everything?"

"You'll figure it out," she said. "God, listen to me. I sound like the Voice of Motherhood. I don't know anything either, you know?"

I picked up my son and looked, for the first time, into his tiny face. I recognized neither Judith nor myself: just generic human. Branching blue veins under the red, delicate skin. He was sleeping, lips parted. Tiny tiny lips.

"Cat got your tongue?" Judith said. I don't know how long I'd been staring.

"Yeah," I said. "We just have to be so careful with this little guy." Already I thought I could see my eyebrows and her upper lip, with its wide philtrum. And then something else, which wasn't either of us: first intimation of Danny, himself.

"You're going to be one of the all-time great fathers," she said. "You can teach him all about baseball and Chekhov."

"Enemy wessel approaching, sir," I said. She laughed. "Oops," I said. "Guess you meant the *Cherry Orchard* one."

"All of the above," she said. "He has to have everything in the world." She was talking very drifty.

"You want to go back to sleep, babe? I'll hold him for a while and then give him back to the nurse if you want."

She shook her head, but slowly, and with her eyes already closed. "Don't want to miss any of it," she whispered. Then her eyes flew open. "Peter don't let them put him in the wrong thing. You know people end up getting different babies."

I was confused for a second about why that would be so terrible at a stage when our baby was so undifferentiated from all others. Then I remembered that wasn't the way it worked.

"Easy," I said. Carefully I leaned over, still holding the baby, and kissed Judith a soft kiss on the cheekbone below her staring eye. When I opened my eyes after the kiss, her eyes were closed. "You sleep tight," I said. "I'll take care of him."

And I did, in however half-assed a way.

Until now.

4

I sat at the kitchen table, still in my coat, and listened to Danny trudging back upstairs. I refreshed myself (little joke) with a good big burning suck on the gin bottle and, when my eyes stopped watering, another one. And now heigh-ho for some coffee. Need that coffee, boy, if you're seriously shooting for New Hampshire tonight. So I got up and ran some hot water, dumped I don't know how much instant coffee into a glass, filled the glass with water and stirred the mess with a spoon until the lumps went away, leaving a dingy foam on top. Then I quaffed the son of a bitch like Dr. Jekyll and Mr. Hyde. And sat down again to wait and see if I could feel it take hold. Drank a little more gin while I was waiting. Now what the *hell*, I wondered, was a gun doing on the kitchen table? Then I remembered. I stuck it in my pocket and went down to the basement.

I got down on hands and knees and dragged my suitcase out from under the ping-pong table, little brass tits scratching across the cement floor. When I raised my head I was looking into the single pink eye of a white rabbit. You saw only one of a rabbit's eyes at a time. As with the jacks of clubs and spades, I think it is. What kind of a world must a rabbit reconstruct, with each eye pointing at opposite sides of things? Peter Jernigan, say, superimposed on the wrong wall of the basement, as if in a cheesy process shot. Like Cary Grant drunk-driving in *North by Northwest*.

I carried the empty suitcase back upstairs, made a quick stop-off at the gin bottle, then went on up to the bedroom. Danny and Clarissa's door was shut. Voices behind it: council of war, obviously. What there was to pack didn't take long. I folded the one suit and laid it flat in the bottom of the suitcase. On top of that, the four shirts, one white, three sport. Old sporting Jernigan. On top of them, the pair of blue jeans, the pair of chinos, the long-sleeve crew-neck sweater, the V-neck sweater-vest, socks, briefs. Put the other pair of shoes on top, soles up. Wasn't there a sweatshirt? Gray sweatshirt? Probably in the dirty clothes. And that was it. The rest had been left at Heritage Circle, a whole closet-and-dresserful, now at a thrift store perhaps, waiting perhaps for some frugal Martha-type to come scanning the racks for a bargain to please a thankless man.

I carried the suitcase down and set it by the kitchen door, then went into the bathroom and pocketed the Pamprin. A handful of these would blur me out enough to sleep when I arrived. If I arrived. I took a couple more angry-tasting swallows of gin and stuck the bottle in my shoulderbag. Which I shouldered. And headed up the stairs for the last time, telling myself to look at everything and let it burn in. Drunk and sentimental. You'd have thought this place had been dear to me.

They were still talking in there, but my knocking put a stop to that. Martha opened the door and tried to stare me down. Ooh: stern mother. Clarissa got around behind her. I started to giggle. Old Martha looked like she was right out of Farmer Gray, boy, some kind of barnyard thing where the mother hen's so mad her feathers get all big. Yes, yes, I know the word *bristled*, but I'd rather have something that's blunt. At any rate, old Martha seemed to swell up big and protective and I was laughing and laughing and she was staring down at my dick. I thought she was giving old Dr. Johnson the evil eye, trying to wither him or something, until I looked down and saw that I'd pissed myself, the whole front of the pants and down the left leg. (I dressed left.) And now that I thought about it a minute, fuck if it didn't feel wet down there.

"You are really falling to shit, Peter," she said. And I guess it actually must've looked that way, especially since the pissed pants had only got me laughing more.

So I made an effort and got it together a little bit. Not that hard to do, really. It was like climbing up one level, up out of the laughter level and onto something else. It wasn't that hard, but it wasn't that easy. I don't know how to say it was.

"Hey, I'm off," I said. "Wish me luck." Keeping it jaunty. I honestly don't think I would have pissed myself if I hadn't had that whole thing of coffee on top of everything else.

"What do you mean you're *off*?" said Martha.

"I told you," I said. "Going to New Hampshire. Ayup."

"After midnight and you're starting out for New Hampshire," she said. "In a blizzard, drunk out of your mind."

"Mrs. Peretsky, don't let him do it." That was Danny. I think.

"Another county heard from," I said. This was an expression. I think it comes from politics. County: it would make sense. Like election returns. "What everybody seems to be forgetting is that *I*—ta da!"—and I pulled it out of my coat pocket—"have the *gun*." I gripped the thing with both hands, bent my knees—you've seen this on television, the arrest pose or whatever it's called—and aimed at Danny's big guitar amplifier. They had the tv sitting on it. I was just more or less fucking around; the amplifier was in the corner away from everybody. You want to be very careful if you're going to fuck around this way with guns. They all stood there cow-eyed.

Well, this got me hacked off. Absolutely the worst thing they could've done.

"Lighten *up*, for Christ's sake," I said. Although naturally with a gun being waved around (not that I was really waving it *per se*) you couldn't expect them to get into the spirit of anything.

"Pyew-pyew!" I went, and then I really did pull the trigger, and the gun gave a little pop, just a nasty little snapping pop. And bing, there was a tiny hole in the grille that covered the front of the amplifier. I was in the kind of head where you just think of a thing and do it. Thank God the bullet apparently just lodged someplace and didn't go ricocheting around the room.

"Bones?" I said to Danny. "Do what you can." I moved catlike into the room toward the amplifier. They all edged away from me. That gave me a feeling I liked. "Hey," I said. "Now I like *this*."

I laid my hand on the amplifier, as if taking its temperature or something. I turned to Danny again and said, "He's dead, Jim." Not a laugh, nothing. Then Clarissa burst into tears. Martha put an arm around her. "Hey now," I said, motioning with the pistol. "Away from the door, okay?"

They all obeyed. I thought, If only I could have taken charge of them like this a little sooner. Although this really wasn't the way to run a family. What you actually wanted was moral suasion grounded in quiet authority. Clarissa was sobbing away; Martha had her in both arms and was glaring at me, nothing left but contempt. So actually, if you think about it, I was already helping to begin the healing process. Only kidding, folks.

I backed into the doorway, looked at Danny. "Train's pulling out, big guy," I said. "Change your mind?" He looked down at his feet.

"Dad," he said. "Don't do it, okay? I mean if you're really going to go, get some sleep now and do it in the morning, okay?"

I shook my head. "No can do, big guy."

"Listen," he said. "Dad, *please?* You're really scaring me. It's like Mom, you know?"

"Mom was Mom," I said. "And never the train shall meet." The train, I said, imagine. "Last chance Texaco here."

"Danny," said Martha, taking an arm from around her daughter and laying her hand on Danny's forearm. "Just let him go."

"Oh *really*," I said. "Sick. Very sick. Big guy, piece of fatherly advice. She likes it up the heinie."

She threw Clarissa off and came at me. I stuck the gun right up in her eyes and that backed her off, you bet, like a cross backing off a vampire. She stood there, her whole body swelling and shrinking as she breathed out and in. An amazing sight, assuming I wasn't just imagining it. With the gun in my right hand, never taking my eyes off them, I crouched and felt around for my shoulderbag with my left hand. Finally I located the son of a bitch and reshouldered it. This was some midlife crisis, boy, if *that's* what this was about.

"Want everybody just stay in this room," I said, backing out the door. "You don't come out until you hear the car drive away." I looked at Danny. "Think you can handle that, big guy?" He stepped closer to Martha, then reached out and took Clarissa's hand. "You're the man of the family now," I said.

Wouldn't even look at me.

"Dad," he said, "just go if you're going, okay?"

"Rrrighty-o," I said, and slammed the door right in their foolish faces.

There was the suitcase, sitting right by the kitchen door where I'd left it, like faithful Old Dog Tray. God's sustaining mind had kept the son of a bitch there while I was busy making my adieux.

Outside, the snow was still coming down like a bastard. I threw the suitcase in the back of the car, the shoulderbag onto the passenger seat. Car started up the way it had years ago, when it was young. And then I remembered I still had the God damn gun in my pocket. So one last ethical conundrum: on the one hand, Martha and the kids might need it to protect themselves if what's-his-name took it into his head to come back; on the other hand, Danny had asked me to put the thing where Clarissa couldn't get at it. Maybe he'd actually meant where *he* couldn't get at it.

I got out of the car, leaving the engine running, and trotted back to the house. I burst open the door and there was Danny standing in the kitchen, bottom teeth working away at his upper lip, obviously afraid to come any closer, yet so glad his father had changed his mind and turned around.

"Here," I said, holding up the gun.

He looked at it.

"This belongs to Mrs. Peretsky," I said. "You see she gets it, okay?"

"We don't want it here," he said. "Could you just take and throw it away someplace, Dad?"

"You really might need it," I said. "Not going to deprive my own flesh and blood." And I laid the thing on the table. As a gesture of trust, the way a dog will turn its belly up. And because he really might need it. And because better him than me.

The next thing I remember is fishtailing up the hill, making it over the crest and then not being able to stop at the stop sign and skidding sideways across Maple Avenue. Then being on some highway, I assume the Garden State northbound. I was the only car out; everyone else must have been home safe from their holidays. Snow was coming at the windshield the way stars come at the viewing screen of the Starship Enterprise. And I remember wondering if that might actually have been where they got the idea: old Gene Roddenberry or somebody just driving along somewhere in the wintertime and thinking, *Hey*. At least it was cold enough so the snow wasn't sticking. That kept the going reasonably good: instead of lying there wet and heavy it blew around, grainy white clouds swirling on the blacktop, making the road look bottomless. Better not look at *that* shit too much.

Afraid to listen longer to the white noise of wind, tires and engine, I fumbled one-handed in the dash for the Walkman. Then steered with my elbows to get the things adjusted over my ears. Whatever was already in there would do. What it turned out to be was Webb Pierce, so on we drove with all those songs going—"Missing You," "Wondering," "There Stands the Glass," "Backstreet Affair"—each one such a sad, if necessarily sketchy, story, but at least a story with contours you could hang right on to, thing by thing by thing.

5

Every stink that fights the ventilator thinks it is Don Quixote.
—STANISLAUS LEC

They wrote this on a piece of paper torn from a spiral notebook and taped it to the wall above my bed. I'd been here a week then, long enough for them to think they'd gotten the hang of me. Hey, no problem, they said when I asked what the fuck *that* was doing there: you don't want to have it up you don't have to have it up. Catch was, though, that if you took it down you had to choose something to put up in its place. That's the rule here. Well, of course I knew better than to get into all that. I considered trying the old IITYWYBMAD routine on them. Probably would've worked, too. These people, are you kidding? But after I'd explained that I wasn't *really* asking them to buy me a drink and we'd all had our little laugh, I would've been in for a round of the let's-talk-about-its. So I just left the son of a bitch up there, radiating its timeless truth. Whatever the fuck it *was*. The waves and particles penetrating the old skull and doing their healing work. I mean, these are people who believe in words.

I do the minimal shit you have to do to keep them off your back. Daily shower, make your bed—surprisingly difficult at first with only one of your opposable thumbs—and go to meals and to group. Resist any of this, I find, and you're in for the let's-talk-about-its. Did I already say Uncle Fred has been up to visit a couple of times? He's the only one I'll see. And I don't have a lot to say, even to him. Especially when he starts with the messages from Danny.

I watch all the tv I can, which they try to discourage, though I don't see how they could control a fucking zoo like this for two hours without it. Read books and magazines from the little library they've got, which is how I've been able to stick in those long passages from this and that. (Obviously no one could recall these things verbatim.) So when I say I read *x* on the train or *y* at Uncle Fred's apartment, you can be pretty sure it was just something I found in the library here and transcribed to stretch this thing out as long as possible. My horror-hand helps too: eight-finger typing, at least in this five-and-three configuration, is probably as slow as straight hunt-and-peck.

But obviously, pad my story as I will, I can't keep this going much past today. I mean, unless I write a thing where I go, *So I put a piece of paper in the machine and typed the following: "I ended up driving all night. The snow eased off after a while—or, more likely, I'd driven past the edge of the storm—and I just kept going. Stopped for gas where you get off the interstate, then . . ."* So today or tomorrow I'm going to have to think up some reason I can't show this to them right away. Tell them I need to change the names to protect the innocent? See, the problem is, fuck with them *too* much and you're out of here completely. It's happened twice in just the time I've been here: the guy who wouldn't go to group and the guy who kept screaming. I just feel I'm getting closer and closer to a real crisis here. Keep harking back to *Jon Nagy's Television Art Book*: what looks like a road just going and going and going to the horizon is really two lines coming together.

So I do it their way. Mostly. *I've found that my way doesn't work*: boy, do they love it whenever somebody comes out with *that* one in group. Then you see those sober little nods of the head meaning *Better late than never*. Fuck if I'll go *that* far to keep them happy. And there's other things I won't do: one, see Danny; two, shave; and three, buy into this pretense that we're all little first-name humans here going soul-to-soul. I'm So-and-so and I'm an alcoholic. I'm Such-and-such and I'm a drug addict. I'm Somebody Else and so forth and so on. But when it comes around to you, you have to give them something, if only name and spiritual disease. That's the rule here. So what I've figured out is this. I stand up and say: Jernigan.

A NOTE ABOUT THE AUTHOR

David Gates writes about books and music for
Newsweek. He lives in New York City and in a
small town upstate.

A NOTE ON THE TYPE

This book was set in a digitized version of Janson. The hot-metal version of Janson was a re-cutting made direct from type cast from matrices long thought to have been made by the Dutchman Anton Janson, who was a practicing type founder in Leipzig during the years 1668–1687. However, it has been conclusively demonstrated that these types are actually the work of Nicholas Kis (1650–1702), a Hungarian, who most probably learned his trade from the master Dutch type founder Dirk Voskens. The type is an excellent example of the influential and sturdy Dutch types that prevailed in England up to the time William Caslon (1692–1766) developed his own incomparable designs from them.

Composed by PennSet, Inc., Bloomsburg, Pennsylvania; printed and bound by Fairfield Graphics, Fairfield, Pennsylvania; designed by Mia Vander Els